NICE ENOUGH TO MURDER

By E. S. Russell

NICE ENOUGH TO MURDER

SHE SHOULD HAVE CRIED ON MONDAY

Nice Enough
to Murder

E. S. RUSSELL

PUBLISHED FOR THE CRIME CLUB BY

DOUBLEDAY & COMPANY, INC., GARDEN CITY, NEW YORK

1971

All of the characters in this book
are fictitious, and any resemblance
to actual persons, living or dead,
is purely coincidental.

Library of Congress Catalog Card Number 77-144293
Copyright © 1971 by Enid Russell
All Rights Reserved
Printed in the United States of America
First Edition

For Stan, of course.

And for my parents, who have often wondered
what really happens in schools.

Deprivation of identity, not frustration, leads to murder.

Erik H. Erikson
Childhood and Society

NICE ENOUGH TO MURDER

PART ONE: BEN AND EVERYBODY ELSE

CHAPTER ONE

There are almost as many ways to prepare for a journey as there are people who plan to make one. There are almost as many items deemed essential to take as there are people who pack them. And almost as many places to go to as there are people who hope to reach them.

But, whether it derives from hope, fear, love, greed, anger, happiness, duty, or revenge, there is only one mood in which all plans are formed and implemented, and that is determination. It usually grows slowly.

Moreover, not every journey covers physical distance, for the immediate world in which the planner lives can be quitted merely by modifying one of its aspects and making it a new one.

And not every destination can be found upon a map.

For instance, of the several people at Manton High School in Manton, Massachusetts, planning to exchange one world for another, one packed a gun and aimed for freedom. Another began to formulate, in a highly professional and sincerely apologetic letter, the damning phrases of blackball. A third gave good advice but sought none for himself from the proper source. Two more prepared for a honeymoon and talked of everything up to but not quite including murder. Another longed to commit it. A seventh waited to be told what to do. An eighth began to wonder if living just a little longer were worth the price of dying many times. And Benjamin Franklin Louis, principal, A.B. (history, summa cum laude), Phi Beta Kappa, A.M. (guidance, with distinction), Ph.D. (history, with distinction), worked and worried at his desk on this lowering mid-October afternoon and reminded himself grumpily of the meeting he would have to attend before he could go home to Jane.

"If there really is a god and the last really do get to be first," she had said once, "then someday school administrators will be among the elect. But," she had added ambiguously, "I doubt it." Jane took a dim view.

In the literal and restricted sense Ben already was, having been elected—*dragooned* would be a better word for it, he grumbled— to referee a dispute among the members of the guidance staff. He glanced at his watch and sighed irritably. It was growing late and he was tired and woolly-headed from smoking the horrible peach brandy tobacco that Jane had barred from home. Furthermore, he was not quite finished with the task before him and he did not want to go to that meeting or anywhere else until it was done.

He riffled through the pages and put them down again, knowing that this next lecture would be an excellent one and wondering why he felt so dissatisfied with it. Restless, he spun round and looked out of the window. The morning sky had been a matchless immaculate blue. Then, for no good reason that he could see, there had been a shower at noon. And now the sky was heavy and menacing, black with rain that would soon begin to fall. All in one piece, it looks like, he thought, and turned back to the sloppy desk and sighed gustily again.

He packed his Monday pipe, for solace, but a glance at the soap-stone statue in front of him increased his vague depression.

Jane had bought the little Victorian figure exactly one year ago to dress a set in the school's television studio where Ben and others gave closed-circuit lectures to the schools in Manton and surrounding towns, and Ben had become attached to the maidenly innocence of a lost era, and kept it. Eternally young, forever holding her book (Tennyson, most likely!) half hidden in the folds of her flowing gown, she taunted him with the fact that another year had passed, that *he* was a year older—suddenly. Forty-seven. He scowled at the saccharine dreamer and tightened his sagging waist and forced his attention back to his work.

He saw, after some ten minutes of careful checking, that there was only one gap in it, pertaining to nineteenth-century scientific techniques, discoveries, difficulties in general, for which he would need a bit of information from Bert Shrag, chairman of the science department. He would get it in the morning. Which was fudging on the research, he supposed, but the preparation for this lecture had already taken a lot of time and there were a thousand other things to do.

His depression widened and deepened, and he stayed in his chair trying to put his finger on the cause of it. He wasn't all that tired. The weather wasn't all that bad. He wasn't sick, although an appalling percentage of the school was. The buildings were still standing six weeks after opening day. And nothing was wrong at home (except Jane's temper because he was going to be late again).

What in hell am I worrying about? he asked, exasperated. He put all his antennae out and became aware that his consciousness was nibbling at the edges of a formless sour anticipation.

He thought back over the years. What could happen that hadn't already happened within his personal experience? Girls got pregnant. Kids smoked marijuana on school premises. Staff members were caught *in flagrante*, or damn near—but he veered hastily from memories of the scandal and tragedy of two years ago. Kids got stabbed, kicked, punched, or shampooed in the toilets by upperclass fascists, or left parts of themselves in the labs and shops.

Okay, so what? Even a school like this one, in a relatively posh town like Manton, was a community like any other community and offered its inhabitants the same kinds of things. Violence, lust, bigotry, and other forms of human stupidity. Yes, and the good things too, which made everything somewhat more than merely bearable. Maybe I am a professional chauvinist, as Jane likes to say, but by god! I wouldn't change places with anyone else, he declared. But he felt just as uneasy as before.

And then his eye fell on the calendar where seven consecutive dates, nine days away, were heavily outlined in red ink, and he realized immediately what was the matter with him.

Something—*something*—might keep him from that conference in San Francisco on curriculum development in history, to which he had been invited as a consultant. Invited, hell! The Foundation had sought him out and wouldn't take no for an answer! Generous fee, all expenses paid, and—the lily-gilder—the opportunity to see one of the most exciting cities in the world. (No wives, naturally, even if they footed their own bills. Oh well, it was tough on Jane, but he'd tell her all about it.) To be asked to that particular conference was a plum. To be invited to join that classy gang was a professional accolade. And I'm godnwell going, no matter what! he swore ferociously. He laughed silently at himself, knocked the dottle out of his corrupt pipe, and got up and stretched his long thin body, grunting with the pleasure of it.

All at once his good temper was restored. Why do I always feel better, he asked the girl with the book, when I discover what a selfish jerk I am? But he reached for his jacket without waiting for an answer. There is a limit, after all, to how much self-knowledge one can bear.

He risked a relapse by straightening his tie, since it caused him to think about Allen Magrue who spent a fortune on his clothes and looked like a tramp. And this very naturally led him to think about Joyce Bellows who, rumor had it, seemed to have a "thing" for Allen. Fast work, that, he commented grudgingly, since Allen had joined the staff only two months back. But even then his mood did not falter—noticeably.

He had nothing against Love *qua* Love, or against marriage and children either. He had been enjoying their benefits for some years and planned to go on doing so for as long as he possibly could. The trouble was, when Love hit an eminently eligible *female* staff member, who happened to be indispensable to *him*—and Joyce was one of several he had without morals or scruples pirated away from someone else—she would marry and resign sooner or later. In which case, where would he find another such treasure to take her place? And if she were unhappy, if the *affaire* went sour, how would her competence be affected if she stayed? He had so far been incredibly lucky to keep Valentine Shrag *née* Cobb, who was too busy creating artists in the art department to go home and create kids, thank god! And even though his magnificent secretary Iva Solomov had left to marry Dixon Stevens, she had found Opal Castle for him first—and Opal was as like Iva as to make him suspect that the latter had simply replicated herself in the office copy machine! But how long would his luck hold? Last year had been bad enough with Joyce on sabbatical at the University for her second doctorate. Simon Wills had had a coronary and then double pneumonia on the strength of it, and Joyce had divided her time between high school and graduate school to keep the guidance office from collapsing too. It had been a miracle of planning and endurance, and he would never understand how she had done it, or cease being grateful that she had. But a sabbatical was one thing. Marriage was something else.

Anyone close to a school administrator knows that Love is one of that deprived creature's crucial concerns. He may regret that there is all too little of it in the world. But when it fragments or diminishes the even shorter supply of professional competence, he can only regard it as an adversary.

Accordingly, Ben almost sat down again to fill his pipe and agonize over the future of his guidance department if Joyce married Allen.

No. If he did, he might sit there for a week and never even get his bag packed, let alone go to the meeting up in Joyce's office. He sighed once more, put pipe and pouch into his pocket, and reluctantly left his sanctuary.

The five members of the guidance department were sitting in their chairs as though, minutes or hours or days or weeks ago, the last word spoken on the subject of their dispute had malignantly frozen them.

"Okay, what cooks?" Ben said, taking his place at the conference table in the main section of the office and filling his encrusted pipe with the poisonous beloved mixture. His hands trembled imperceptibly in the preparation of this reliable armor against conflict, for he had immediately sensed in the familiar room a quality of tension that was new and disturbing. He encouraged his own tiny conflagration with rhythmic vigorous puffs, and, as rank smoke wrapped him round in a ghostly bandage, Simon Wills came out of the collective trance and went to crank open a small window in the wall of glass.

Simon always moved his grandfatherly body with caution now, but despite his economy his damaged heart began to beat too rapidly. Frightened, and frightened of being frightened, he put a pill under his tongue and excused himself. "Anything you want is all right with me," he said, walking gingerly past several large cartons stacked near the door. "You don't mind, do you, Joyce? I could stay if you really—"

"Oh, we're used to it by now, Simon," she said cheerfully. "We'll carry your load as usual. You're better off home now, before the weather gets worse."

If it was a dig, it was clearly unintentional and had just as clearly been said many times before, Ben thought, judging by the lack of reaction in the others. They all seemed unconscious anyhow. But Ben was not, and he sensed Simon's humiliation as the older man let go of the doorknob and took an indecisive step toward the table.

"Really, Simon, it's quite all right," Joyce said patiently. "There's no point in your staying. We can manage perfectly well without you. We know how you feel, and you've given me your vote—which is all I care about at the moment."

She had said no more and no less than she meant and her words and voice were unexceptionable. But again there was that cutting thrust. Simon's face, as soggy and yellow as a dumpling, hardened as if it had been lying around for a week. He nodded and shut himself out.

The click of the latch released the others into consciousness. They smiled almost shyly at Ben but avoided looking at each other. He gave them his neutral face, although his lungs and liver were beginning to play musical chairs with his intestines, and remained silent. There were times when his silence, which had earned him the reputation as the best nonverbal communicator in Greater Boston, catalytically created a problem-solving environment for combatants. But Ben, an able administrator, was an eclectic: there were other times when he grabbed battlers by the hair and told them plainly what he wanted them to do. This was certainly not the time. He would have to find out first what the trouble was. That he did not know was not surprising. Implicit in his administrative style of sharing responsibility with his staff was the penalty of often being the last to know what was happening. But that there should be trouble among this group was unthinkable. Given what he knew about them, serious discord here was nothing less than unbelievable.

Take Simon's departure, for instance. None of these four would have insisted that he stay and needlessly risk another seizure. They liked and respected him and each other, and Allen Magrue's arrival in August had appeared to increase their mutual loyalty, their morale, and their accomplishments. They were excellent people and complemented each other profitably.

Moreover, because they continued to teach, they were on good terms with the rest of the faculty. "I want you each to keep one class," Joyce had said on taking over years ago, "although it will make things really tight for you. But if you preserve your identity —your origins, so to speak—we'll disarm a lot of staff opposition and defensiveness to our kind of specialist." It had proved a wise strategy and done much to unify the school.

So what cooks? Ben asked them again, silently. In the long seconds that passed he scrutinized them apprehensively.

Opposite him sat Allen Magrue who was forty-five and looked twenty years younger. His face was almost unmarked, as though the mature structure was just emerging after a prolonged static interval. Yet there was a remembered pain in the gentle hazel eyes which gave his seeming youthfulness an odd and endearing vulnerability.

He was also very unkempt. Fair thick hair tumbled like a boy's over a high forehead and level brows. There was an unshaved patch on his chin. His well-tailored suit was unpressed and dusty with chalk. His collar was turned up halfway round his neck, his silk tie was askew, his forty-dollar shoes scuffed and unpolished. Such disregard for his appearance and belongings was unstudied and added to his attractiveness, although even those who knew him best, and loved him, would have liked to hire a valet to follow him through all his waking hours and keep him neat.

His other salient characteristic was the impulsiveness with which he lunged at people like an uncoordinated warmhearted puppy. When in a group, parts of him seemed scattered everywhere—a hand on someone's arm, an arm about someone's shoulders, his face bent down earnestly and eagerly as though the better to join in conversation. Guileless, sensitive, dedicated, generous, he did from time to time annoy those who gave of themselves warily in bits and pieces. One person in the school hated and feared him and would have fled from him if she could.

To Ben's left at the end of the table was Helen Chadwick, a well-fleshed, wholly feminine woman of forty, with a wry sense of humor and a largesse of spirit that sustained enormous competence and unfailing serenity. It was ironic that everything about her, so bountifully scaled and made for giving, for mothering, should be a casualty of a profession dedicated to children and dominated until very recently by women. Yet she would never disintegrate in the bitterness and frustration common to aged spinsterhood, which she had often contemplated calmly. She knew without complacence that hers was a temperament that accepted life as it was. The good things were good and you enjoyed them gratefully. The bad things—well, you made your adjustments without rancor, and for the rest all you could do was to hang loose, as the kids said.

Jane Louis had put it differently. Helen Chadwick, she said, had a talent for happiness, and why were men such damn fools— and what kind of men were they, anyway?—to have passed over this lovely woman? And Ben had told her to mind her own business and not rock his boat.

But looking at Helen now, at her widely spaced gray eyes under the smooth broad brow, at the heavy chestnut hair that waved graciously back into a coil at the nape, Ben briefly experienced Jane's anger at this waste. Was Helen's reward after years of service to be the continued loneliness of scratch meals at her kitchen table, and an unshared bed? Or at best a sterile relationship with another unwanted unused woman?

Turning to Joyce Bellows at his right, Ben realized for the first time that he and Jane had never thought of her in this way. Although she was two or three years older than Allen Magrue, she too looked very young. Scarcely five feet tall and delicately boned, she had the transparent skin and fine silky hair of a child. She was also as expensively dressed as Allen but so exquisitely groomed that tidiness seemed to emanate from her very core. As if, Ben thought in surprise, all thoughts and emotions and physical processes, even the subconscious and autonomic ones, were ordered, channeled, and controlled by an extraordinary will power. She was very pretty. But for that control she would have been beautiful.

Ben was astonished by his enlarged perception of this woman with whom he had worked so closely for eight years and about whom he knew almost nothing. Her profound contributions to the school had, like Helen's, been so unstinting that until this moment he had never remarked her reticence about her personal life. A reticence so extreme that she might as well have left no trace in the evening shadows but the light scent she wore, and materialized in the morning when the Unitarian Church on the Common struck eight.

Well, he thought, since opposites attract, it stands to reason that Joyce rather than Helen should have bagged Allen Magrue, for no two people were more dissimilar than they. The notion made him unaccountably irritable.

David Ross moved his chair away from the table with an abrasive sound that made Ben jump. He saw that David's thin clever face was darkly flushed under his stiff gray hair and that he seemed about to explode from tension. But then he always did, as if his small wiry body even in repose were a bomb with a short fuse that was permanently alight. No one really minded his temper. It was just "David's way," they said affectionately.

"Let's get on with it!" David said in his staccato voice. "We all had plenty to say before Ben got here!" He regarded the cartons with brooding fury.

"Okay," Allen began, thrusting himself forward so abruptly that he was nearly halfway across the table. Joyce Bellows winced and drew back. "To put you in the picture, Ben, it's this. Joyce wants to record therapeutic counseling sessions with the kids on audio-video tapes, to evaluate our performance. She also wants our counselees to evaluate us in writing. But with all due respect, this is one time when I feel I should dictate staff policy." His smile took the harshness out of the challenge to his department head.

"It isn't staff policy!" David Ross interrupted, snapping and hissing. "Willy-nilly we're getting University-honed along with Joyce! To hell with it!"

"Aren't you being rather defensive?" Joyce said in her soft melodious voice. Her eyes brimmed with tears.

Tears! Ben said to himself. From her? From Joyce? What *is* this?

Magrue made a soothing gesture. "I wasn't thinking about myself—and neither was David," he added out of loyalty. "An approach like the one you're pushing would be very tough on some of the kids. We're the only ones they've got to rely on, Joyce. You know that. Your idea may seem good but it's lousy in practice. I've been in on it before and I know. Kids like Tony Evans or Tim Lunn shouldn't be put in the position of evaluating us. It's a blessing they've got the sense to want to come to us at all. Through the grapevine they find out enough about the guidance staff to decide which one of us they want to open up to. But let them start evaluating us as to competence and whatnot, and they'll have a good excuse to work off spleen and get vicious and personal and solidify their resistance to us at the very same time that they're asking for some help. It just doesn't work. We'd never get to first base with them. It would become a game for them. We'd be one more of the Enemy for them to try to shoot down. We'd be hoist with our own petard."

"Joyce's petard, not ours! Not mine!" David said bitterly.

"What are you talking about?" Ben said.

"Joyce's Administrative Performance Project! New and Radical Ways To Supervise and Evaluate Guidance Counselors!" David spat out upper case as though it had given him a bad taste. "When she gets through this year, we can call her Dr. *Dr.* Bellows! God knows what we'll be called!"

"*You* knew about Joyce's project?" said Ben, who only knew that she had chosen to do a performance project rather than a thesis. But that she of all people should have publicized her project to her colleagues gave him such a jolt that he almost dropped his pipe. But now he had one clue. It was easy to understand David's anger and the underlying guilt. Ben knew as surely as if he were inside David's head what the little man was thinking.

David Ross liked Allen and had shared Joyce's enthusiasm for him when they had met last spring. There had been other fine candidates for the position Simon Wills had all but vacated, but they were women, and there were too damned many women already in education and specifically in this department, David felt. Another one would wreck the balance here whether Simon retired or stayed on. Poor Simon! He wasn't using a quarter of his smarts any more. Because of his heart condition he would no longer work with the worst problem boys who needed a stable older type. He wouldn't even talk about them! And David felt increasingly that he himself needed a man to talk to in this field. Although he was as knowledgeable as the average counselor, he held minimum paper credentials in guidance, less than Helen did, and far less than Allen who was well along in his doctoral work in psychology and who had already explained to him a lot of technical Freudian stuff that had been very helpful. It was easier to ask Allen for assistance than go to Joyce, who had gotten her doctorate in psychology years ago and was now on the last lap of a second. Administration, this trip. As wonderful as she was, she always made him feel inadequate, and he didn't want his counselees to tear him apart in formal written evaluations and make things even worse! If only he were as good in counseling as he was in science! Second in ability to Bert Shrag, as a matter of fact. But with a wife and four kids he couldn't take more than the required three credits every five years to maintain his tenure, or return to full-time science teaching and lose his differential. So all in all, Allen was a welcome addition and a hell of a nice guy. But he was new here. And every time David went to him for help or backed him in any way, he felt disloyal to Joyce—which made his reaction to her scheme now seem disproportionate.

Ben knew all this. What he did not know was that David felt even more uncomfortable because Joyce and Allen had been sparking and flaring at each other for weeks. It wasn't that Allen was bucking for power or being insubordinate, either. It wasn't that. Maybe they were in love. Could be. David wished he hadn't hinted it around to so many people. But if they were in love—and he hoped to Christ that Joyce would break down and loosen up for once!—he could understand why Allen was being so hard-nosed about the whole damn business. It was tough on a guy to work for a woman, and tougher if he loved her. But whatever it was, there was a weird undercurrent between them that he could not define or explain, and it served to heighten his feeling of being lacking.

He put a cigarette between his lips and opened a matchbook. It was empty and he flipped it into a wastebasket. It missed and fell to the carpet.

"God!" he said crankily. "Anyone got a match?"

"I do," Joyce said. She turned over the flap of her alligator handbag with a deliberation hardly warranted by its size or weight, took out several matchbooks and shot them across the table, and then left the bag opened flat. A small gold pin gleamed on the grosgrain lining.

Allen Magrue saw it and the blood drained from his face. Helen Chadwick also saw it and gasped. They glanced at each other and looked away as though scorched by the brief contact.

Neither Ben who was fussing with his pipe nor David who was stowing away the matches saw this small interchange.

And none of the four caught the complicated expression of satisfaction and regret on Joyce Bellows' set face as she carefully closed her handbag and put it under her chair.

"I'm surprised, Joyce, that you announced the topic for your doctoral project. People usually don't," Ben said, fishing.

Her eyes were candid. "I mightn't have except that it didn't seem fair to ask for something like student evaluation and everything else without explaining why I wanted it. It will certainly give us all more work."

"I wouldn't exactly say you explained it on your own hook," Helen said mildly. "David—"

"David smelled a rat!" Ross interrupted again. "I'm getting cynical, skeptical, and paranoid in my old age!" He sprang up and began a rapid circuit of the table. "And who wouldn't? We don't get watched and rated twice a year like ordinary people, oh no! With us it's four times—by our academic department heads *and* by you, Joyce! And now, on behalf of the Great God University, you want us to submit to further assessment! By kids who don't know their ass from their elbow most of the time, let alone fantasy from reality! I say no to that! And you can quote me in your top-secret monthly goddam journals! Tell the dons on your *ad hoc* committee that I'm a low-down sonuvabitch who's out to spike the wheels of your progress into the higher echelons!" He almost kicked the cartons as he approached them but gave them a hate-filled look instead and flung himself back into his chair, hardly able to breathe because of the anger, shame, and guilt that clogged his throat.

They stared at him. Even for David Ross, this was going too far.

"Ben, how do you feel about student evaluation?" Allen said.

"In general I'm for it. We can learn a lot about ourselves and what we're doing—what nerves we're hitting—by listening to kids."

"Thank you, Ben. That's what I said." Joyce was quietly triumphant.

"Well now, wait a minute, Joyce," Ben went on. "I said in general. But in *this* case I'm inclined to agree with David and Allen. There are only two reasons why giving counselees a printed form to fill out on you would serve their purposes or yours. If it's genuinely therapeutic to them and helpful to you. I don't think it would be either."

"Absolutely!" David cried. "What's the biggest problem in evaluating the effectiveness of counseling? The single fact that we can't *quantify* our effectiveness! In other areas we give tests, we have certain fairly good standards—even in creative writing, Allen, wouldn't you say?—against which to rate a kid's performance. As far as our teaching performance is concerned, it's less easy to measure the factors that make a good teacher. The way we dress, the way we speak, the amount of creative productive control we exert over classrooms full of all different kinds of kids, our personalities —here's where evaluation can get dangerously subjective. But even so, it can be helpful, and it often is.

"But how the hell do you evaluate a counselor's performance? How can you measure his effectiveness? If we have good follow-up programs, we can find out what's happened to the kids who came to us. Or if a kid suddenly gets the message and changes his behavior and his values so that right in school we're lucky enough to view his growth, then we know we've done something right, something helpful! But for crissake, Joyce, you know it seldom works out like that. It may take months—years!—before therapy takes effect. And we don't have any follow-up except occasional word-of-mouth news fourthhand. Or maybe we see in the paper that a kid we counseled once is now being tagged for the presidential Cabinet or was just arraigned on a rape charge! But over a school year, what goes on?" he demanded of them. "There aren't enough of us to cover all the kids who need help. And how often do we see the kids we *do* see? Once a week? Twice a week? Once a month is more like it! So each time we see them, we've got to re-establish rapport."

"But—"

"I'm not finished, Ben! I might as well cover the waterfront for you. Apart from the inadequate time we have with the kids, do we get to see their parents? Not a chance! They're afraid to be seen here, and even if we had the money to *pay* them to come, they wouldn't talk about themselves and the extent of their responsibility for their kids' messes. And do they back us up at home? You're damn well told they don't! They don't really want to know anything—they wet their pants when we even give their kids a group IQ test! And IQ tests of any kind aren't much good anyway!

"So here we are with our hands virtually tied behind our backs
—and Joyce thinks she can get a fair reading of what we're doing
and how well we're doing it! With counselee evaluation of us—
and watching us on TV *and* listening to us on mikes—*and* record-
ing the whole kit and caboodle on audio and video tape! To hell
with it!" By now he was panting and scarlet.

"Take it easy, David," Allen said softly.

"I'm damned if I will!"

"David, please. Please. This won't help us," Helen said.

"What's the matter with you two?" David demanded. "What're
you holding back for? If you want Ben's help, don't snow him!"

"I wasn't trying to," Allen said. "But I couldn't see a place to
get a word in edgewise. Okay, I agree with all you've said. But I
want to make it clear that it isn't supervision and evaluation—in
general—by Joyce that I'm against."

"That isn't what you said before!"

"It is, David, I only qualified it a little. If Joyce wants to use
tape recorders and mikes during counseling sessions, or a TV
camera and receiver, or even a one-way screen, that's okay with
me. I've worked with all that stuff before and it's a damn good way
to learn. Cameras and tapes don't lie. We may think we look or
sound one way or another, but how we—and the kids too—are
perceived by others is recorded impersonally. So we all get a chance
to get clued in on a detached view of ourselves. It's an excellent
means to supervise and evaluate—and to learn. After all, what
Joyce is proposing is only a means to an end, not an end in itself,
project or no project. As far as I'm concerned," he added, giving
Joyce a charming grin, "you can even sit in the same cubicle with
us."

"I've agreed to all that too," Helen said.

"I have not!" David snapped. "I can just see my rating now if
Joyce had used a tape recorder or TV—or sat in with me and
Vinnie Dean the other day! I thought I was following his lead
and advancing at a safe pace, but I moved a little too fast in one
touchy area with our violin *virtuoso* and he damn near knocked
my teeth in! He would've, too, if it wouldn't hurt his bowing arm!
It could happen to any one of us, and it has. And what's the al-
ternative to hitting—my god, even murdering!—one of us? Murdering someone at home—or committing suicide! Patients of the

best psychiatrists have done it! Look at Marilyn Monroe! But when our bell rings and the forty-five-minute hour is up, do we get a chance to stick with it 'til the danger's past? No! We have a class to teach, or another kid coming in for a session. Or money to collect for the Red Cross, for godsake! I've been sweating my tail off worrying about Vinnie, wondering what he's going to do before I see him again! *If* I see him again!"

"Look, David," Joyce said, "I've never denied being in the same boat—"

"Magnanimous, Joyce, very, very generous of you! But who supervises and evaluates you when *you* get into a jam?" David said tightly. He pointed to the manila folder under her hand. "And never mind what libels you've written about us in that journal of yours! How objectively do you write yourself up? How much do you tell on yourself to your professors?"

So that's what that folder is! Ben thought, horrified. My god, how much worse is this going to get?

"Knock it off, David. Also cool it, baby. You know Ben supervises all department heads," Allen said easily. "And the Superintendent goes after *him*, and the School Committee and the community at large go after the Superintendent, poor bastard. And what Joyce writes in her journal for the University is her own business." He ruffled David's hair affectionately and the little man grinned shamefacedly at him.

"We all get our lumps one way and another," Ben said quietly. "Sometimes I think the only free agent in this system is Rocco Tomasello. There are times when I'd give a lot to change places with him."

Even David relaxed at this. Everyone knew the school's *premier* custodian, and liked him. And jumped when he told them to.

"Allen, what did you mean about qualifying your agreement with Joyce's plans? We've gotten away from this a couple of times," Ben said. His insides were churning.

"Oh Christ!" David muttered, but they paid no attention to him.

"Well," Allen said, "to sum it up, I'm against counselee evaluation altogether. Joyce can count me out on that, University or no University. I'll go along with the mikes and TV and tapes, though, as I've said. But I'll pick the kids for these methods of evaluating and supervising my performance as a counselor. Some kids—some adults, for that matter—are so skittish that you can't even take notes while they're talking. They're so paranoid, they can't cope with the sight of a pencil and paper. It takes months to develop enough trust in them so that you can at least write something down, let alone use a TV camera or a mike and a recorder. With kids like Tony Evans or Timmy Lunn—well, I told Joyce I'd see them alone. No monitoring during sessions. No discussion of them afterward. They insist on complete privacy. I can't promise them they'll get it—and they won't come otherwise, not any more —and then violate their confidence by letting Joyce in. They want her out and she'll have to stay out."

"Over my dead body," Joyce said. She was smiling and seemed relaxed, but she was as determined as he. Her tiny hand patted her manila folder meaningfully.

Helen Chadwick stirred uneasily and only Ben saw the angry light in her eyes. He stole another look at her and a tremor of alarm ran through him. All at once he began to suspect that something was being discussed that no one had said a word about.

"Oh come on, Joyce," Allen said, laughing. "Unless I've been talking another language, you know I'm all for you and what you're trying to do. But with those two kids you're—" He stopped suddenly and flashed a glance at Ben who was smoking his horrible peach brandy tobacco as calmly as though he were on the plane to San Francisco.

"She's what?" David broke in, trying to salve his conscience. "If it hadn't been for her, God knows where those two and a few more would be today! Death Row, probably! Why wouldn't she still be concerned about them, even if they're your babies now? After all, Al, she's been working with them for three years!"

"I know, and I agree. It put me in a hell of a spot, but what could I do? Kids can refer themselves to whichever counselor they want. And if kids like that actually want help, what are we supposed to do if they want to make a change and see a man instead of a woman?"

"You're right, Allen," Joyce said. "But the point is only that I insist on basing my first evaluation of *you* largely on your work with those two. This has nothing to do with the University, Ben. It's just the usual evaluation after six weeks of school. Also, I wasn't expecting to keep those boys as my counselees. I always said they should have a father figure—"

"And they couldn't relate to anyone as short as me!" David said ruefully.

Joyce laughed with malice. "Oh David, stop feeding your neurosis! They're in your chem class. You had to remind them of that last year, remember. You can't counsel the kids you teach."

"I know! I know! Sorry again! What do you think, Ben? After all, Helen and Simon and I haven't asked for special preference. The policy ought to be clarified." And he was angry again. "And something else ought to be clarified! This whole bit on Joyce's project! None of this fancy stuff ever came into the picture until Joyce picked it for her doctoral work! Why do we have to be roped in? I will not do it, Joyce, and that's *final!*"

"That isn't fair and you know it!" she said, her fair skin nearly as red as his. "My *ad hoc* committee won't approve anything just because it happens to accommodate what you consider my selfish needs! Ben, you're close to the University. Tell him! He won't believe me."

She was not merely angry. She was pleading. Incredible! Ben told himself. He wondered if anyone who knew Joyce Bellows had ever seen her behave like this. Reluctantly he said, "If you did what other degree candidates have had to do, first you had to review—thoroughly and in writing—the professional literature on your sphere of interest. In your case, I know there's almost nothing on methods of supervising and evaluating guidance personnel, which in itself supports your doctoral interest in the subject. And then you had to write a position paper describing and justifying your thinking and planning of such methods. And your advisers put you through some damn tricky hoops before giving you the go-ahead. And they'll make you sweat every step of the way until you finish. They will not tolerate anything that smells like makework." He felt like a junior instructor in front of a slow group. "And when you're all done you'll be a fully fledged administrator. You can drop guidance altogether and be a high school principal too!"

"I know all that," David grumbled. "What I'd like to know is the blow-by-blow account of the perils of Joyce in that folder she carries around day in and day out!"

Ben felt that he had to let this pass for now. "About Allen's wanting to work without supervision of those two boys, Joyce—do you have some reason for wanting to stay with them?"

"Yes, Ben, I do. I'm trying to keep them from dropping out, for one thing, whereas Allen—but if you don't mind, I'd rather discuss it with you some other time. It's—it's getting late. This is as far as we ever get, unfortunately. The others felt you might be able to help sort it out—or change my mind. But the more we go over it—"

The telephone rang and she said excuse me and went to answer it. "Yes, Tom. Tonight is fine. We'll be leaving soon. You have all the instructions? And the table? Wonderful. Wonderful. I can't thank you enough. I'll see you tomorrow."

She came back to the table smiling and David looked at her suspiciously.

"Well. As I was saying," she went on, "the more we talk about it, the more convinced I am that I'm right, the more determined I am to do it my way."

"That was Tom Quinn, wasn't it," David said furiously. "He's going to set up those boxes of equipment, isn't he? And you're going to issue a fiat, aren't you?"

"I've done it before," she said, smiling at him. "And we've got the best department in the area, in spite of all the things that hold us back."

"Which is your way of saying that department heads have the right to make unilateral decisions regardless!"

"They do. I do. I will again, David, whenever I'm sure I know what's best. If you don't like it—" She shrugged slightly. "But really, David, be objective. Helen and Simon have accepted the plans and so has Allen. His—reservations are between him and me and I'm—certain we'll straighten them out. You're the only one opposed *in toto*. So I don't see how you can say my decision to go ahead full steam is unilateral."

"Could I say something?" Helen said. "I don't want to be misunderstood. I just want to add that in the past it was clearly understood that *we*—Simon and David and Allen and I—that *we* made the appointments for evaluation! That *we* chose the cases we'd discuss with Joyce!" She was speaking directly to Ben now and her voice rose steadily. "That *we* chose the kids we'd counsel during those appointments! Via notes or tapes or anything else! It's not because of her doctorate that we're being pulled into a mess! It's only that Joyce wants her own way as usual! Allen's feeling about those boys is justified and everybody knows it! And if you knew as much as you think you do, Joyce, you'd know why!" she cried, swinging on her superior. "As nice as you are, as wonderful as you are—to those boys you're pure poison! It has nothing at all to do with your being a woman! Allen was just too polite to say it any other way!"

White with shock and pain, Joyce stared at her.

"I'm—I'm sorry, Joyce. I didn't mean to hurt your feelings," Helen said, her eyes glittering with tears. "You've been marvelous until—" She stood up. "Forgive me, please, everyone. I haven't felt well all day. I think I'm getting the flu too." The thick coil on her neck bobbled and loosened as she ran out holding a handkerchief to her lips.

The others gazed at the door she had all but slammed as though expecting a teletyped explanation of her behavior to appear on it letter by letter. If she had committed murder before their eyes, and lately in her dreams she had, the act would have been no more at odds with what she was than were her anger and her tears.

"She must be sick! Don't you think she's sick?" Joyce pleaded in the appalled silence, and wiped her eyes.

"Almost everybody else is," David said briskly and went to the door. "I'm sorry, Joyce. You have been great. Everyone knows that. But this time—" He made a gesture of finality and disappeared.

"I think it's my turn," Ben said, scraping out his pipe. He rose wearily and closed the window. "I'd like to talk some more with all of you tomorrow or later in the week, but I think we'll have to give it a rest for the moment." He stopped, studying the titles in Joyce's extensive professional library while seeking the words he wanted. "I'd like you to hold off on that equipment a while, Joyce. If you have some time tomorrow, drop into my office and give me a rundown on things." He didn't want to make a directive more specific than that in front of Allen Magrue. Nor did he, when Joyce shook her head stubbornly, want to sit down and start all over. This was not the time. "You two can straighten out your area of disagreement without me, though. It doesn't seem too great. I don't think you need me for that."

He was wrong, as it happened. If he had stayed and pressed the issue, he might have gotten to the heart of it. If he had outstayed either of them, he might even have scotched the problem on the spot.

But because he thought he knew what it was, not a disagreement over policy but a veiled battle of wills between two people who were in love and who had the bad luck to be working together, he left them to it.

His reproof to Joyce he would save for her ear alone. Like the White Queen he could believe six impossible things before breakfast. But he could never believe at any time that someone like Joyce would have been rash enough, tactless enough, to announce the subject of her administrative performance project. And, what was infinitely worse, to keep in the school, in an identifiable item like that manila folder, even an enciphered note meant for the diary she was obliged to submit monthly to her advisers at the University.

For in that diary must be entered every aspect of her planning and development of the work she had chosen: everything from an abstract describing its nature and purpose to a highly detailed and subjective—and therefore conceivably damaging—record of her staff, their backgrounds, their personalities, their physical descriptions, and their reactions to her and to each other, particularly where these reactions disclosed weakness of character.

If the material in that diary were read by anyone but Joyce and her advisers, a lot of fur would hit the fan. It had happened once, he remembered, in a school system out West with another degree candidate.

And with David in his enlarged state of tension, and Helen clearly jealous of Allen's attention to Joyce, it could happen here.

I don't mean, he told himself hastily as he entered his office, I don't mean that any of *them* would try to get at that journal! God forbid! he said, crossing his fingers. But Joyce is right about David, and David is right about himself. If what I just saw isn't a bud of paranoia growing on him, then I've never seen one. And I've seen more than one!

There was a serious ramification to the conflict between David and Joyce. If neither would back off and compromise, then one would have to leave. No department could contain such dissension and continue to function. And if their quarrel were not resolved soon, it would spread and infect the rest of the faculty. Ben had seen that, too.

His blood turned to water as he considered the bind every administrator dreads: being forced to choose between two fine if very different and valuable people. He did not want to do it and he did not see how he could. And he knew that he would not be able to dodge it. That Joyce rather than David was more useful to the school was not the point. There were reasons why he needed and wanted them both, and he would have to find the way to keep them both.

One thing was plain. The onus was on Joyce. Her stubbornness was not merely incredible. It was unjustifiable. She had enough support from the others to accomplish her aims without dragging David into something that would obviously destroy him.

Oh god! Ben groaned, half drowned in pity—and self-pity.

He sat down at his desk again to go through his lecture notes, and then he looked at his calendar and felt better. Nothing was going to mar this week's anticipation of the splendid week to follow, he decided on a strong surge of cheerful determination. Nothing was going to keep him from flying to San Francisco. Not Joyce's love affair with Allen Magrue. Nor the fuss created by her graduate work. Nor David's tantrum, which was nothing unusual for David, only just a little more so. Nor the growing absence list because of Asian flu. If necessary he would close the school, declare it a disaster area, and dump it on the Red Cross and the Governor of the Commonwealth. And while he was away, Joyce and Allen could get married and have their honeymoon if they felt like it. Just so long as Joyce was back in school when he was! And she would be, he thought happily, because that's basically the kind of person Joyce is!

Cheerful, smiling, unaware of what was brewing all about him and under his feet, he locked his office door and went home to Jane.

Rain or no rain—and it had begun, a violent full-fledged nor'-easter—he might at least have stopped to get his wife some flowers. It would have solved one of his problems.

But then again, maybe it wouldn't. Jane was pretty determined too.

CHAPTER TWO

The moment Ben left the guidance office the storm broke, howling and whining round the corner room and flinging great ropes of rain against the glass-paneled walls. But the silence between Joyce Bellows and Allen Magrue absorbed all sound, and indeed it separated and enclosed each so completely from the other that they would have been equally warm and dry outside, and as hopelessly alienated.

Within his cocoon Allen was very conscious of his situation. He was tired but his shoulders lifted proudly. He loved and was loved. And in his pocket was an airline reservation dated two weeks from today, along with a document explaining the reason for its purchase. The document had come last Wednesday and he had bought the ticket that night. Childlike (such pleasure did this regular trip give him), he carried document and ticket around for a while before putting them safely away until it was time to leave.

But the ticket would bring him back again, to a world he had chosen in April, lived in happily since July, and come simultaneously to dread and to love three short days before. Rocketing since then on alternating bursts of joy and astounded frustrated anger, he was still without a plan. The ticket and the document had clearly been of no use to him where Joyce was concerned. They had not been acceptable evidence of his probity.

He would have to find something else. Or do something else.

But one thing was certain: He was going to stay in Manton and get married. And he would do his damndest to live happily ever after.

With an enormous effort he forced himself through the wall of silence and regarded Joyce with a bleak smile. "That was a nice touch, Joyce, that pin on your bag. What did you expect me to do when I saw it? Faint? Run out screaming? Fall on my knees and confess all?"

She shook her head reproachfully. "It's been there a long time, Allen."

"Pardon my bluntness. I hate to call a lady a liar but I don't believe you. You made quite a production out of showing it. In all the times you've worn that bag you never pulled a stunt like that before."

"I wasn't sure before. Not until Friday. I told you."

"Oh god! So you found you knew me when! So what? So did a lot of other people. What does it prove? I've got proof, genuine proof—" He took an envelope from his pocket but she waved it away contemptuously.

"We've been through this already, Allen. Talk is cheap. Words are cheap. It isn't what we say that's important, or the official papers we carry. It's our observable behavior that means something. And what I saw you do on Friday with Tony Evans—"

"With—?" His face went blank with thought, and as he recalled the little incident his eyes focused and hardened with baffled fury. "Christ, you're fantastic, Joyce! The kid fell and I caught him. So you put two and two together and get 1944! And two minutes later you tell me to resign or you'll blow the whistle on me. Forget the extenuating circumstances! Forget the hell I went through getting myself cleared away! Forget the fact that the information you had was up to and including my court-martial and you never knew a damn thing after that! You talk about proof! What kind of proof is a lapel device on a handbag?"

"I know what I saw. I know what I know."

"I wonder if you do," he said slowly, eying her with clinical detachment. "I wonder if you really know, deep inside you, Joyce. Not about me. About you. Or is your suspicion of yourself so unbearable that the only way you can handle it is to foist it onto me? To project it, in other words. There's a dangerous and significant aspect to your intransigence, Joyce. People call it paranoia. You've used the word correctly about others."

He said this very gently, inviting her trust while mocking himself for the hope implicit in such a minute effort. For he knew that no therapist, not Freud himself, may entertain optimistic expectations of a patient even after months of careful work. And he knew that a stone wall would have answered him sooner on this or any other private matter. So it did not surprise him when, with no change in her color or manner, without a word, she went into her office to put things away and lock up. He followed her.

"Tell me something, Joyce. If I were to agree to go along with all your graduate work—if I let you come in and evaluate my performance with anyone you like—would it make any difference?"

She said composedly, "Are you suggesting that I'm taking some kind of revenge because I think you're blocking my work?"

"It's a possibility." But he did not believe this.

"Are you actually challenging *my* professional judgment? What none of you seems to realize is that I'm doing something I've thought about for a long time because it needs doing. Of course I'm killing two birds with one stone! But if there weren't any justification for doing the project, I wouldn't do it—doctorate or no doctorate. I'd choose something else. I'd have to. And if I were stubborn enough to try to do it anyway, my advisory committee wouldn't endorse it!"

"What are you getting so touchy about? I know that," he said impatiently. "We all do. That wasn't what I meant."

"I don't care what you meant!"

"Maybe you ought to, Joyce. Because the question should be clarified. For everybody's benefit."

"What question?"

Again he looked at her as though she were a specimen. "The question," he said slowly, "is why are you so frightened? To put it another way, why am I so threatening to you? Or, why is it so necessary to you that I leave?"

She stared at him as if he had said something insane and embarrassingly self-revealing, yet the tears that flooded down her cheeks were entirely for herself. Standing before him like a child who has been harshly and unjustly taken to task, she covered her face with her dainty hands and sobbed.

He watched, fascinated, as she tried to press her misery back into herself. She cried wrenchingly yet tentatively, he thought with pity, like someone who had not cried for many years and had forgotten how.

Presently she turned her back on him and dried her eyes. "I'm sorry but I've had enough! This has become intolerable to me!

Misinterpreting my motives! Questioning my professionalism! Insinuating that I've lost my value! That I can't do my job! No one—*no one!*—has ever treated me like this before!" She swung on him, shouting, "And none of this happened until you came and I remembered what you were—and are! You've poisoned my department! You've worked on David with your boyish charm until he's out of his mind with suspicion of me! You've turned my boys away from me! With your capacity for stirring up argument you've frightened poor Simon away from all my staff meetings! I will not simply stand by and let you destroy me and my work and my staff! How dare you ask me your insulting *quasi*-psychoanalytical questions? I know all I have to know! It's clear to me why you have to leave!"

"Possibly. But there's one thing you don't know," he said calmly. She was like an infuriated mouse in a limitless maze. Deliberately he added another blind alley. "I love Helen and I've asked her to marry me and she said yes."

She blanched and stepped back as if he had struck her. "I don't believe it," she whispered. "She couldn't. She couldn't do this to herself. She doesn't realize—"

"She realizes."

In the space of a moment or two she seemed to have removed herself to an immense distance from him. So profound was her effort at concentration and control that he looked at her and blinked and looked again, surprised by the fact of her physical presence. And then as though nothing unpleasant had passed she gave him a straightforward answer to the question he had asked on following her into her office.

"All right. The answer is no. It's too late. Your arguments were logical, better than David's. But they don't ring true, they're a mask."

"Coming from you that's rich, Joyce. You can clothe your use of your TV and mikes and tape recorder in the finest jargon, but it's all specious and you know it. Because things are slipping away from you, aren't they? And your Big Brother technique, approved and unsuspected by the University, is a last-ditch stand to keep your empire intact."

He was beyond help. She shook her head slightly. "I know your real reason for opposing me. You know why I'm suspicious of you.

That and everything else go together. I don't see how they can be separated. The only thing I can say is that I'm sorry. I've never been sorrier for anything in my life. If you resign, I'll cover for you and I won't say another word to anyone. You can say you've decided—with regrettable tardiness, for which you apologize—to study full-time. You have to sooner or later anyway, it's a University requirement. Otherwise I feel I've no choice. I'll have to inform the Superintendent."

"And when do you plan to do that?"

"Allen, that's up to you." Her lovely voice was filled with sadness. "You know me well enough by now to know I don't like fuss and discussion and exposure. This is inexpressibly distasteful to me."

"To you!" He clutched the shock of hair on his forehead and combed it back nervously with his fingers, making it messier than ever.

For an instant they pleaded silently with each other. But it was utter stalemate: For either to grant the other's wish was to wreak self-destruction.

Then she turned back to her desk and locked away the manila folder containing the diary of her graduate work-in-progress.

"Foolish," he said scornfully. "There must be dynamite in there. Be careful it doesn't blow up in your face."

"It won't be there long. I have an appointment and I don't want to carry it around in all this rain. But whether you believe it or not, there isn't anything in it that's—you know. Even if I weren't going to the University I'd be ready to give Ben my first evaluation of you and Simon and David and—and Helen." A constriction as from pain caused a momentary shift in her features. "I only have to write up the forms. I've discussed the material with each of you. All you have to do is sign them. Naturally yours will indicate your opposition to me."

"What else did you say? That I'm a menace to youth?"

Again she was white with shock. "Oh Allen, do you think I'd do that? Without giving you a chance? Why do you insist on misunderstanding me? All of you! Simon doesn't matter, poor Simon! But David—and *Helen* . . . I don't see what I've done to deserve such treatment from her. After all I've—" She stopped abruptly and shook her head as though to rid it of an unworthy thought.

Then she arranged her face in a brittle smile. "We'd better go, Allen. It's dreadful out. Traffic will be murderous."

He looked at his watch and groaned. "I've got to be at the airport in an hour! God! I'll never make it in that mess!" He went out hastily, saying, "I'll see you tomorrow" as casually as if they were winding up an ordinary meeting and ran to his cubbyhole of an office for his coat and brief case.

A hulking boy in black jacket and high-heeled boots was sitting on the floor, waiting for him. He unlocked the door and yanked his coat off the hook, tearing the loop.

"Sorry, Tim," he said panting. "Not now. I told you I had a meeting and then an appointment. You should've gone home on the bus hours ago. It's a lousy day. Come on, I've got to take off."

"But what she say? What Bellows say when you told her? I ain't lettin' that bitch near me! She ain't gonna muscle in between me 'n you. You tell her I said so?"

Magrue locked the door, then put a hand on the boy's shoulder and shook him playfully. "Look, Tim, just cool it. Don't worry about it. We'll work it out." He hurried to the stairs and the boy gazed after him resentfully.

"Can yuh gimme a ride at least?"

Magrue stopped at the stairway door and turned. For all Tim Lunn's size and defiant dress, he was as lost and defenseless as a baby, as rooted in his misery as if he were standing waist-deep in a bog. Magrue's heart swelled with compassion. He could have become what that boy was now.

He set his brief case down and went back. "I'm going the other way, Tim. Any other day except today. If I didn't have to meet that plane, I'd drive you to Timbuktu! You know that. If you're going to trust me, then trust me. Start now. How about money for a taxi?"

"Nah. I got dough. I'll go see Quinn down cellar. He'll ride me or maybe loan me his car. Or I'll go find Tony. But when'll yuh be here tomorrow?"

"The usual. Hey, give me a break, fella! If I don't get out of here, I won't have time to get back!" He was rewarded by a responsive gleam in the hooded eyes. This time he left without hindrance.

His thick hair was soaked to the scalp before he reached his car, and raindrops stung his cheeks and rolled down onto his shirt collar as he watched Joyce Bellows drive out of the parking lot. His eyes narrowed but he was not too worried yet. He had a few other strings for his bow. If talking with Joyce didn't work, there were other ways to bring her down. Figuratively speaking, he said to himself as he turned on the ignition and wiped his face on his sleeve.

But as he drove away a rhythmical screak—the windshield wipers rubbing along the glass and completing each semicircle with a little thud—sounded contrapuntally to three words lodged in his mind.

Presently he was nodding his head and tapping his fingers to a little song that went: "Bri-i-nngherDOWN, bri-i-nngherDOWN, bri-i-nngherDOWN!"

CHAPTER THREE

Over in Building Two, in the chemistry lab on the second floor, Tony Evans stopped washing the counter, put down his rag as if it were an egg weighing a ton, and listened. All was quiet except for the muffled sounds Mr. Flanagan was making at the other end of the corridor with push broom and trash bin.

Safe.

He unbuttoned his work shirt and took out something that he had wedged uncomfortably between ribs and belt.

It was a large pistol, powerful, black, shining with oil and care. Several small notches on the smooth grip were probably only the result of many years' handling. But the boy preferred to think that each had been made over the dying body of the Enemy—guts falling out, head half blown away—by a coldly steady soldier's hand that knew how to kill and keep score. He wished that his could have been the hand. After all, his best friend Tim Lunn said it was okay to kill people if you were in the army. Maybe. He'd like to believe it. Tim was a creep, though, so maybe he was wrong.

He fondled the ugly weapon, his eyes blank and dreaming, his sensitive fingers seeking out every crevice as he totted up the list of his own enemies and wondered which would get the first notch. . . . When you got right down to it, it wasn't so easy to tell who your enemies were. Take his ol' lady. Or his ol' man, that lousy beerbelly. Or his ol' school shrink, Miss Bellows. One day they were for him, did nice things. Next day they weren't. Lately they seemed more against him, it looked like. He just didn't know. He wasn't sure of anything any more. Except Mr. Quinn, the engineer down cellar, was always good to him. And Mr. Magrue, his new shrink, was real cool. So far, anyways. All depended if he could make Bellows butt out. . . . Well, I'm seein' her in the morning.

I won't *tell* her anything, like before. Only that she's gotta eff off and leave me be.

His hand curved round the grip, his trigger finger stroked the gentle crucial arc lightly, yearningly. He looked down at the hand as if it belonged to someone else. It was a good hand, long and thin but strong, and he liked the way the powerful cords rose so close under the skin and ran down the thumb. A good hand to draw. He ought to of tried it before. Tonight, maybe.

There were fingerprints on the grip and barrel, oily smudges that indefinably reduced the gun to the level of a common tool and robbed it of its significance. He wrapped his cleaning rag around it and polished it, careful of the trigger, and then uncovered it and admired its special beauty.

The rattle of a bucket outside the room jolted him out of his dreaming and he stood rigid with fear and guilt, for a moment unable to think, to hold fast to his plan.

"Hey! You done yet, kid?" the custodian called impatiently.

He couldn't put the gun back inside his shirt, under his belt. His hands wouldn't work and there wasn't time. His jacket pocket wasn't big enough—and anyhow it was down in Mr. Quinn's office closet. His eyes danced crazily, desperate to find a hiding place. His leg pressed against the hoodlike brass handle of the drawer below the counter.

As the custodian came in he was industriously cleaning the countertop, doing his job, scrubbing hard at an ancient stain. And feeling pretty calm too, because in a second he'd take the key and lock up as usual, and that would give him time to go back and open the drawer and get the gun out and shove it in his pants.

"You comin'?"

"Yeah, Flanagan, I'm done, just about." Another careful swipe of the counter.

"*Mr.* Flanagan, *Mr.* Flanagan. And don't you forget it, *Mr.* Tony Evans, or I'll bust your mouth." But the voice was not unkind.

He smiled shyly. "Yeah. I'm sorry. I'm done, Mr. Flanagan. Want I should lock up?"

"No, I'll do it this time. Forgot my brush down the hall again. You get it, I'm pooped. Meet you at the stair."

"But—" and he sagged with alarm. Once the door was locked

he couldn't get back in 'til morning. And for more than one reason he couldn't take the risk.

"You hear me? Get with it, for crissake! It's almost five-thirty." There was nothing he could do. Except get back up here first thing tomorrow before it was too late. Pale and sick with fear, he went past the custodian and down the hall to fetch the brush.

And Flanagan thought, What the hell's buggin' him this time? and shrugged, inspected the room with a glance, and closed and locked the door. Time for supper, beer, see the kids did their homework, and then TV. After a long day what more did a man want to think about?

"You want a ride, kid? Rainin' like a s.o.b.," Flanagan yelled over the noise of the engine room as they approached Quinn's office. A large sturdy table stood outside the door. "Well, well, what's this? Hey, chief, you gettin' new furniture for your home away from home?"

"Why not? I'm gettin' tired of the day-core," the engineer grinned, lying flat on his back on a cot covered with a flowered spread.

The boy slipped in behind Flanagan and took off his chino work clothes. He would have preferred to go home in them, because of the storm, and change to his "good" clothes in the morning, but his mother would kill him if he walked in looking like his old man —a washout, a failure. Money or no money, she didn't want him working down here with the men.

"I got just the word for you, chief," Flanagan said with friendly scorn. "Sybarite." He pronounced it *sigh*-barite, with a certain relish. "Y'oughta be ashamed, a man your age." He picked up a gay but grimy cushion from the cot and bounced it on Quinn's broad chest. "Okay, how about it, kid? You want a ride?"

"Hey wait a minute, Flan," Quinn said getting up hastily. "Would you gimme a hand before you take off? Help me get that table over to Three? I promised Miss Bellows I'd do a job for her when they all cleared out."

"Ah Christ! Can't the kid—"

"I gotta go," the boy said. "If I ain't home by six my ol' lady'll have a fit." She would anyway, he thought hopelessly.

"Even so," said Quinn, "I ain't got a master like you guys do. Listen, Flan, just help me with the table and open her office. You don't have to stay. I'll make sure to lock up. What the hell, another few minutes is all."

"Oh—okay. Got a dolly?"

"In the storeroom. Thanks, Flanagan, you're a sweet kid. Listen, Tony," he said as he went out, "you can leave your sack here if you want."

"I'd rather take it," the boy said, buttoning his shirt. He took a big brown shopping bag out of the closet and set it on the floor. His hands clenched as Flanagan opened it.

"What's this junk?" Flanagan said, poking around. "You an artist?"

"It ain't junk!" But there was a note of pride in his voice as he knotted his tie neatly. "I like t' fool around with paints 'n stuff."

"Heyyyyy! No kiddin'! You got hidden depths, kid. This stuff's not bad!"

"He really is good," Quinn said in a proprietary way as he came back with the dolly. "Okay, Flan, let's go. An' I'll do somethin' for you someday."

"I ain't doin' it for you, yuh lazy lunkhead. Miss Bellows is somethin' else," the custodian laughed as he upended the table onto the dolly. "Okay, kid, see yuh next week or so. Yuh done a good job. Only take my advice and cheer up. Yuh look like death warmed over. Things ain't so bad. Hey! Don't forget your sack!"

"Yeah, Mr. Flanagan. Thanks a lot," the boy muttered. He snatched up the shopping bag and fled. But he did not take the bag home with him. It would be safer in another place.

"What's eatin' him this time?" Quinn yelled, stopping at the storeroom again to get a hammer, nails, and other small tools.

"Who knows? It's up one day, down the next with them kids. He ain't so bad, though," Flanagan yelled back. "What's this table for?"

Quinn, the sybarite, let Flanagan trundle the dolly and went ahead to hold open the heavy door to the quieter section of the basement where were many large shops and workrooms. With the noise of the engine and boiler rooms behind them, it was possible to speak in a normal voice and Quinn told the custodian what he knew of Miss Bellows' plans.

"She'll do anything to help the kids. All that equipment's out of her own pocket too," he said as they approached the door to the south tunnel.

"Christ, I hate this place," Flanagan grumbled.

"You an' everybody else," Quinn agreed, helping him ease the dolly down the steps. "And kids come down here to *neck*, for god-sake!"

Once in the tunnel they could not talk over the reverberating thunder caused by the dolly's bare wheels. Nor did they want to, in this depressing place.

It was painted a dreary gray, filled with stagnant air, and dimly lighted on one side only by small caged bulbs spaced an economical fifteen feet apart. Along the other wall ran a number of pipes encased in insulation resembling orthopedic casts which had, predictably, been punctured by sharp instruments, no doubt for the purpose of relieving intense itching.

Because of its width the tunnel was divided all the way down the middle by a massive supporting structure in the shape of a series of xs. Each apex of the resulting triangles had been filled in for additional strength, leaving square apertures through which even a large body could easily pass from one aisle to the other and which were responsible for the bizarre sound effects created by the dolly.

They sighed with relief as they turned the corner near the other end and went up the ramp into the cafeteria. Timothy Lunn passed them on the stairway to the first floor.

"What's that for?" he said, backing into a corner of the landing to let them pass. He did not offer to help.

"Thanks a lot," Flanagan said sarcastically. Of all the kids Miss Bellows had given into the charge of the maintenance staff, this was one kid he had never cottoned to and never would. Which was a shame, and funny too, because he looked enough like Quinn to really be his son.

"You're gonna be on candid camera, Timmy," Quinn joked. "How'd you like to help me set up?"

Something in Flanagan's expression warned the boy to disclaim curiosity. "Nah," he said. "I'll wait for yuh down cellar," and took the rest of the steps in one graceful bound. He was smoking and reading a magazine when Flanagan came down again, looked in suspiciously, said good night, and went out into the rain.

Then he ran all the way back through the tunnel and up to Miss Bellows' office in Building Three to make himself useful to Thomas Quinn. He began by pointing out that the door could be opened or locked by adjusting the buttons under the latch as well as by a key, which presented cheering possibilities. "Boy! I'd like to get in them files someday!" he said, eying the confidential record cabinets hungrily.

"So wouldn't I!" Quinn laughed, making a joke out of it. "Must be some red-hot readin', way you kids talk." Privately, though, he was worried about what was in Tim's file. Tony's too. Or rather, what was in them that he didn't know about. Miss Bellows had discussed some of the boys' difficulties with him, in fact she had clued him in on all the boys who worked part time with the maintenance staff so that their efforts at rehabilitation would be coordinated. But sometimes he wondered if all the things he did were right. "C'mon, Tim, hold this roll of wire. Pay 'er out slow while I staple."

Little by little the boy became deeply alarmed by the implications contained in the microphone wire Quinn was tacking up from each counseling cubicle to the control panel on the new table behind Miss Bellows' desk. He knew about the equipment, of course. Quinn had told him it was coming, and Allen Magrue had explained further and had reassured him that its use would be entirely optional. But Miss Bellows had told him otherwise, whereupon he had threatened to withdraw altogether from counseling. It looked now as though she was going to win out. The reality in what he was doing had a lot more punch than Mr. Magrue's "I'll talk with her again" routine.

So what am I gonna do now? he asked himself. But Quinn kept him too busy to think clearly, and he was in any case too scared and angry to think at all. When the job was finished he hustled the empty cartons into the corridor and anxiously watched Quinn fuss with the latch and close the door as though the engineer was creating a permanent barrier between him and the new equipment that menaced his safety and his future. He met Quinn's fatherly chitchat with surly grunts, and for ten minutes after they returned to Quinn's office he brooded and said nothing at all.

And Thomas Quinn, chief engineer first class, who had only moments ago talked himself out of worrying needlessly, began to worry again, starting with Tim Lunn and going on into everything else.

For a long time things had gone along fine for him. Clear sailing. Good berth here. Less work all the time (the job he had just done for Miss Bellows was child's play, and a personal favor anyway). A crew of pretty good kids—surrogates, Miss Bellows called them, for the sons he'd never had—to help shape up into decent able-bodied men. And himself a surrogate too, a father figure, she'd said, to fill in for dead ones or for ones who'd jumped ship (like Timmy's old man) or for the worst ones of all, the fathers still present and listed on the family manifest (like Tony's) but absent all the same.

And then the bastards down Town Hall had fouled him up but good. They were right to save dough where they could by closing down the school's generator and plugging into Edison, so that what remained in operation in the engine room no longer justified their keeping someone of his high rank and pay. He'd said so himself a few years back when the change-over was first discussed. No one could say he didn't know his job and wasn't a fair-minded man besides. And they'd been fair too, giving him time to look for another berth, with full pay the past month in view of his extra service with the kids. Now if they'd just change their minds and grant his appeal to stay aboard at his current rank and pay! Sure, he could take a cut in both and stay on. He had the seniority. They could bump one of the second-class engineers. Only, he wasn't alone now—if you counted the kids as family—and he couldn't afford it. And if he left he'd be alone again, and a man nearing sixty didn't want to be alone any more. And kids were kids. If he went someplace else they'd forget him, they'd stop coming after a bit, it'd be too much trouble to manage the money and transportation to look him up in a new job. But the way it was now, he was mostly always on watch and available, or else in his little apartment nearby, and they went with him places. And sometimes for a special treat when they'd been really good he'd give them the keys and money for gas and tell them, like a father would, to drive careful and have a good time.

He sighed heavily. Nobody could say love (in its broad clinical sense, Miss Bellows said) was enough.

"Hey, Pop. Awright with you I take the car this Saturday?"

There! You see? On x number of dollars less a week he'd have to stop being so openhanded.

"What you got in mind, Timmy?"

"Nuttin' much. I and Tony thought we'd go see a show. Maybe go down the new Government Center in town." After a pause he ventured, "Wanna come? It's gettin' colder now." Calling Quinn *Pop* always got a little more out of him, and reminding him of physical discomfort was sure to keep him home. Not that he wasn't a good Joe, and Tim liked him about as well as he could like anybody. But it was more fun alone with Tony, and anyways Tony wasn't being his old self last few days. Magrue wasn't going to win over Bellows now, no matter what he said, because she could listen in on anything over them mikes up there. And then do whatever she wanted. *If I come there any more, which I won't, and Tony neither.* The thing was to get Tony away awhile from the school and Quinn and Bellows and even that goddam bag of his, and work on him some more so they could go ahead with the plan. He grinned a sly malicious grin and Quinn looked at him sharply. He changed his expression but it was too late.

Quinn wasn't having any of his ingenuous face. "You goin' shootin'?" he said severely.

"No! Honest!" He was, too. His .22 rifle had to be kept at the Rod and Gun Club where he could use it only when one of the members had time for him, which wasn't often. At least the police hadn't taken it away altogether, after catching him with it on the street last year. He'd had Quinn and Bellows to thank for that.

"You promised."

"So I promised!"

"You about to go back on your word to me, Timmy? You thinkin' of sneakin' that rifle out without permission?"

"Aaaaaah!"

"This is important, son. You gave your solemn word."

He hated it when the ol' man gave out with the Christer crap. "What's it *to* yuh?" he said angrily.

Unwisely, because he was worried, Quinn lost his temper too. "Whaddyuh mean, what's it *to* me? You know damn well. I promised Miss Bellows last year we'd work together on this gun thing. She could make it hot for me if there's any more of it. An' you know goddam well now isn't the time for me to get fouled up. I got my job to think about, even if you don't."

"That lousy bitch! She's tryin' to wreck me. Me and Tony both, that bitch!"

"You know why. You keep on the way you were, she'll have to take steps. An' she can, too, even if you're goin' to Mr. Magrue now. She's the boss."

"I'd kill her first," the boy muttered. "*I* got what it takes."

He did, too. Gun or no gun, he was as strong as an ox and as agile as a cat.

"You don't mean that. If it wasn't for all she done for you, you wouldn't be sittin' here now, you punk kid. You think every school runs like this one does? I got friends in some, and I know they don't. Kid steps over the line and first thing you know, he's in the brig. An' for what you tried to pull off that time you 'n your bunch jumped me in the tunnel, horsin' around, vandalizin'—"

"I been goin' straight and that bitch knows it. She's just out to get me. Pesterin' all the time. But there's nuttin' she can do t' *me* an' she better not try! An' *you* better not either! You say one word to her about my *attitude*"—he was fed up to there, hearing about his attitude—"and I'll have somethin' to say to her too. 'Bout that gun you got in your desk. I know all about that deal."

Quinn's mouth was dry. "You ever say anything to her in one a your sessions? Or to Mr. Magrue?"

"No. 'Course I dunno what she put down afterward. Boy, I'd like to read her stuff! Magrue he don't put nuttin' down. He promised. But that bitch is all the time carryin' her notes around!"

"What about Tony? He say anything?"

"I ain't sure. Gimme the car Saturday an' I'll get the chanst to find out." His tone was deliberately pacific now. There was a lot at stake. He even managed a smile.

"We'll see. How about it, son? Do your best, rest of the week, and then we'll see. Okay?"

He's practically beggin' me, he's so scared, the boy thought, savoring his power. "Okay," he said quietly, adding for good measure, "listen, Pop, I'm sorry I got sore. I didn't mean it." But he couldn't keep *this* up much longer. He rose to leave.

"Okay, son, I believe you. Where you off to?"

Jesus! Same as Bellows! He said, "Maybe over Tony's. You leavin'?"

"Can't tonight. Late shift."

"See yuh then."

"See yuh, Tim boy."

After the boy had left Thomas Quinn opened the bottom drawer of his battered old desk. I should of taken it home long ago, he told himself, reaching down and feeling around in the clutter. I can't afford a mess like this. I must of been crazy.

But the gun was gone. He took everything out of the drawer and then emptied all the others and then he turned the whole office upside down. But the gun was gone.

"Well, looka choo! Don't tell me yuh workin' for a change!" This was Rocco Tomasello, the school's chief custodian, on his way out through the engine room to the back parking lot.

"Aaaaaah, eff off, Tomasello!" Quinn said furiously.

The Roc's fuse, always smoldering, ignited the main charge in fine style. "Yah!" he jeered. "Yuh lazy bastid, wit' yuh cot 'n pillers 'n blankets 'n percolator 'n hot plate 'n ice chest 'n radio— an' yuh hands onna machines an' yuh head up yuh t'roat! A little honest work'ld kill yuh!" and took his virtuous way home after a day's toil that would have felled another man half his age and twice his size and three times his strength.

Thomas Quinn sat in the mess in his cozy nest in the cellar, his big body slack with something close to terror, his pale skin green. What was he going to do now? Selling Tony Evans a pistol had been just another of his well-intentioned bribes, material proof of his trust and affection for one of "his" boys. If any of this got out, he'd be sunk. And it wouldn't be Town Hall or the school department who'd torpedo him, either.

It would be little tiny Miss Bellows, head of guidance. Funny, when you thought what a very fine gal she was, to realize that you hung between her and the deep blue sea. And she'd do it, she would have to tell on him, because it was right. She wouldn't be what she was if she didn't. He accepted this because it was true. In her place he would do it himself.

But it was equally true that he would have to keep her from doing it.

Helen Chadwick put down the potato peeler and picked up the telephone—and instantly burst into flame, glowing like a human votive candle. "Darling!"

"None other!" said Allen Magrue. "Look, sweet, will you be disappointed if we can't make it? Don's plane is half an hour late and he won't be landing for another twenty minutes, but his Nashville flight is supposed to take off on time because of the weather pattern. I just checked. We wouldn't have time to come home and eat with you and get back. Have you done much yet?"

"No, darling, it's only steak."

"Save it for tomorrow then. Damn it, now I'm sorry you didn't come with me although not even a house fly should be out in this muck! My big brother didn't have to eat your cooking to know how wonderful you are. He could have found out just as easily at the restaurant here."

"I'll meet them all at Christmastime. Besides, it's just as well for your sake. You'll have enough to talk about without my being there. Is there—is there anything he could do?"

"I doubt it. He's more of an engineer than a lawyer these days. But he may have an idea or two. It'll be all right, sweet, we'll make it. One way or another," he added grimly.

"I put my foot in my mouth this afternoon, Allen. I almost blew it. But I just couldn't bear it! You were so reasonable about the whole thing. So fair and logical. I'm sure Ben thought so too. And the way she—she sat there rattling her saber! All of a sudden I was terribly scared. And the funny thing is, I'm not even sure why."

"Well, I am. I think I am, anyway. I'll tell you later. I want to mull it over some more. But everyone thinks you have flu—except Joyce. I told her about us. We had a little talk after David and Ben left."

"Oh darling! Was that wise?"

"I don't think it matters any more. Anyway, I had an idea and I thought it was as good a time as any to try it out."

"Oh Allen, do you really think she's written about—about you in that journal?"

"No. She doesn't want to tell anybody. Herself last of all. She said the next move was up to me, and I believe her. The damnable irony is that she's really a very wonderful gal! No, she wouldn't consciously lie about anything and certainly not about that. David's the one who's terrified. He tried to pass his anger off as a joke but that manila folder of hers is an intolerable threat to his position. I'm just the middle man who made it all happen. It would've happened eventually anyway, from what I see. But God knows what he'll do if she doesn't shut up about that journal and take it home!"

"Can't you talk to him, darling?"

"I've tried but he's literally unable to believe me. He'll get mad at me too if I say any more. The more she pushes, the more he does. Sort of on the principle that it takes one to know one," he said dejectedly.

"One what? You're being very cryptic."

He hesitated, and she knew that his face had gone taut with distress, that he was greathearted enough to have charity for those who believed him to be the cause of their suffering. And indeed he was. Only last Friday he had said so, and he had just said it again. She didn't understand it. "Never mind, darling, forget I asked," she said quickly. "Tell me some other time. I just wish—"

"Your every wish is my command, fair lady."

"I was only going to say I wish I knew as much as you do."

"Sometimes I wish I *didn't!* It's not easy to be a single-minded vengeful bastard when you're stuck with the *gestalt* of a problem! Look, sweet, I've got to hang up. This place is a madhouse. Four people are lined up waiting for me to get out. What do they care how much I love you—and want you! Damn! I'll call you later if I can."

She held the warm solid receiver as though it were his hand and then reluctantly cradled it and put the steak away. But she did not mind. It was one of the last solitary meals she would give herself, there would be only a few more. She laughed softly as her capable hands went about their business without any help from her, leaving her mind free to count the remaining weeks. She felt cushioned in love, and love was all the sweeter for having come so late. Not even the horrible dreams she had dreamed for three days could spoil it, nor could all the blood she had spilled in them violate it.

Allen.

It had happened so fast. It had begun in the last place that any teacher would have expected. You welcomed the newcomers and talked shop and ate the obligatory hot dog and potato chips and never dreamed that Ben's annual ice-breaking August picnic was about to prove any different from the others. A staff party was a staff party even if Ben and Jane Louis gave it.

(She laughed with wry affection. Ben would have canceled not only the picnic but the whole school year if he'd so much as suspected the least hitch in his jealous plans for his staff.)

No trumpets had blared, no rockets had gone off on the instant of their meeting. What had happened had been more reassuring and more satisfying—a quiet mutual recognition of the significance and the necessity of each for the other. That was all. And this awareness, this shared sense of discovery had grown steadily, without one word of love spoken or vow offered. . . .

Until last Friday.

Just as well that their offices and classrooms were in separate buildings, and that they did not meet too often in the guidance office: Professional behavior was a value in itself and came before anything else including professional competence. Knowing now why Joyce had been looking cross-eyed at Allen since the picnic, she was glad that they had been so discreet.

She supposed she ought to be grateful to Joyce for having brought them together all the sooner and beyond any question of separation. Barring death, of course. It would have happened in happier circumstances, perhaps—she had a feeling about this after they had traced together the various happenstances that had led him to Manton—but nevertheless it had happened, because of Joyce. . . .

She had had to pass the door of Allen's little office in Building Three last Friday. He was sitting at his desk, blind with misery, deaf to her greeting or the sound of her characteristic slow step which he had very soon distinguished from hundreds of others. And she had decided to risk the speculation and gossip of the bystanders by going in and closing the door. And listening.

And when she had come out again, she was engaged to be married on Thanksgiving Day, and heartsick and incredulous at what she had been told.

Still, it was with a measure of serene faith that she looked ahead to her life with Allen. But she was not placid. A good teacher is by definition anything but placid, and Helen was an excellent science teacher. And, being one, she was well acquainted with synergism: She and Allen together could accomplish more than the sum of what either could do singly to destroy the threat to their happiness.

Joyce had not entered that threat in her private journal or on the school evaluation form or—as yet—on any other piece of paper. But she had fastened it inside the flap of her expensive handbag.

The question is, Helen said to herself, what are Allen and I going to do about it?

"I don't like this," said Dr. Muir. His spare face sharpened with concern and his neat pointed beard quivered as he examined the graphic record of Simon Wills's tiring heart. "What have you been up to?" He looked like a Velasquez model, a seventeenth-century Spanish grandee, and the upcountry twang that came out of his patrician head was startlingly incongruous. At his nod the nurse removed the electrodes from Simon's chest, helped him up, and left the room.

Simon shook his head and put on his shirt.

"Explain this then!" the doctor challenged, flapping the graph at him.

Simon shrugged. "If I were doing any less, I'd—I might as well be—out altogether."

"'Tisn't work I'm talking about! My word, no one ever died of work in your line! It's attitudes—if you don't mind my borrowing from your professional vocabulary!"

"Not at all. Go right ahead."

"I don't like your sarcasm—or your self-pity!" Muir snapped. "And I don't like the choices you're making. You say Joyce Bellows is making demeaning remarks about you. You're a bleeding heart for boys you won't even work with. You want to round out thirty years of service for a few extra retirement dollars you won't even live to enjoy at this rate! You've chosen to stick with a job—under a woman you've come to hate—that frustrates and upsets you at every turn. My word, Simon! Never mind whether she's right or she's wrong. What matters is that you're in the wrong place if she can strip you so easily of your self-esteem. Or if you think she can. Find something that fits your age and your needs, Simon! Resign now, or your stubbornness will make Lydia a widow in six months!"

"If I quit, how many years will you give me? Provided I have that bedside manner of yours to ease me over the rough spots!" Simon said quizzically.

"You want a guarantee? Bah! Besides, patients like you don't deserve any bedside manner!"

Simon laughed. Ethan Muir's bedside manner consisted of the verbal equivalent of sandpaper and a bull whip. But he said seriously, "If I quit now, I'd be dead in a month and you know it. No, Ethan. You may be right and I'm a stubborn old fool. Even Joyce may be right and I'm a useless one. But I'll stay with the school even if I die in it—and I probably will! That coronary and then the pneumonia I had cost me a hell of a lot over and above my medical insurance, and every week that I can hang onto the job will help Lydia when I'm gone. She deserves it—I've given her little enough all these years—and it'll be better for her than having me underfoot all day long if I resign now. But I'll tell you something. The satisfaction I get from knowing how Joyce feels about my continuing presence is better than medicine."

"How do you know how she feels? In my view you haven't the perception of a two-year-old!"

"That's nice to know. Put it on my tombstone, Eth'. But Joyce is so infuriatingly sure of herself about most things that it's—shall I say heartening?—to see her sweat for a change between humane feeling for my situation, expressed in her inimitably charitable way, and annoyance because covering for me isn't 'professional.'"

"Well then, put her out of her misery!" said Muir, sitting down to make an entry in Simon's folder. "Resign."

"I'll give it some thought," Simon promised equivocally, and left.

David Ross announced his homecoming with a vicious slam of the front door that sent his children scurrying for cover.

"Oh god! Dr. JekyllandHyde is here!" Flo Ross murmured and poured bourbon into a tall glass. For fifteen years she had handled everything like a top sergeant blessed with the disposition of a saint. If not for her, David's stomach would be as full of holes as a strainer, his children all to pieces, his marriage a shambles, his career at a dead end. She smiled complacently, put his highball on the table beside his favorite chair, and gave him a motherly kiss.

"How did the meeting go?" she said, settling her plump comfortable body on the couch. "Dinner can wait 'til you unwind."

"The meeting was rotten! Ben agrees with me, I'm sure of that."

"Of course he does. You've been right all along."

"Damn right I'm right! And Allen's on my side—more or less—and so is Helen. Simon doesn't care about anything except holding onto himself for one more year."

"Then it's all settled?"

"Not the way you think. Joyce has the bit in her teeth. I've never seen her like this before. There's something—I don't know what it is, and it's driving me nuts! Allen looks at her with those bedroom eyes and she blushes like a kid and they're still on opposite sides of the fence! Neither one will give in about those boys I told you about."

"It's love. And about time too."

"I'm all for it, hon, but what's happening to *me* meanwhile? I feel I'm being sacrificed on the altar of her ambition! She's always gotten her own way before—very nicely too. You couldn't turn her down on anything without feeling like a coldhearted brute. She's a power-wielder *par excellence*. There's nobody in her class except Ben. But lately . . . I don't know what it is. She's just —different, that's all. God, I feel lousy!"

She stroked his hair and went back to the kitchen. The whole business bored her to tears. "I'll get things ready, sweetie. I don't care what you say. You look better already."

"But what am I going to *do*? Tomorrow she'll have that goddam equipment set up and I'll be evaluated and supervised right out of the guidance department!" He got up and followed her, waiting for some sort of direction. In a moment he had it although he didn't immediately recognize it for what it was.

"There are other schools," she said.

"Not here there aren't. I've no intention of commuting and buying a second car. We can't afford it and we don't need it, not when we live close enough to school for me to walk every day. And we aren't moving. I like it here. And I'm not giving up my seniority. And I won't work for anyone but Ben and Bert Shrag. Bert's the best science man in New England."

"But you could be science department head up in—"

"I *told* you, Flo! Their salary schedule's way lower than Manton's. I'll always make more with my split program here than I would as department head in that jerkwater town! We can't afford it, and I wouldn't go even if they did offer me more money. Everything's the way I want it here. It was, anyway, until Joyce started her doctoral project. Why the hell didn't she do a research thesis instead!"

"Well, why didn't she?"

"Because it's more interesting this way, she says. Never mind that she's *been* administrating all these years! She wants to show her committee just how well she can solve staff problems, set up new programs, all that jazz. Then, as Ben says, she can be a principal too! Or a superintendent, even!"

"Well, when she marries Allen, we'll all be happy."

"I don't think so. She's not the type to bow out. Maybe twenty years ago. But even then I'd doubt it. Joyce likes to control things. A house and kids wouldn't give her enough scope. I'll tell you something, though. If she ever pushed kids of her own the way she's pushing a few at school, she'd get the same results their parents have now! Still . . . she's so damn good and she knows so damn much that she *must* have an ironclad reason for doing what she's doing. That's driving me nuts too! If it were anybody else, I'd say she was using damned poor technique. . . ."

"I'm glad our Ricky doesn't have anything to do with that gang. Tony Evans and his cronies . . . still and all, they're Allen's concern now, aren't they?" she said, carving turkey as competently as a chef.

"As his counselees they are. As a matter of department policy— well, the outcome of that battle affects all of us. There won't be any battle anyway. She said in front of all of them that I'd have to go along—*or else!* My whole world is falling apart!" He was more petulant now than bitter.

She thought he was being childish. Why couldn't he learn to compromise? You couldn't always have your own way. David talking about Joyce like that was the same as the pot calling the kettle black. Her mouth watered as she arranged the turkey slices on the platter. Fresh-killed fowl beat everything and when it was time to eat, you put everything out of your mind and ate. She laughed the problem away. "Oh well, maybe she'll be hit by a truck, hon. Or—

what's that expression Ricky learned in English? Something about hoisting something?"

He had looked up the quotation rather than ask Allen for an explication on *Hamlet* as well as Freud, and explained it to her.

She looked dubious. "I don't think that applies to Joyce, hon. How could someone as lovely as she is cook her own goose?"

"It applies to everyone," he said sententiously. "Given the right combination of circumstances." He nibbled a bit of turkey meditatively. "The question is, how can I help her do it?"

She reproved him with a quizzical motherly look.

"Oh, in a manner of speaking, I mean! Joyce is too nice to be done in. I'll work something out somehow. Think I'll see Ben in the morning. Come on, let's eat. I'll call the kids."

By the time he went upstairs to bed he felt reasonably calm. But always at the back of his mind was the half-serious question he had posed in the kitchen. In what way could he help Joyce to defeat her purpose so that he might preserve his own? Was there a way?

There must be a way!

Slowly through the early hours of sleep a part of his mind grappled with the problem. He dreamed of Achilles' heels and belling the cat. He played Red Rover Come Over, but Joyce wouldn't come over and somebody—some unrecognizable figure— hoisted her onto a petard shaped like a matchbook and carried her over. And then Allen said, "*Her* goose is cooked!" And when he looked at her he saw that she had plainly been done in. And then Flo elbowed him aside, said, "Oh perfect! She's done just right!" and began to carve neat slices.

He awoke sweating freely and tiptoed downstairs for bourbon and a cigarette. But as he poised the whiskey bottle over the glass, the intuition that had wakened him and then slipped away now teased the edge of his mind again.

He could not explain it, or the plan it suggested, or precisely what his part in it should be. But all at once he thought he knew where the key to Joyce's downfall lay.

The inexplicable sense of triumph that filled him—inexplicable because it too derived from his limited background and understanding—was immediately followed by a surge of anger that seemed to corrode his bowels. He corked the bottle and dosed himself with bicarbonate instead, but presently he was bent in half, grunting with pain.

To sleep now was impossible. Restlessly he turned the pages of the evening paper and read without comprehending a word. An ancient horror movie on television was not bad enough to be good. He switched off the set as though it were at fault and padded silently about the living room, a hand over the fire in his belly. The clock on the mantel ticked off the minutes of sleep that he was missing but the last thing he could have done now was to lie down and let the pain engulf him. If he could walk—or, better, jog. Loosen up.

In the rain?

Why not. He wasn't going to melt!

He went quietly down cellar for his work pants and old sneakers, put a hooded poncho over his pajama top, and let himself out the back door.

When he returned, there were three hours left to this extraordinary night. He crept into bed like a thief and listened to his wife's heavy breathing.

Yet, when he came down for breakfast, Flo said, "Well, baby, things can't be as bad as you said. You were sleeping with a smile on your face."

He could not understand that either, because of the thoughts he now harbored and the measures he had taken to ease his pain so that he could fall asleep at last.

CHAPTER FOUR

Allen Magrue left the phone booth and ran through the crowded terminal to the Gate 6 waiting room. He could run for the next twenty minutes and not expedite the holding pattern of the planes stacked up in the dismal sky. But walking was out of the question. In spite of everything he was too excited and happy to walk or to sit down and read or to buy another drink at the airport bar. He stared out of the window, panting from his run, sweating a little, hearing the circling planes roaring like infuriated bees denied safe entry to the hive. But all he could see was himself, crying, as by a trick of the lights the raindrops seemed to dribble down his cheeks.

He smiled sadly. Joyce would love to see him cry, in a manner of speaking. She would wish him to be contrite, frightened, a suppliant. A whipped dog, leaving belly to the ground. Then she would be safe again. But on another, deeper level she would want him to stay and go on working—successfully, of course, as he had been doing. For his success would validate her own, and she would still be safe. Safer, perhaps. He wasn't sure yet, and he might never know. It would depend on what happened in the next few days. Maybe.

But never mind her now! he told himself. The important thing was that despite the meeting and Tim Lunn holding him up and the storm and the traffic, he had been inside the terminal two minutes before Don's original time of arrival. *He* wasn't the one keeping Don waiting! It would have been inexcusable of him, no matter what the reason, after all the trouble Don had taken, spending extra time and money on this dogleg to Boston just to see him for a couple of hours.

He had been late so many times before. Always he had been the

last one, tagging behind, disorganized. And like the boys he counseled now, operating on an undercurrent of diffuse anger that had
colored everything he did and said and was. But for minor dif-
ferences like dress and speech he might very well, he thought
again, be what Tim Lunn and Tony Evans were now.

But he had not been late or angry for a long time. And he never
would be again. Except for Joyce. Except for her. But that was different! Forget her now! He squared his slumping shoulders and
straightened his collar and tie.

A sense of extraordinary joy filled him. Helen's voice was still
in his ear, and Don was coming. For a little while he forgot everything else. He even stopped thinking. He only stood there and
gave himself up to happiness.

The woman watching him from behind a pillar would never
have guessed as much, for he kept mopping his face with a
wrinkled handkerchief and glancing at his watch, breathing quick
shallow breaths as if he were deeply agitated.

He *is* an attractive man, Joyce Bellows thought regretfully, peek-
ing round at him. I've never denied it.

But now her soft virgin lips thinned as she looked at him and
wondered what sort of person he was meeting. Whoever he is, she
thought, I hope he gets in here before Grace does so that I can
get a look at him. She knew beyond question that Allen Magrue
was waiting for a man, and if she were right (and she almost always was!) she would write to the Superintendent tonight or tomorrow. She had put it off too long out of a grossly unprofessional
desire to be kind and fair. In this instance she had been wrong.
But she would not mail the letter without showing it to Allen
first. She owed him that. It was the *correct* thing to do.

She would have to tell Helen Chadwick too. It meant breaking
her word to Allen, but in the circumstances she could hardly allow
Helen to be duped and hurt by this charming liar. What she had
to say was not, after all, casual malicious gossip. To keep it to herself was to be not honorable and discreet but guilty of deserting a
treasured friend.

She decided to lose no time calling Helen. Allen's back was
turned. She slipped away from the pillar and melted into the tide
of people which swept her away and deposited her in the lee of a
booth. She closed the door and sat down gratefully, feeling light-

headed and rubber-kneed. Her head ached and she leaned back, glad to be so safely isolated for this moment of rest. Then she put a coin into the slot and dialed briskly.

"Helen? It's Joyce. I was worried about you but I couldn't call before. Are you feeling better?"

"Why—yes thanks, Joyce," Helen said warily. "I'm—I'm sorry about this afternoon. I must have sounded unstrung. I hope I'm not coming down with flu. It was nice of you to call." It was abrupt, even ungracious, but it was the best she could offer.

"You don't sound at all your usual self. I want you to stay home tomorrow just to be on the safe side. You may want to anyway when I—"

"When you what? What is it, Joyce?"

"I've something upsetting to tell you. I don't know quite how to say it. I wouldn't hurt you for the world, Helen. But if I stand by and say nothing, I could hurt you more cruelly by—by default. . . ." She paused and took a deep breath. "Allen told me after the meeting that you're going to marry him. I can't let you do it, Helen. I can't let you do this to yourself!"

Helen stared at the telephone.

"Helen? Are you there? Helen?"

"Yes. I'm—still here. I think I know what you're going to say. But please don't say any more."

"But I must! I can imagine how you feel—"

"Can you?"

"—but disappointment now is better than heartbreak later. You see, I know all about Allen—"

"Do you? What makes you think I don't?"

"But—"

"Joyce, please don't say any more. We've been friends for a long time. Don't spoil it. We'd both lose too much."

"I'm only thinking of what's best for you!" Joyce said angrily. "I've only got your best interests at heart!"

"If you have, then drop it. Oh damn! My supper's burning! Look, I've got to hang up, Joyce. I'll—I'll see you tomorrow." Her heart was pounding but she smiled faintly as she looked again at the tuna fish sandwich on the table. Even Joyce couldn't have ended a fantastic conversation like this one more tactfully and quickly.

Presently the smile faded along with her anger and resentment as she began to reflect on Joyce not as friend or superior or even as a menace, but as a fascinating clinical puzzle to which Allen thought he had the solution. But she could make nothing of it. Indeed she could hardly articulate the general observations with which all case studies begin. Detachment was difficult because she was too close to Joyce in one way and too close to Allen in another.

Patiently she put the matter aside and ate her simple meal and waited for Allen to call. Or to come.

Her heart began to pound again, with happiness.

Balked again, hurt, and angry, Joyce went back to her pillar and looked for Allen Magrue. He was moving restlessly through a gathering crowd although the plane had finally landed and was rolling toward its stand. When it came to rest and the staircase was wheeled out to its open door, he looked round impatiently (guiltily, she judged) and went back to the window.

She withdrew behind the pillar, looking flushed and lovely and feeling dizzy and nauseous. Someone hurrying by pushed her roughly against the pillar, then lost his balance and fell, grabbing her sleeve to steady himself. She stumbled and turned irritably at the touch of the strange hand.

"Sorry, young lady! That was a chain reac—Joyce!" Painfully he got to his feet. "Uh-oh! Done it again! Back's out!"

"Why, Zachary! Of all people! I've been trying to catch you for two days—but not like this! Are you all right? Oh, your poor back! I'm so sorry."

He was a rotund elfin-faced little creature only a few inches taller than she, with an infectious rippling laugh and a merry grin that showed the space between his front teeth. If he were cast in a movie as Dr. Zachary Inman, University professor of abnormal psychology and a psychiatrist of note, which is who and what he was, he would be panned as the only unbelievable actor, and he would laugh and agree. He himself had said once that he looked like a grocer out of Malamud by Bellow and that this was the secret of his success.

He giggled now as though everything—the terminal, the storm, meeting his old student, his slipped disc, his pain—were a vast fantastic joke, and she laughed with him although she wished that he had not come. She stepped back to look again at Allen Magrue, and the doctor, an insatiably curious character, forgot his pain long enough to follow the direction of her gaze while marking its intensity.

"That's Magrue, isn't it?" he said, standing on tiptoe to make sure. "Hmph!" he snorted in E flat. "Small world. He's a good man, Joyce, a very able guy. We're lucky all around. You've got him on your staff, I've got him in class, and all of us have him in Manton. His background's tremendous, better than yours. You're both overtrained for a high school—if that's possible, which I doubt. Why don't you two latch onto my clinic? We could use people like you." And I could keep an eye on you, he said to himself. There was something disconcerting about her these days.

"Thanks, Zachary," she said so coldly that his eyes nearly popped out of his skull.

"What's buggin' you, gal?"

"Nothing I can't handle. I wanted to talk to you about—about something, but I changed my mind. Allen's yours for the asking, as far as I'm concerned. As a patient."

He snorted a third higher. "You diagnosing again? Or did the lecherous sonuvabitch make a pass at you?"

"Oh, Zachary! Don't be absurd! And I don't have to diagnose him. He'll do it himself—unwittingly—if you take time to watch him."

"I don't have the time. And I happen to know he doesn't need it anyway. Look, I'm here to personally escort a visiting fireman to an all-night rap. Call me at my office at eleven tomorrow. Okay? You'll call?" He looked like a worried gnome.

"I'll try."

"Hmph! If you'll take my advice—which you won't, you never have—you'll stay in bed tomorrow. I don't like the way you look. 'Bye." And he limped away, massaging his spine.

She was glad of his characteristically abrupt departure, for now the passengers were pushing and shoving in out of the rain. She came round the pillar just in time to see Allen Magrue throw his arms about an older man and hug him. And then they were pounding each other on the back and, finally, shaking hands. Their faces glowed. As they turned, arm in arm, Allen saw Joyce and stopped in dismay.

"Well, for godsake, Joyce! Why didn't you say something! I didn't know you were coming here too! This is—"

She paid no attention to the other man. Her pretty lips were tight, her eyes hard. "There was no reason to, Allen. We certainly couldn't have gone together, and in any case I had—have my own plans." And then she was interrupted in her turn as a voice behind her shouted her name.

"Let's go," Allen murmured to his brother and steered him hastily away.

"Good-looking gal. Who is she?"

"A mixed-up dangerous gold-plated bitch. And my boss. Tell you when we're out of this jam."

"Joyce! Darling!" said Grace Wickham, hugging her younger sister. "What an adorable man! The one with the hair in his eyes. You haven't told me about him. Oh, I'm so glad to see you!" She paused, scrutinized Joyce with a maternal eye, and put a practiced hand on her forehead. "Hot. I thought so. Something's the matter even if you aren't going to tell me. I don't like the way you look at all. It's a good thing I came."

"I'm glad too, Grace. Come on, let's get your bag. It's late. As a matter of fact I don't feel quite right. Half the school was absent today. I may have caught the bug too."

The ready admission of something even this personal startled them both.

CHAPTER FIVE

Two of the school's travel planners missed the boat on Tuesday morning. Because of the heavy rain which had not abated in fourteen hours, Tony Evans' bus arrived late at his corner and by the time he reached the lab in which he had left the gun, the door was shut on a busy class. Sick with fear, he cut his appointment with Joyce Bellows and all his classes and spent the morning shuddering in the plenum chamber.

What with the Ford's wet plugs and flooded carburetor (which never worked any better on a fine summer day), Ben Louis was also delayed in getting over to that same lab for the information he needed from Bert Shrag, the school's walking encyclopedia of science. Better to wait 'til class is over, he decided, and began writing the speech he was going to deliver in San Francisco.

But Joyce Bellows had been very much beforehand. As feverish from determination as from Asian flu, she put under the main office door five copies of a memo she had written the night before and was up in her office at seven-thirty to inspect the installation of her equipment.

Excited but shivering in her wet coat, she looked into each counseling cubicle and saw that Tom Quinn had done a praiseworthy job. The yards and yards of microphone wire were almost invisible, and the microphones so discreetly placed that they could not possibly upset either party to a therapeutic session. Miss Bellows thought so, anyway.

She hung her coat and severely tailored suit jacket in the closet and continued her inspection.

On the large table that Quinn and Flanagan had put behind her desk were the audio and video recorders and their control panels. As agreed, Quinn had left Cubicle One's audio tape on

In-Put but rewound it to signal that he had tested the microphones and found them satisfactory.

She switched to *Play* and laughed as the familiar voice said, "Mornin', Miss Bellows, an' I hope when you hear this, it really is a nice day. Rain ought to stopped by then or there won't be any left! Everything's shipshape an' no trouble at all, so we'll weigh anchor now. Anything you want, just gimme a ring below decks. Okay, son, let's—" The message ended abruptly. Still smiling, she turned off the machine and started out of the office to see the camera. She was halfway there when the import of Quinn's last words shook loose her complacency.

Okay, son, let's—

One of her problem boys had helped Quinn last night. How could Quinn have been so reckless? All her boys wanted urgently to know what their records said about them. There wasn't one who didn't tear the locks out of the confidential record cabinets with his suspicious angry eyes the moment he walked in! Which one of them had been here?

But with Tom Quinn stapling wire all over the place, who would have a chance to break into the files?

Nonsense!

Or her desk?

Impossible!

But suppose Quinn had left the office to get something he needed?

No. He was a superb workman—when he worked. If he had forgotten something he would send the boy for it.

Still . . .

There seemed to be nothing wrong with the locks on the big file cabinets. They were old but the locks were subject to little use. As a rule only her secretary, Gert Kane, opened them, getting the key from the safe in Jack Hardy's office as soon as she arrived and returning it immediately afterward. Joyce of all the staff had her own key—naturally!—although she rarely used it. Their security measures were cumbersome but satisfactory; there had never been any reason to change them.

And then she remembered Allen Magrue's warning about the folly of leaving her graduate journal in her desk. She ran back into her office.

Standing, she could at first glance see nothing wrong with the lock, but bending to examine it closely she found unmistakable signs that it had been tampered with. There were fresh scratches on the dark green paint where none had been before—Joyce had an automatic comprehensive eye for details like this—and one side of the keyhole was raised. Minutely, but raised all the same. Its edge was rough and fluted.

Staring at it incredulously, feeling the violation as a physical thing, she felt for the key ring in her handbag and selected the desk key with sure fingers. It jammed slightly in the lock but then went home and turned easily enough. Mechanically, like one mesmerized, she pulled out the drawer.

Again, a casual glance suggested that the manila folder was as she had left it, lined up with the right-hand corner. But like everyone else in the world Joyce had seen James Bond set his shrewd tiny traps. After Allen had gone yesterday afternoon she had placed a 3 x 5 pad in the middle of the folder and penciled two almost invisible dots at the pad's bottom corners. And then she had opened and closed the drawer several times with normal force to see if the pad had moved. It had not. And it certainly wouldn't be jarred out of position at the cautious hands of an intruder. It would move, she had reasoned meticulously, only because no one but she knew of the penciled dots.

And the pad had been moved. A mere fraction of an inch, true, but moved all the same. There was no other sign of interference but no other was needed. Whoever had forced the lock had read the diary.

It was unlikely that Allen with his active social life, Joyce thought, employing a bitter euphemism, would have had time or inclination to break into her desk sometime during the night. Besides, he was interested in only one entry, and she had told him truthfully that she had not made it, and he had believed her.

As for Simon, well, Simon didn't give a damn, and he didn't have to. And he wouldn't have known the journal was here anyway. Poor Simon! He was quite useless now, of course. A shell of a man. The sooner he left, the happier she would be. If he were not on the verge of retiring, she would have seen to it that he resign and take his illness and incompetence somewhere else. She would have to soften the description in her journal of his condition. After all, he had been so very good, once. And he was taking care of much of the busy work for her and the others, leaving them free to concentrate on important matters. Still, it was sad. . . .

And—Helen? No. She knew whatever Allen knew. Therefore she would not have done such a thing on his behalf. And she did not have to—she never would have cause to—on her own.

But David regarded the journal with fear, even loathing, as if it were a live thing. Poor David! Anything new, the slightest change, frightened him profoundly. She had written this down, and told him too. He was behaving very badly, and she had told him that as well, if not so baldly. But in her journal, only a small part of which had been repeated on the incomplete evaluation forms clipped together in the folder, she had also described him as a definite paranoid type with delusions of persecution, showing signs of breakdown, and contributing to his worsening illness by staying in guidance for which he was entirely unsuited. She had not told him this, but she would when she was sure. After yesterday's meeting she was almost sure. How could she not be!

If he had broken into this desk his behavior would clinch the diagnosis and she would take steps. For now she would watch and wait and say nothing to anyone.

Persuaded of the soundness of her logic and forgetting that David had never seen or expected to see the folder out of her reach, she closed the drawer and rubbed her aching eyes, still resisting the certainty that she was ill. I can't be sick now! she told herself. I can't give in now!

Perhaps it was only the dream and her broken sleep that had caused this exhaustion. . . . No, it was more than exhaustion. It was depression, and she felt now as though it had lasted all her life and would never end, never . . . never. . . .

Oh god, oh my god, what's happening to me! If I can't restrain myself, if I don't protect myself—

I've never acted this way before! Crying. Pleading. Shouting. It's dreadful and disgusting and unprofessional to be so uncontrolled!

And that dream—it's come back! After all these years . . .

I won't think about it!

She went to the window and pressed her hot forehead against the glass, resting and listening to the rain patter and the wind.

. . . time to get ready for bed . . . go to the beach . . . take a shower . . . try on a new dress. . . . And always, whenever she undressed in the dream, her body *was not there*. Like H. G. Wells's invisible man, when she took off her clothes she was without substance. Sometimes only an ear was gone, or an arm, or a leg, or her head, or her breasts. But always, part or all of her body vanished when she undressed—

And then she would wake up terrified and turn on all the lamps and run to the long mirror—as she had done last night—tearing off her pajamas to see if she were still whole, still perfect. And convulsed with fear, in that horrible instant before looking, that she was not.

The vivid memory shook her again, and again she withheld from herself what she had given to so many others, a recognition of fear and an understanding of its source. She could only despise herself for weakness.

"This is ridiculous!" she said aloud. "All *you* ever needed was hard work!" The sound of her voice calmed her, the old formula mobilized her defenses, and now it occurred to her that she had not yet looked at the television camera. With hysterical purpose she ran out of her office.

The small camera was mounted on a tripod in the first cubicle. Using the measurements of the little room, she and the salesman had adjusted the lens to focus on counselor and counselee if they sat side by side in a specified position. It was evident from the chalked circles anchoring chairs and tripod to the floor that Tom Quinn had carefully followed her diagram. An extra-long cable ran slyly along the baseboard moldings to the viewer in her office.

She switched on the camera and went back to turn on the viewer. Right on target! She nodded, pleased, and switched on the video recorder. When the tape reel began to turn and the needle to fluctuate, she went back to the cubicle, closed the door at the very instant someone unlocked the door to the outer office, and sat down facing the round black eye.

"Good morning, Miss Joyce Bellows!" she said brightly, addressing it. "This ought to cheer you up!" And it did. Instantly she was filled with euphoria, which swept like a healing breeze through her aching feverish head, leaving her with a marvelous sensation of soundness. She was in control again. She was all right now. She had been, before. She would continue to be. "Tom's a wonder," she went on. "Now you'll see everything, hear everything, know everything! And with Allen and David gone and Simon soon to go, I'll work with Helen and put this department back on its feet again!"

And then, her eyes gone blank but her movements quite matter-of-fact, she undressed quickly and turned to one side then the other, displaying to the camera her small perfect breasts and her arms and back. Then she climbed onto the chair and the camera's gaze slid over her buttocks and down her lovely legs. She revolved slowly, stood still a moment, then jumped down.

It was only when she began to struggle with her stocking clips that she found herself half-dressed.

Deathly pale, she fell onto the chair. "What have I done? What have I done? What's happening to me? What is this? What have I done?" she muttered, begging the camera for answers. The empty eye stared back. "Ahhhh . . ." she whispered in panic. "The dream! The dream! Oh god . . ."

Exhausted and sick, she pulled herself up and finished dressing. Her hand shook as she reached up to turn off the camera. "Dreams lie. Cameras don't lie. Now I'll see. Once for all," she told it as she pushed in the Stop button and then opened the cubicle door.

She almost fainted at the sight of Allen Magrue standing behind her desk, his hand on the video recorder. At her cry he turned. The normal set of his features was nearly obliterated by compassion.

"You were all there, Joyce," he said with supreme gentleness. "I swear it. Were you afraid part of you was missing?" His quiet voice drew her to him.

"Yes. Yes," she whispered eagerly. "You know? You've dreamed it too?"

"No. I know about it, but it doesn't fit my hang-up. It never did. I never had that one. I told you."

"I don't believe you! I-don't-believe-you!"

"I know you don't. For your own sake you'd better try to."

"Get out! Get out of my sight!" she screamed.

"I'd be happy to," he said evenly. "I stopped the tape just as you—just at the right time, so you can play the first part back. I'm sure it works. You paid enough." He went to the door but turned and blurted, "And you'll pay more! For godsake, Joyce, don't go ahead with this! Don't do this—to yourself, to me, to any of us! Even you can't swallow your ostensible reason for it—not now. Not any more."

"Get out! How dare you talk to me that way! Get out!"

"Well, well," said David Ross affably, coming in with Timothy Lunn. "I hope I haven't missed anything. Morning, Joyce. Sorry to say it but you look a bit under the weather. Hi, Al, brought you a present." He winked at the boy, tossed some papers onto the secretary's desk, and sat down at the conference table, unabashedly curious. Simon Wills came in a moment later, looking gray and deeply tired, and went over to the copy machine, carrying a package of paper and a stack of envelopes.

"Morning, Tim," Allen said. "You're a bit early, fella. Take a seat in one of the cubicles. I'll be with you in a couple of minutes."

"You tell 'er yet?" the boy asked.

"Yup."

"So?"

"So? Sew buttons. Go in and wait, please."

"Not a chanst! Not here I ain't! I ain't even gonna tell yuh the time in fronta them mikes!"

Joyce Bellows stood in her doorway.

Allen said deliberately, "Oh, they're up too? Well, I don't blame you, Tim. After all, I said you wouldn't have to be bothered with them. We'll go to my office." He gave the boy a friendly push. "Go on ahead. I'll be along."

"You'll do no such thing!" Joyce cried. "I forbid it! Tim, go into the first cubicle. I want to talk to you."

The boy's eyes flamed with hatred. "I don't talk t' you no more. I talk t' him. You can't tell me what t' do!"

"Tim!" Allen began, but Joyce ignored him and advanced on the surly boy.

"You'll do as you're told if you want help from this office! I am the head of this department and I make the decisions! I said I wanted to talk to you. Go into the first cubicle."

He looked down at her, considering her. A provocative grin spread over his face. "No. An' you can go t' hell," he said softly. He ducked away from Allen's angry lunge and darted into the corridor.

"Goddam you, Joyce!" Allen said in a low voice and ran after him.

His face pink and his eyes bright with anger, Simon left the copy machine. "I can't stand this!" he said, and for the first time in days his voice was sharp and vigorous. "What are you trying to do to that boy, Joyce? And to Allen? What right have you got to interfere—and publicly! What's gotten into you? If I hadn't seen this, I wouldn't have believed it!"

"What difference does it make what *you* believe any more!" she said coldly. "You're out of it. You took yourself out—months ago!"

"It was a mistake, I can see that now. So I'm putting myself back in!" Simon said firmly. "You can't keep that boy from Allen. You can't block his bid for an identity he can live with. If he wants to drop out of school and enlist, he should be encouraged to enlist. It's the only thing his father ever did that was and is socially acceptable. It's the only thing—the *one thing in his life* that he's got to hang onto! It could be the making of him. It's—"

"I know better than *you* do, Simon, and I know *him* better than you do!" she said contemptuously. "I don't agree with you at all."

"We'll see who's right. We'll see," he said quietly. "I'll finish that work later, David. Tell Gerty. I'm going over to the science office." He walked out slowly and heavily, a hand pressing his chest.

David whistled softly. "Getting it from all sides, aren't you, Joyce! Too bad. Say, got a scissors?"

"What? What?" Her voice was toneless.

"I said *have you got a scissors?*" he repeated with exaggerated care as if she were a foreigner or an idiot.

"Scissors? What for?" She looked at him dully.

"I've got a kid coming in a couple of minutes. The mike goes."

She didn't understand him, that was plain. Well, she would in a second. He went into the cubicle tacitly reserved for him and yanked the microphone off the wire. "Here, Joyce. This is yours, I think?" he said, coming out and putting it into her nerveless fingers. "Okay, Allen's right. I'm too paranoid to work with this sort of thing. That's your reading of me too, isn't it!"

"So you *were* the one," she whispered.

"The one what? Well, it doesn't matter. No mike, no paranoia. Simple. Morning, Gerty, how's the gal?"

The secretary was backing into the office holding her streaming umbrella at arm's length. She laughed. "If I were made of sugar, part of me would have melted by now! My feet for sure!"

"You're all there, don't worry about it," David joked. Out of the corner of his eye he saw Joyce gasp and cling to the door frame. The look on her face alarmed and shamed him. "Listen, Joyce, you ought to go home. You look like the last rose."

Tears spilled down her pale cheeks but her voice was surprisingly steady. "I'm expecting Tony Evans. When he comes send him in please, Gert. I won't take any other calls from anyone until he leaves. Say I'm with a client."

Quietly she shut her door on them and they looked at each other, the secretary speechless with surprise, David obscurely frightened by what he had done.

But it's working, whatever it is, he said to himself and went into his cubicle.

At nine o'clock Jane dropped into Ben's office. His revolting Tuesday pipe was going full blast as he considered the first of the day's pressing matters.

> After giving serious thought to our discussion yesterday afternoon, *read Joyce's memo*, I have decided to go ahead with my plans regarding the use of audio and video equipment during counseling sessions as well as counselee evaluation of the guidance staff. As of November 1 . . .

"Oh boy!" he said, ignoring his wife and puffing away worriedly. Joyce had wasted no time. After heading up guidance for eight years she should have known better than to do a thing like this! Well, the flak would begin in earnest now. And when she recorded it in her journal and submitted it to her University committee, they'd tell her off.

But I think I'll beat them to it, he said to himself, and reached for the phone. Gertrude Kane told him that Miss Bellows was in conference and could not be called away. He put the phone down quietly and then said, "Goddam it to hell!"

"Uh-huh," Jane said, shaking out her coat. "What a day! And what a stench! Phew! Ben, you ought to be arrested."

"So write a letter to the School Committee."

"What's the use of that? Even Amanda Raus smokes a pipe on occasion. I'll get further with Art Hudson. He's got more than enough probable cause to make a lawful arrest. Peach brandy, my god!"

"Not a chance. Art owes me for solving the Houseman case for him. He'd never touch a hair of my head."

"He won't have to, the way it's going," she giggled, kissing his rapidly ennobling forehead. "Anyway, in my experience, gratitude is just another way people express resentment because you're smarter than they are. You'll have to keep stoking the furnace so Art's regard for you burns pure. Which is more than can be said for that miserable pipe."

"If you mean I should give Art more solutions to more murders, perish the thought. And never mind about my pipe. I only smoke it to save you the trouble. What's up? Aren't you meeting the set crew?"

"Yes, but they aren't here yet. Probably the rain has pulverized them." She picked up the girl with the book. "I want to use this little lady again, unless you think someone'll remember her from last year."

She kissed him again and left. An hour later he opened his door cautiously, hoping to sneak out unobserved and get over to Building Two. But his senior secretary, Opal Castle, nailed him immediately, even before his other secretary, poor Mrs. Duffy, had hoisted herself off her chair. Despite his determined good humor he felt a twinge of alarm, for the papers Mrs. Castle held looked thick enough to ground him for six months. Reluctantly he went back to his desk.

"I promise not to take long," she said in her light sweet voice, and indeed she never did. "They're all important items, but some," she added with unconscious prescience, "are more important than others. First, Mr. Magrue has Reserve Training the first two weeks in November. I've already gotten a sub for his English class. And I'll have to drum up some more. The absence list is awful."

Her quiet competence soothed him. He could see the Golden Gate looming.

"Next, the Central Office called about the trash on the lawns and walks. The Forestry Department can't do anything about it before two weeks at the inside. Mr. Tomasello's been complaining for days because of the mess and he's threatening to clean it up himself, union or no union.

"Next, someone stuffed a roll of toilet paper into one of the johns in the 200 Block and tied the flusher lever down, and the intercom wires under the floor were shorted. But that doesn't have anything to do with anything. I just thought you'd like to know."

"Thanks," Ben said wryly. "My god, that's some stunt. What'll those kids think of next?" He would be horrified and not a little impressed when he knew. "Well, it does mean something, though, apart from everything else. Jack will have to find the money to replace that roll of paper from the contingency account. More likely he'll just buy one with his own money! How's he coming with his moving? We sure can use that office, and he'll be glad to have peace and quiet."

Jack Hardy, the business manager of the Manton School Department, was in process of moving to the Central Office where space had been found for him.

Mrs. Castle laughed. "He thinks he'll be all moved over by next Tuesday or Wednesday. Most of the personnel files and things are there already. He said you'll have to be responsible after that for the key to the guidance office private files whether you like it or not.

"Next, you've had several calls from Mrs. Evans, Tony's mother, but every time she's called you're out of reach. She's angry and suspicious, she won't state her problem, she refused to talk with Miss Bellows, and she said she won't talk to anyone but you." She handed him a slip of paper with the Evans phone number, along with an official envelope. "And this is from the School Committee for Mr. Quinn."

He accepted both as if they were a new invention that would explode in his face. "Anything else?" he said morosely. If this were a sample of things to come, he might as well tear up his plane ticket.

Mrs. Castle hesitated, then said apologetically, out of compassion (for him), "Something went wrong with Mrs. Cory's pregnancy last night and she can't come back. In fact she has to spend the next six weeks in bed."

He stared at her as if she were responsible for this most unkindest cut. "It's—it's not fair! Six weeks in bed? Seems to me she's already spent too much time there!" Mrs. Cory was his finest history teacher, and in her infrequent absences Ben was the only one who took her place.

The state of California broke off and sank under the smiling waters of the blue Pacific.

Mrs. Castle began to giggle and put a hand over her eyes. It was an application of pressure in the wrong place. Suddenly she was bent in half, sobbing with laughter, and her papers scattered on the floor.

Ben grinned sheepishly, then roared until he was limp. "Okay," he said, picking the papers up. "But I'm not licked yet." He sighed nevertheless. "I'll see Quinn now. Then I'll be with Bert Shrag. If Mrs. Evans calls again I'll be in the science office in Two."

The mantle of his overlordship hung heavily from his burdened shoulders as he went out. Mrs. Castle said loyally, "Don't worry, Mr. Louis, I'll find a good sub for Mrs. Cory." And even poor Mrs. Duffy, who had lumbered up over the difficult terrain of polished tile, suppressed the plaintive "Oh Mr. Louis!" that was always on her lips and let him go in peace.

He met Joyce Bellows and Allen Magrue coming up the stairs from the basement and alarm stabbed him again because they seemed to be engaged in mild argument. But maybe it was only the distorting acoustics of the stairwell. He crossed his fingers, for luck. And then, although it was part of his survival code never to cross a bridge until he came to it, he crossed one that wasn't even built yet. As far as anybody knew, he thought.

"Well, you two! From up here it sounded like a lovers' quarrel, hahaha," he burbled, joining them on the middle landing.

A peculiar expression swept over Joyce's pretty face, and Magrue, whose tie lay like a scarf over his shoulder, looked startled, then thoughtful, then pleased. There was an odd pause and then he said, "I'll see you later, Joyce," and winked at Ben as he went up.

"Glad I caught you," Ben said, disappointed that they hadn't taken him into their confidence. "I called you a while ago but you were busy. I want to talk with you alone, Joyce. It's important. That memo of yours—"

He was interrupted by Timothy Lunn whose hefty body vaulted the banister from above, landed as neatly as a cat a couple of steps below them, cast a defiant look at Joyce, and disappeared into the basement before they could stop him.

"One of my biggest worries, Tim Lunn," Joyce said. "A war lover. I've already—had a chat with him this morning. And Tony Evans was supposed to see me. I've been downstairs looking for him. They're both uptight about my new regime and I must say that a double dose of paranoia this early in the morning is exhausting."

"This may not be the time or the place, Joyce, but I'm telling you now to lay off those boys. I want them left entirely to Allen," Ben said sternly. "Whatever he says about them is the way it has to be. *I* want it that way. I hate pulling rank, but I'm doing it now. And when Allen goes off to Reserve Training—"

"Is that what he told you?" She laughed, her tone tinged with something he couldn't quite identify. "No. There's something I can do for them that no one else can. Certainly not Allen."

"Joyce—"

But she only sighed and rubbed her forehead. "For once I'm not looking forward to a new day. I don't feel up to par. I can't remember any other year when a virus hit us so hard and so soon." She started slowly past him.

"We'll have to sit down and go over this, Joyce. But I think you'd better stay home a day or two. I can't afford to lose you." She only waved her hand listlessly and left him.

He went down the steps thinking how easy it was for successful therapists to develop what he called the Messiah Complex which combined concern for their clients with enjoyment of the dizzying effects of power-wielding. Was it Voltaire who had said that pity was a sign of vanity? Or to put it another way, that compassion was a veiled synonym for arrogance? He could not remember but he knew he must not let the matter drop. As Allen Magrue had said, he too had his regular evaluation of department heads to make twice yearly, and he would give Joyce a write-up that would stand her on her ear.

And then as he entered the south tunnel and the skin on his nape began to crawl, he forgot about Joyce. He hated the south tunnel. If it had not been raining so hard he would have gone through the gym and across the driveway to Building Two.

To Ben the worst thing about this dogleg tunnel was the angle some ten feet from the entrance ramp where the tunnel turned sharply to the right and continued for two hundred forty feet to the door into the older building. Hugging the wall and feeling like a jerk for doing so, he approached the angle with reluctance, his hard leather heels resounding eerily. He would have loved to play cops and robbers here when he was ten. Now, a decorated combat veteran, he shrank from the admittedly idiotic anticipation that something horrible lurked behind that corner. He did not permit himself to peek round it, but after making the crucial turn he ran like a rabbit (for exercise, he told himself) into Building Two and took the mazelike path to the engine room.

Left, then right, and again right down the long corridor past the classrooms and shops, and through a door, where heat smote him and noise blasted his eardrums. Then left again past the entrance to the boiler room, and into Quinn's domain, wondering how some men could move so comfortably and securely among the equipment that unceasingly assaulted every sense and cell of the body. His, anyway. But the firemen and engineers, most of them old navy men, looked on these leviathans as friends and they loved the stink of the oil, the roar of the forced-draft fans, the blinding fires in the twenty-foot-high boilers, the fierce energy of the huge machines, even the thick gleaming grease with which they lovingly massaged their monsters.

Quinn was not around but one of the watch engineers emerged from behind the great black panel board at the far end of the room and called to him. Despite the fact that most of the machines were now dormant, the air shook with noise and Ben was unable to distinguish a word.

The engineer came over to him with a rolling gait and planted his feet widely as on a heaving deck. "Mornin', Mr. Louis. If you're lookin' for the chief, he won't be back 'til next shift."

"Oh. Well, would you give him this for me? I'm sorry I missed him. Thanks, Mr. Garvin," and he handed over the School Committee letter denying Quinn's appeal and terminating his job as of October 31.

He was glad to have gotten rid of it so quickly and he hoped that Quinn wouldn't come crying to him again. There was nothing he could do about it, and no reason why he should. No need for

Quinn to be so uptight about it anyway. With all the urban renewal going on in Boston he could have his pick of jobs.

He trotted up two flights of stairs to the lab where Bert Shrag was teaching physics and looked through the glass panel in the door. Bert was talking with a few boys at the far end of the front counter, their heads clustered in serious involvement. The others were slowly clearing up.

Bert straightened, went to the board and wrote something on it, then turned to speak to a boy who was standing at the sink.

Good, Ben thought, his chest heaving gently, Bert's about through. I'll just wait out here a min—

And then his breath stopped, his blood congealed, and his body turned to stone as the blast of a powerful gun rattled the glass through which he stared with horror.

CHAPTER SIX

"But what were you *doing?* I don't get it! What the hell were you *doing* that you could miss a thing like that?" Police Chief Art Hudson would demand later of Bert Shrag in the hospital.

Bert was winding up a two-hour lab that had gone off exceedingly well. It was the kind of day that made a teacher's life worth all the crap, he said later. He had been feeling happy and grateful—

Why?

WHY? Because you never could tell about kids—about how much talent was buried under the sludge! Because you never really knew how good *you* were until you'd lit a fire under a bunch of cretins and dunderheads! Because a sense of communion covered the lab like a tent and everything was first-rate—

And suddenly the ear-shattering BLAM, followed by a fraction of silent time in which every head turned like an obedient compass needle toward the boy in the sink. But only Ben Louis, outside but in a direct line with the sink, and Bert Shrag, opposite it, saw the front of the boy's head fly off in bits and sprays of red and white and gray and brown which were blood and bone and brains and hair.

At almost the same instant Bert clutched his left arm as the emerging bullet struck him too and jerked his short stocky body round to the left. He faced Ben now but did not see him. His eyes blind with shock, his ears ringing from the weapon's sharp report, his face and hair and collar and lab coat revoltingly spattered, he staggered back under this double baptism under fire and slammed into the wall. This additional assault on his nerves caused his knees to buckle and he fainted, sliding down the wall into the position of a sunbather relaxing under a benign sky.

And during that paralyzed moment, too short to measure by ordinary means and too long to be forgotten, the boy simply stood—without his face—before falling into the deep stone sink, hitting it with an indescribable disgusting sound. The terrible head was now mercifully hidden yet the posture of the body was shocking because the feet dangled, pathetically, a few inches above the loose moccasins out of which the boy had been lifted by the enormous impact. The legs twitched and then were still.

All of them, and Ben still rooted in the corridor, remained fixed like a museum diorama ("And here, ladies and gentlemen, is an example of the unparalleled barbarity of American education a thousand years ago!")—all of them for an interminable frozen moment as dead as the boy in the sink.

And then every head turned again to another boy two tables behind the jackknifed body.

He was holding a big black pistol at arm's length and staring at it. Then his stiffening fingers opened like the sepals of a bud, and the bud ripened with supernatural speed and dropped a ghastly fruit onto the tiled and barren floor.

There is no such thing as an instinctive reaction, Ben said afterward, because he was aware as he rushed into the lab of thinking slowly and deliberately, I will not have any hysterics around here, and, Where in hell did Vinnie Dean get that gun? Nevertheless he admitted later that he had no idea of what he was going to do until he had done it.

"Quiet!" he commanded, although his sudden appearance had shut every mouth. "Take your seats! NOW!"

Two teachers ran in almost at his heels. Because of his height, and because he was not only the last person they expected to see but also the first they would seek in an emergency, they did not notice the dead boy or the unconscious teacher so relaxed against the wall.

"Is anything—Oh Ben!"

"There was a terrific explosion or something—"

Ben whirled and blinked at them: Simon Wills, fat, sixty, coronary case. Helen Chadwick, beautiful, Rock of Gibraltar.

Good! he thought, his mind amazingly clear. He literally stared Simon out of the lab.

"Simon, get back to your class!" he said harshly. "See to it that your kids leave by the far stairs. There's been an accident. I want absolutely no traffic here. None anywhere near this lab! Understand?" Simon nodded and left gladly.

David Ross sidestepped him at the door. "Ben! What the—"

"You free?"

"Yes but—" His quick eyes darted, his clever face sagged. "Oh Jesus!"

"Close that door! Helen, look after Bert. And wash him, for godsake!" He swallowed convulsively. "Can you manage?"

"I can manage," she said steadily and set about it.

The clattering of stools whirled Ben around. "I told you kids to sit down and shut up." Silence. He considered them. "You and you. I want that door glass covered. Towels, tacks, tapes—now!"

He went back to the gun on the floor and planted a stool over it and then he said to David, "Call Mrs. Castle. Tell her to check the schedules and use the PA and cancel any classes that are supposed to come in here today. They can go anyplace else that's free. I'll buzz her in a little while. You call Chief Hudson. Tell him you'll wait for him downstairs at the side of this building."

Ross nodded. He looked down at Bert who was beginning to stir and moan with pain. Fresh blood reddened the lab coat. Her face pale but composed, Helen was carefully cutting away the sleeve and the shirt sleeve underneath. Then Ross edged past the two boys who were covering the glass panel in the door and went quickly away.

Ben knew the boy who had fired the gun. Vincent Dean, one of the finest kids who'd ever been born—if his parents would leave him alone!—and first violinist in the school orchestra. The boy's long sensitive hands hung slack between his thighs and he swayed dizzily as Ben reached him.

"I thought . . ." he whispered. His lips were dry and stiff and he licked them slowly as if to do so were painful in the extreme. "I was . . . only . . . playing . . ."

"Whom did you see, Vinnie?" Ben said in a low voice. "Whom were you shooting at?"

"I—don't know . . . I was pretending . . . My parents . . ." His eyeballs were distended with shock.

"Vinnie, is that your gun?"

The boy barely managed to shake his head.

"Where did you get it?" Ben said gently. He put his hand lightly on the boy's shoulder and Vinnie looked up at him with glazed eyes. Slowly, slowly, he lifted the terrible burden that his hand had become and pointed to an open drawer under the counter. Then he shuddered under Ben's hand and leaned against him, sighing like a tired baby, his fuzzy cheek pressing against Ben's belt buckle, and Ben's arm automatically encircled him and held him close.

"Who's the other one?" he whispered to the nearest boy.

"Gerald Rosen," was the whispered reply.

When Chief Hudson arrived ten minutes later the smell of gunpowder and the sickening smell of fresh blood had dissipated among the familiar odors that impregnate every lab, but twenty-two boys were still motionless on their stools. Helen was still ministering to Bert. What was left of Gerald Rosen's face was still draining into the stone sink. And Ben was still holding Vinnie Dean, rocking him tenderly and patting his skinny back to keep him from disintegrating too.

CHAPTER SEVEN

When Hudson's round pink face appeared Ben groaned in relief. His arm was numb, his knees weak, his stomach in knots. But a fresh reserve of strength pulsed through him. I've never been so glad to see anyone in my life, he thought, and realized that he was smiling.

For Hudson looked as if he had just been taken out of a gift-wrapped box, and Ben knew that at the end of a long day he would look no different. There would be no lint on his serge jacket, no fingerprints on the black bill of his cap, and his trouser creases would be able to cut a cake. His compulsive cleanliness was the butt of amiable joking among his friends. But it was never the butt of ridicule: His compact heavy body was packed with integrity and on his arrival the monstrous tension in the lab abated.

Hudson for his part was flabbergasted by the bizarre scene. He had viewed violent death in many forms and places and he had been told what he would find here: a boy's dead body half out of a sink, its legs dangling, and Bert Shrag, wounded and out cold. (Bert was conscious now and holding a tourniquet on his arm, his square face pallid but clean from Helen's gentle sponging.) But Hudson had expected chaos. His large jaw dropped at the sight of all those boys on their high stools, quietly looking at carnage.

"My god, I don't believe it!" he murmured, clutching the strap of the camera bag that hung from his shoulder. If he had read a description of such a scene in a detective novel, he would have flung the liar in the trash. But then, Ben knew his onions, no doubt about it. Hudson awarded him an approving nod.

He put down his camera bag and went to squat next to

Bert who said hello weakly. "You okay, young fella? There'll be an ambulance along in a minute. Your wife's been notified and she'll go with you."

"With—? In the same—?" and Bert fainted again. Helen grasped the tourniquet firmly as his hand fell away from it.

"He means all of them together," Hudson said to her in a low voice and motioning to the dead boy. "No chance. We have to wait for the M.E. but even if he were here now they wouldn't be going to the same place anyway. Bert lose much blood?"

"Enough. The bullet's still in there but I hope it didn't hit the bone. I guess it just ran out of steam. From the way he looked he must have been standing opposite the—the—" She bit her lip. "Actually I think it's mainly shock. Bert's really a tough nut," she said affectionately.

"Look, Miss—uh?—Miss Chadwick, why don't you get out of here? I'll watch him. Looks like you've had enough." He eased himself down onto his immaculate knees and braced Bert, and Helen got up stiffly and wobbled out.

A strident bell signaled the beginning of the next period and the arrival of Police Sergeant Sam Lang and the stretcher-bearers. Strong competent hands lifted Bert (Hudson jumped up immediately and brushed off his trousers), covered him, and bore him smoothly out. Lang, less imaginative than Hudson, said hello to Ben and surveyed the room impassively.

Ben said in a strangled voice, "Sam, we need another stretcher. For Vinnie."

Hudson nodded to the sergeant who hurried out. "I take it *he* did the shooting?" he said repressively.

"Art, it was an accident. He found the gun in the drawer here. It's a Luger—no wonder it went off! It's under this stool. But Vinnie's out of the picture and I won't let you question him now. I want him under a doctor's care as soon as possible. I'll call his parents. And I want to get the rest of them out of this room!"

Hudson's gaze, alert and thoughtful, swept over the boys looking for signs of strain. There were none. But even while he gratefully noted the fact he pitied them, thinking, TV and movies have made death more real to them than the real thing: They've grown up with violence, they're used to it! And I'll never be, not if I spend another thirty years in this racket!

"You'll be out of here shortly, boys, but I'll take some pictures first," he said as he assembled his equipment. "These your assigned seats? Right."

The flash bulbs glared two, three, four times as Hudson moved from one angle to another.

"Now take the places you were in when the gun went off. And the direction you were facing. Try to remember what you were doing then."

Awkward and self-conscious, they avoided each other's eyes as they rearranged themselves. Presently all was quiet.

"That's it?" Heads nodded and he frowned. "Looks like none of you saw anything."

"That's right, Art," Ben said. "I was at the door. All of them turned at the same time."

Again the flash bulbs glared.

"Here, fellas," Ben said as the ambulance attendants and Sergeant Lang returned. But he picked up Vinnie himself and set him down with infinite care on the stretcher. He stroked the boy's hair and whispered, "It'll be all right, Vinnie, don't worry," and knew that the boy would suffer the memory as long as he lived. Then he turned to the others. "Any of you know anything about that gun? Have you seen anyone with it? Or with any other gun in school?"

"Any collecting or trading going around here?" Hudson said.

No, sir. No, chief. Their eyes were large with the drama of it.

"Anyone absent today, Ben?" Hudson said tightly.

"Everybody's here today, sir," said one boy. "I remember. Mr. Shrag said it was the only class in school where someone wasn't absent."

"Well, that's something!" Hudson commented ironically.

Ben went to the PA panel and signaled his office as Helen Chadwick came back. "Opal, about that schedule—"

"It's all right, Mr. Louis," his secretary said calmly. "All taken care of. Mr. Shrag's class goes to math now in 108."

"Thanks. Get me the phone numbers of Vinnie Dean and Gerald Rosen. I'll be down in a few minutes." He looked at Helen and marveled. She had been made for tasks like these—for mothering and protecting and loving. Jane was right. What fools, how many fools, had passed her by? "Helen, will you take this group to

108? Thanks. Boys, I want your word that you'll keep from telling
any tall tales. This is a terrible thing—but it was an accident. Is
that clear?"

"Some hope," Hudson said cynically when they had filed out.
"Sam, give me a hand—"

"Art, I don't think I can stand to see that face again," Ben said.

"Then go look out the window," Hudson said unfeelingly. "I'll
only be another few seconds. I want to talk to you in your office
and Keefe will meet us there when his boys are done here. If they
ever come! You can take me down through the basement."

Because you don't want to get your uniform wet! Ben said
soundlessly. He leaned against the windowsill and stared unsee-
ingly at the storm as Hudson and Lang lifted the poor bent body
out of the sink.

"Oh my god!" Hudson muttered. Ben's breakfast rose sour into
his throat.

Lang whistled. "Christ!" he said, adding as though Ben
were someplace else, "Mr. Louis did damn well, considering. But
I guess he saw a lot of this in the war."

"The fly boys," Hudson said acidly, "don't see their targets. They
just drop the junk and run."

Ben clenched his fists, because it was true and because he had
hated doing it.

Hudson screwed a flash bulb into its socket and gave it a vicious
twist because he was so depressed and furious over this senseless
tragic accident.

One flash.

Ben bit the insides of his cheeks.

"Turn him over."

Another flash.

"Nice neat hole," Hudson observed bitterly. "Christ! For his
parents' sake why couldn't it have been in the front! Cover him
with something and let's blow!"

"The gun, chief," Lang said, showing him the ejected cartridge.

"God, I forgot!" and Hudson moved away the stool under which
the Luger lay like a caged and dangerous animal. One last flash,
and he had done. "Okay, Ben, let's get out of here! Sam, wait here
for Keefe."

While waiting for State Police Detective Lieutenant Inspector Peter Keefe to join them, Ben called the parents of Vincent Dean and Gerald Rosen to make sure that someone was at home, and Hudson dispatched police officers to inform them in person of the tragedy and direct them to the places where their sons, one living, one dead, were to be found.

Keefe came into Ben's office shortly afterward.

"There wasn't much to do up there," he said, sitting down and grunting as his perennially aching feet were relieved of the weight they carried. "What's going to take time is finding out where that gun came from. One thing'll make you happy, Ben. Donnelly was sure no fingerprints except the Dean boy's are on that gun. The chances would be a thousand to one we'd find any, contrary to what people think. So we won't have to turn your school upside down fingerprinting everybody in it. But that makes it harder for us. Any ideas?"

He still looks like a banker, thought Ben, who had not seen him since the Houseman murder two years ago. Keefe was portlier now but serene and imperturbable as ever, a perfect foil for Hudson with whom he had often worked on Manton's felony cases. Observers unfamiliar with procedure assumed, from his tact and deference, that Hudson was his superior here, but Keefe was in fact in charge of all personnel investigating a crime in Hudson's bailiwick.

"Place is probably crawling with guns!" Hudson charged unfairly because he was so upset.

"You're absolutely right, Art!" Ben flared. "This school is a sinkhole of vice and corruption, and every day I stand at the door and the kids check their gats—"

"All right, all right, take it easy, you two," Keefe said.

"Sorry, Ben!" Hudson barked.

"Yeah. Okay. Me too. God! Nothing in my training prepared me for this thing, and I don't know that it'll make a better administrator of me either! And seeing it—" His jaws clamped round the pipe with an audible crunch.

"Tough," Hudson said tactlessly, "but it was lucky you happened along. But where did that gun come from? Who put it there? How long was it there? Why was it left there?"

"You ever hear any rumblings of gun collecting among the kids, Ben?" said Keefe. "Any trading?"

"No. Lots of boys have a rifle, of course. And many fathers are vets. One of them might have picked up that Luger as a trophy during the war and done some target practice with it. You might check with the Rod and Gun Club. Someone there might have seen it. It won't be easy though. Members can bring guests and I don't think they have to sign a visitor's book."

"Well, it's for damn sure that Luger's not registered," Keefe said. "It was illegal to keep one and bring it back here. But it'll go over to the gun registry anyway. Only—if there *is* anything in the registry, it'll take a week or more to find it."

"Well, I doubt if any of my parents would leave a handgun around loose," Ben said, aware that he was being illogical in view of the horrible things he had been anticipating the night before. If there was one thing he had always been convinced of, it was that anything was possible, anything at all.

"Ben, you know better than that!" Hudson said, astounded by his illogic. "You of all people! How many crackpot parents have you known over the years? A lot of them are worse than their kids!"

"I know. I wish I could forget it! Okay. All I can think of at this point is that the Luger was stashed in that drawer just as accidentally as it was fired. I can't believe that anyone who knows about guns would deliberately leave a Luger lying around! Someone who doesn't know beans about guns in general and Lugers in particular—like Vinnie!—can't tell whether it's cocked or loaded. Why the hell was it designed without a hammer!" He blew out a noxious cloud of smoke that made Hudson gasp. "Okay. All I can offer at this point is that the gun must have been left there after David Ross was through yesterday. It wouldn't make sense any other way. Bert was in there yesterday doing lab work, which means the drawer would be open and someone would see the gun. And it doesn't make sense to think a kid would see it and say nothing about it. And David was only giving a lecture-demonstration. He's a very fussy guy and when he lectures he wants to see every head turned his way. And they always are, believe me! And no one else used that room."

"We'll see his group anyway, Ben," Keefe said. "If it's all the same to you. But if they're clean, then someone left it—a visitor, a custodian, a teacher even!" He was silent for a moment and then said, "We'll need a complete list of all personnel here—everyone —and a list of your problem kids. You've got a few, I'll be bound."

"Yeah," Ben said glumly. "But some of them are very cooperative in school. They reserve their mischief for outside."

"That gun was *in* the school, Ben. Not outside," Hudson said. "So give us your list of possibles. And get your staff together. They may have seen something or heard something and they're handling it quietly to give a kid a chance this early in the year." He bounced out of his chair and adjusted his jacket and heavy black belt, then blew on the visor of his cap and shined it on his sleeve.

"Art, I've never seen you look lovelier," Ben needled. Hudson's crack about the air force still rankled.

"A-a-a-rrrgh!" Hudson said.

Keefe rose with a grimace as his big body pressed down on his crushed arches. "We'll see Ross's class now. Then we'll see what we can get from the Rod and Gun. Get us that personnel list as soon as you can, Ben. We've got a lot of people to see."

"Hold it a minute," Ben said and signaled Mrs. Castle over the intercom. "Opal, ask Mr. Hardy for a complete personnel list—yes —everyone, even in the cafeteria—the works. The police need it. Soon as possible. And get on the PA right away. Cancel all clubs, chorus, everything. I want the kids out at two-ten and I want all teachers in the auditorium immediately after the buses leave. With their rank books. This is urgent. Thanks." He led the way out of the office saying, "It'll be a while before you have the list, Pete. Our directory isn't printed yet—not 'til the end of the month when all staff are set for the year."

In Ben's presence they interviewed David Ross's class, and Hudson griped afterward, "Those kids are pure as the driven snow! They never even *heard* the word gun!"

"Looks that way so far," Keefe said comfortably. "By the way, Ben, how come Shrag's class are all boys? And Ross's too? It just hit me. Don't girls have brains enough to take physics and chemistry?"

Ben smiled in spite of his woes. "Those are slow groups, Pete. The senior girls are all in honors physics."

He was glad to see them go at last. He went back to his office to ring up Joyce Bellows and ask for a list of the toughs and troublemakers. He had his hand on the phone when Mrs. Castle buzzed him on the intercom.

"Mr. Louis, there's a reporter here. Mr. Albert Shedd."

Oh hell, Ben thought. That little jerk. "Ask him to come in."

But Al Shedd's style precluded invitations, which was one reason why Ben disliked him, and he breezed in in a studied manner reminiscent of Hollywood 1935, which was another reason why Ben disliked him.

Ben regarded with distaste the cocky Tyrolean hat and dirty trench coat which Shedd affected, and said hello. Beyond that he would not go.

"Well, come *on*, come *on*, Ben, *give!* Something like this doesn't happen every day!" Shedd cried, clearly wishing that it did. His piggy eyes glittered. "What's the story?"

"There isn't any—story," Ben said stonily. "A boy found a gun in a drawer. It went off accidentally. A boy was killed and the teacher wounded. The affair is—regrettable but the school is operating normally. The police are investigating. That's all."

Shedd scribbled hastily, saying, "Don't kid me, kid. I hang around the boiler room and engine room a lot. Remember the time one of those guys had some action down there with some of your beauties? I'll bet you a plugged nickel—" He stopped and looked at Ben slyly.

"You'll bet me about what?"

"You tell me something, I'll tell you something."

"I've got nothing to tell."

"Well, there must be something in this. I got the names of the kids involved from your secretary—the fat one who quivers and cries. A boy named *Dean* kills a kid named *Rosen*. Very loaded ethnic-type situation you could be sitting on here!"

He was plainly trying to bomb something out of Ben, but Ben had had enough. He shot out of his chair, knowing that he was taking a risk. An administrator needs a good press almost more than he needs a good staff. Nevertheless he shouted, "You try printing a filthy thing like that and I'll do whatever I have to do to break your filthy neck!" and propelled the little man out of his office.

"But Ben! I know something!" Shedd exclaimed. He was actually enjoying himself immensely.

"I don't give a curse what you know!" And Ben slammed the outer door in his face. Trembling with fury he instructed his secretaries to give no information to anyone and to refer all inquiries to him.

When he had simmered down he called Joyce's office. Gert Kane informed him that Miss Bellows had been disturbed by Tony Evans' failure to keep his appointment and that she had gone home very early anyway because she had not been feeling well.

"Oh. Look, Gert. She keeps certain folders separate from the others. You know the ones I mean. Evans, Lunn, that bunch."

"I'm sorry, Mr. Louis. She took them with her when she left."

He thanked her and put the phone down. That's funny, he thought. If there's a connection between one of those kids and what happened over in Two, it's almost as though she had known what was going to happen.

But that was impossible. Or was it?

But why would she take the folders? They were not off limits to him or to the police. She knew that just as well as he did.

Well, then, what the hell was going on here?

He picked up the phone again and dialed an outside line.

"Joyce? Ben Louis."

"Oh, I'm sorry," said a rather familiar voice, "but she can't come to the phone now. Can I take a message? Oh! Mr. Louis! Joyce has spoken of you often! I'm her sister, Grace Wickham."

Ben was so astounded that he almost fell off his chair. He had known Joyce for eight years and more and had assumed that she was an only child. My god, if she's kept this sinister information under her hat, he thought, what else is she hiding! He managed to say, "You sound almost exactly like her. How is she feeling?"

"She's asleep now. It's just a twenty-four-hour bug, I think. She wasn't feeling well when she met me at Logan last night. She actually tried to do some work when she came home this morning —she said something about writing an important letter—but she had to give it up and go to bed. Very likely she'll be back tomorrow."

"I hope so, for selfish reasons." He outlined the events of the morning, the information requested by the police, and the need for the confidential folders.

Mrs. Wickham gasped. "I'm terribly sorry to hear this, Mr. Louis. It must be very difficult for you. But I don't know what to say about the folders."

"Would it disturb you if I came over for them now?" Such politeness was perfunctory. His car keys were in his hand.

"Well . . . this may sound strange, but I'd really hate to poke around in her things. It's something nobody's ever done with Joyce. Would it—I mean—in the circumstances I realize—well, could you possibly wait until later today? I'll bring them myself."

"I'm afraid that won't do, Mrs. Wickham. I must have them immediately. They shouldn't have been taken out in the first place. I'll be right over. Save you a trip in this weather."

Gone were his plans for his trip to California. Apart from everything else, he would have to fill in for Mrs. Cory until his secretary found a decent sub. He drove away wondering when his own stamina would dribble out, and he almost wished for the comfort of a sickroom of his own. The wind whipped his old Ford and rain covered the window like a thick gray towel. He shivered hopefully. But he knew that he was not sick, only very tired, and that all he wanted now was to be home with Jane.

Later he found that he might as well have stayed in school and let Mrs. Wickham bring the folders to him. They yielded nothing that he did not already know. But where were the blow-by-blow transcriptions Joyce had made of crucial sessions? He had never read them but he knew that, with her phenomenal memory, she had often reproduced accurate accounts of as much as an hour's talk with some of her boys. They were almost analogous to X rays.

Had she destroyed them or kept them now that these boys were seeing Allen? And if she had, what possible reason could she have had for doing such a thing?

But aside from that, and the fact that she had broken a school security rule by taking the folders out of the building, that confidential material was Allen's business and should be available to him at all times.

Puzzled and irritable, he went to the large lecture hall to talk with his staff about the tragedy, about guns, stealing, behaviors suggestive of guilty secrets.

The meeting, like the folders, was unproductive except that it increased his growing tendency to snappishness. The staff were spiritless and unresponsive. Nobody knew anything. Nobody had seen anything. Nobody had heard anything.

God!

And Allen Magrue on one side of the room and Helen Chadwick on the other were noticeably withdrawn. No doubt Allen was concerned with his girlfriend's health and Helen was exhausted from her labors over Bert Shrag. Well, he thought with mounting frustration and even anger, I'm concerned about Joyce too! And furthermore, I witnessed that accident! And moreover, I've got this school to run!

He closed the meeting by pleading with them all to search their memories for the least trifle that might have caught their attention since school began, and to come to him as soon as possible.

Then he called the hospital to inquire about Bert Shrag and was told that Mr. Shrag had undergone surgery and was resting, but that visitors would be permitted after supper for a short time. He left a message for Hudson that he would meet him there at seven. Then he looked round his smoky smelly office, regarded without favor the million matters awaiting him on his sloppy desk, said to hell with it all, and went home.

"Here, darling," Jane said, handing him a generous dose of scotch. "Feel like talking? Or should I go and cook dinner? I believe in doing one thing at a time and doing it well." She grinned at him and immediately he began to brighten up.

"Sure," he said and kissed her at length. "But this time try to do both together. I have to leave soon."

"Why can't I ever fool you?" she complained, following him reluctantly into the kitchen. Jane hated cooking.

"Because I'm smarter than everybody else. You said so yourself this morning."

"It was that peach brandy tobacco! I didn't know what I was saying. Okay, what happened?" She began banging and charging about in her customary efficient way, skipping over the great dog

Fee who lay in the entire middle of the floor watching her with greedy eyes and serene expectations.

Ben recounted every occurrence of the day including poor Mrs. Duffy's unbelievable forbearance as he was leaving his office to go and see Quinn and Bert Shrag. "The staff meeting was lousy. I haven't one iota of information to give Hudson tonight and he'll think I'm holding out on him. It seems to me a few people are holding out on *me!*" he fretted, and told her about Allen Magrue whose reputed ladylove was sick-abed.

"Who's he? I can't place him. I remember that name, though. It's an odd one. I think I met him at the picnic. I must've. But even the people I know all looked like one more hot dog to me. All *I* did was barbecue!"

"That's because you do it better than everybody else. Okay, *okay!* Well, Allen's a little above medium height. Dresses extremely well, too. But that's because he's—"

"I know! Because he's single, and it's my fault and my kids' that you aren't," she laughed, pointing a carving knife at his frayed cuff. "What's he like?"

"He's a good man. I'm damn lucky to have him. Nice guy. He's in guidance and English."

She popped a hunk of meat into Fee's slavering jaws. "Oh, now I remember him! He's the rumpled one! Like a little boy, only clean. Like Benjy when he was ten. Appealing. I wanted to stuff his shirttails in. And he's got a habit of holding onto you, sort of, and peering into your face when you talk. Although I don't know that physical closeness is a guarantee of *genuine ongoing communication,* as you *educationists* say! Well . . . I always like to be able to add more dimensions to people," she said thoughtfully. "That reminds me. You know, Ben, I'm always surprised to see Joyce angry or annoyed."

"She's human," Ben observed with measurable accuracy. "And when did you last see her angry?"

"A few days ago. Friday, I think. Magrue was with her, which is why I remembered it, although I didn't remember his name at the time. She certainly was misnamed. That lovely gentle voice and that relaxed nondirective manner even when she's a bit tense— the way she seemed the other day. And she's got a name like Bellows! She couldn't bellow to save her life."

"Well then, there are at least—" he counted on his fingers— "at least twelve other misbegotten souls to worry about." He grinned cunningly, waiting for her to ask him why.

"Why?" she said suspiciously.

"I've been keeping a list of physicians and things. There's Payne. And Asprin. And Cronkhite—which is German for sickness! And Comfort. Harms. Slaughter. Graves. And Gash. The best one is Friend, though. There's a vet named Bull. My aunt Ray used to see a chiropractor named Limber. And I know someone who goes to a lawyer named Clever. What do you think of that?"

She laughed. "Dinner's almost ready. And I hope you get indigestion!"

And he did, although it wouldn't have mattered what he had eaten or who had cooked it. But the reason for it didn't occur to him until much later.

"You may not believe it," Bert Shrag concluded at seven-forty to Keefe and Hudson and Ben who were almost as weary as he was, "but this morning my worst worry was that horned toad— well, it's a lizard actually—that I've been goosing along since July."

The police officers gaped at him, for although he was pale and weak he appeared rational in his hospital bed. Ben Louis laughed out loud for the first time in many hours.

"He's got ulcers," Bert explained. "It's from those mealworms . . . they have these hard cases . . ."

His eyelids fluttered and all at once he was asleep again.

"We'll be back tomorrow," Ben told the hard-eyed nurse who came to usher them out with a jerk of her thumb.

"Oh goody, we can hardly wait," she said and closed the door in his face.

"Christ!" Hudson exploded as they went down the stairs. "Bert doesn't know anything! You don't know anything! Your students don't know anything! Your staff doesn't know anything! And we don't know anything! We spent the whole afternoon with lists of names from the Rod and Gun and from Hardy—we saw a million people—"

"Oh come on, Art," Keefe said, "it wasn't all that bad."

"Well, all I can say is, it'd take even the FBI weeks to check

everybody out! And I bet they wouldn't know anything either
when they were done!" He gave his uninformative notebook an
angry flick of his elegant nails. "Gun owners. Veterans. Both in
most cases—where the men are concerned. We'd need an army to
get through these lists!" he griped, and wrenched open the lobby
door.

"Mind that puddle, Art," Keefe said. "You'll wet those nice
shiny tootsies—"

"A-a-a-rrrgh!"

Ben laughed again and said good night. But just before he went
to bed he thought of something Jane had carelessly mentioned before dinner, and his slightly improved spirits fell once more.

She had observed a certain tenseness in Joyce when Joyce and
Allen were together. And so had he, he thought uneasily. And
again he asked himself what the hell was going on there. Maybe
the acoustics in the stairwell weren't so distorting after all.

At two in the morning he woke up and went for the bicarbonate.

If he had remembered another remark Jane had made all too
quickly, and if he had awakened her and asked her about it, he
probably would have carried himself back to the hospital and taken
a bed next to Bert's. But he did not remember it for some time,
which was as well. A teacher needs a lot of rest, and Ben was going
to teach several classes on Wednesday and for as long as it took
Opal Castle to find him a decent sub. Eventually he slept.

And all night the rain fell.

CHAPTER EIGHT

On Wednesday morning a letter from the student chairman of the Dance Committee of Manton High School was delivered by hand to the home of the chairman of the School Committee of the Manton Public Schools:

Dear Sir:

May we have permission to hold our Harvest Dance on Friday night as planned? We all feel terribly (*sic*) about the tragedy, but several hundred dollars have been collected and spent on tickets and all other arrangements, and it would be very difficult to change things now. Our faculty adviser Mr. Crayne feels that Gerald Rosen would have wanted us to carry on.

Very truly yours,

Hal Kent, Chairman

"What do you think, Ben?" the Superintendent said over the telephone, to which Ben had been summoned from a delicious school cafeteria lunch of American chop suey and peanut butter sandwiches.

"I'll abide by the decision of the School Committee," Ben said reluctantly, and belched. "Let me know. And now if you'll excuse me, I have two classes to teach."

"Any further developments?"

"No. And I don't know if I'm glad or sorry."

From the unedited minutes of the School Committee meeting

on Wednesday night, recorded by Jack Hardy, business manager of the Manton Public Schools and secretary to the committee:

1) Lawyer, Bldg. Svc. Employees Union, speaking for T. Quinn, threatened will charge MURDER against Supt and Sch/Com if boilers explode because no chief engineer 1st class on premises! (Bluff, and he knows it. As much as admitted case would blow up sooner than boilers ever will! Nice try, though. What the hell is eating T. Quinn?????)

2) On school dance Friday night, a whatthehell attitude in general, along $$-spent-show-goes-on lines. But final say with B. Louis (not present, stomach upset). More trouble due Friday?

3) Rosen funeral Thursday aft. Send flowers *both* families, Thursday morning. (Argument *re* $$—petty cash or private pocket. Collected $3: chrmn, supt, myself. Am to buy flowers, collect from others later. Hahaha. Big joke.)

"What do you want to do, Ben? It's up to you," said the Superintendent early Thursday morning.

"Does it matter?" Ben said bitterly. "Either way the fur will hit the fan."

"You feeling any better?"

"Stomach-wise? No. Now, if you'll excuse me—"

Memorandum:

To: Dance Committee and ALL STAFF

From: BFLouis

In the circumstances the dance will be from 8:30 until 11:00 *only*. We will have the usual police chaperone, but I want the main entrance to Building Three, the two side doors, and the gym's two outer doors monitored AT ALL TIMES.

NO tickets are to be sold after 12 noon Friday. NO

students are to be admitted without a ticket. NO tickets
are to be sold at the door.

ALL students are to be confined to the first floor. I
WANT NO ONE IN THE BASEMENT.

Be in school at 8:00 P.M.

Later on Thursday morning Allen Magrue and David Ross, each
bent on seeing Ben alone, met at his office door.

The door was open and inviting—and misleading. Destroyed by
the recent ferment, poor Mrs. Duffy had left it ajar and bollixed
up a lot of other things as well. And Ben, submerged by history
lesson-planning on the one hand and general school matters on
the other—and stifling in an atmosphere of police suspicion that
pervaded everything like a disease—had, simply, not been able to
get up, walk over to the door, put his hand on the knob, and close
it. He felt that he was being pulled in every direction simultaneously, and his expression on seeing this additional claim on his
time was inhospitable, to say the least. He was not presently interested in the loves and hates and personality clashes of his guidance staff, or even in the possibility (which was not as remote as
might be thought) that there was something positive he could do
for Allen and David at that very moment. He only shook his head
at them.

"Ask Opal to try and find some room on my calendar for you.
Next week," he said dismissively.

"But you'll be in Frisco next week," said Allen.

"Sure. And Hell will freeze over too," Ben said glumly. "Say,
mind closing the door for me? I'm really sorry but—" and instantly
forgot them.

They did not speak to Mrs. Castle but went slowly and indeci-
sively into the corridor like strangers to the building who had
misunderstood directions.

"Hell!" David exploded aromatically.

Allen looked sharply at him. "Where's the bar? Or does home
ec' just provide take-out setups?"

"Something like that!"

"Better make it vodka, Dave. Now hold your water, pal! Keep
it down, for crissake! I'm on your side," Allen said, worried

about him. "Look, Dave, something's bothering you. It sticks out a mile. Is there something I can do?"

David snorted. "Ask rather what I can do for you," he paraphrased sardonically. "I didn't get a chance to ask you about that hassle you had with Joyce on Tuesday. What's with you two?"

"Just—a misunderstanding."

"Just—! If looks could kill, brother, it wouldn't be flu that's kept her home!" He added reflectively, "A consummation et cetera et cetera," which earned him another sharp look. "Well, why not? Hell of a lot neater than shooting!"

"Dry up, David! And dry out too!" Allen warned under his breath as Tony Evans and Timothy Lunn approached them. "Hi, you guys, what's up?" Plenty, from the looks of them, he saw with new concern.

"You free, Mr. Magrue?" said Tony. He was gray-faced and shaking to pieces.

"Nah nah, don't say nuttin'!" Tim muttered. "C'mon!" and pulled him along.

Tony yanked free and gave his best friend a look of bitter hatred. "Leave me alone, yuh creep!" he said passionately. But all the same he followed the older boy like one running for his life.

"What was that supposed to mean?" David said.

"Damned if I know. I haven't seen Tony since last Friday. And we both saw Tim on Monday. I haven't had a chance to get to either one of them. But that reminds me! One of the firemen— Trent, I think—saw you go through the boiler room Monday night. He said to tell you the next time you're passing through at two in the morning to stop by for a cup of coffee. What were you doing here at such a time?"

"Reading!" David said, and left him open-mouthed.

Gerald Rosen was buried Thursday at noon. A small group of teachers and students, Ben among them, attended the quiet services, paid their respects awkwardly, and left as soon as they could.

Before Ben returned to school he spoke with Vincent Dean's parents who stood apart like lepers, pleading mutely for absolution and taking despairingly what there was of that questionable commodity.

"We're moving out," Mr. Dean said sadly. "It's just too hard."

"People forget, Mr. Dean. Things will straighten out soon."

"Not for my boy. Not here. He can't do anything. He can't concentrate, he can't play his violin. He just looks at his hand and cries."

"What have you found out about that gun, Mr. Louis?" Mrs. Dean said aggressively. "It wasn't *my* boy's fault! All he did was—"

Ben's suddenly stony face was an eloquent reprimand.

"What will they do to him?" she said tearfully. "What will happen to him?"

"Legally, nothing. He'll be exonerated because there was no criminal intent. For the rest it will take time. You'll see. The more you cry, the more he will. So take it easy."

"But the gun?" she insisted angrily.

"I don't know. I have no information. I wish I did. I'm very sorry," Ben said tiredly. "If you'll excuse me now, I—have to get back."

There were two more angry calls from Mrs. Evans to Ben Louis, but he was teaching Mrs. Cory's class and was unable to call back.

You'd think, he said to himself resentfully when his secretary had given him the messages, you'd think she hadn't heard about the tragedy at all! You'd think her problem came first! Before anything else!

It had, but neither of them knew it.

Allen Magrue sighed, happily replete, and pushed away from the dinner table. "I think I'll have to marry you in time for Thanksgiving!" he said and gave Helen Chadwick an impetuous hug. "Turkey, stuffing—the works!"

He had showered and changed before coming but looked as if he had been tumbled together in a Mixmaster. She kissed him and straightened his tie. "Greedy. For shame."

"No." Her hands were light against his chest and he covered them with his. " 'There is no spectacle on earth more appealing than that of a beautiful woman in the act of cooking dinner for someone she loves,' "* he quoted in a voice that trembled not with passion this time but with profound gratitude. "Thank you,

* *The Web and the Rock*, by Thomas Wolfe, Chapter 28.

my darling. I'd better hurry. The library closes at nine. I'll call later if I can."

He came instead, when she was pink and fragrant from her shower, her rich hair vibrant from brushing and loose on her shoulders.

"How lovely you are," he said hoarsely and clutched her arms. "I swear to God, I swear it—I'd kill her before I'd let her do anything to hurt you or keep you from me!"

She kissed him and led him to the couch. "Brandy, darling? You look so discouraged. What did you find out?" It would be foolish to tell him to rest, although he looked sick with fatigue. How could he rest now? She gave him a glass of brandy which he emptied at a gulp.

He leaned back and closed his eyes. "Not much. About the same thing Don said. Joyce would be properly discharging her duty to her superior by sending him a qualified privileged communication about me. There'd be no malice involved. The likelihood is that I couldn't win in court if I sued her for libel."

"What about a suit for invasion of privacy?"

"Same thing. But I wouldn't do it in the first place. Private matters should be—private."

"But Don doesn't specialize in this kind of law. And books—you couldn't have read the most recent cases. Aren't more and more suits like this coming into court now? Why don't we see a lawyer who—"

He shook his head. "No. And even if I did win, all I'd gain is a Pyrrhic victory. You know that!"

"Then why don't we go and talk to the Superintendent? He's a wonderful person. We can trust him, Allen."

"No. He'd always have that tiny doubt. I just refuse to take the chance. And anyway, do you really think Joyce would stop there if he told her to forget it? Sooner or later she'd blow it. And what could I say? That her behavior was consistent with her orientation as of this point? The first question her counsel would ask in court is 'Are you qualified to judge?' Well, technically I'm not. And if I brought in someone who was, like Dr. Inman, they'd say it was an interesting opinion. As David says, ours is not an exact science."

"Then," she said slowly, "it looks as if we're in a box. . . ."

Would you consider resigning? Joyce is right, darling. You'll have to be a resident student sooner or later. Why not now?"

"And let her win? Not a chance!"

"Allen, forgive me, but you sound like David at this point. You won't give an inch! And Joyce will probably be back tomorrow, at least for the dance. What are you going to do?"

"I . . . don't . . . know. . . ."

They sat in silence for some time, and suddenly he laughed lightheartedly. "Do you realize that I almost took that job in New York? That I might have missed you? So easily?"

"No. I was waiting."

"But why?" he said half seriously.

"I'm very particular."

"With—all this?"

For answer she opened her arms to him.

"Ben, did I or didn't I take that statue away with me the other day?" Jane said as she struggled into her nightgown.

"What statue?"

"That statue. That soapstone thing. You know." She slid into the immense bed and adjusted the covers. "I thought I left it on one of the cabinets in the TV studio, but I looked in there today and it wasn't anywhere around. I'm sure I took it out of your office. Did I bring it home instead?"

"I don't know. I didn't see it," Ben murmured, exhausted. He fell asleep before he had finished speaking.

CHAPTER NINE

"You look extremely handsome tonight," Jane teased. "I must be out of my mind letting you out loose." But her eyes were anxious and her hands tender as she helped Ben into his best suit jacket. "You're sure you don't want me to go? Maybe you could use another chaperone."

"I don't think so, darling. And anyway, you never liked this sort of thing," he said generously and bent to kiss her. "I'll make sure the kids wind this up by eleven. Ought to be home by eleven-thirty at the latest." Under his fine dark eyes were black stains of tension and fatigue.

"I'll be waiting," she said and watched him trudge out to the car and drive off. "Damn Them," she said with indiscriminate feeling. "Damn Them all." Uneasy, she closed the door and her hand curved round Fee's shaggy neck as she sought reassurance.

Ben was not surprised by the crowd he found at the school, for it had acquired a morbid fascination even for those who ordinarily preferred to be anywhere else at any time. Since Tuesday kids had loitered on the grounds, whispering, gossiping, speculating, gathering in little clots that formed and re-formed like restless amoebae. Tonight almost the entire student body seemed to be here, he estimated wearily as he made a slow patrol of the maze of driveways and paths round and about the three buildings. The parking lots were full, the entrance to the main building—Building Three —was mobbed, the atmosphere was weighted with expectation as thick and palpable as a polluted fog.

As he drove past the back of the main building a second time, he saw Tim Lunn playing handball in the yard behind the boiler room and the repair shop, and looking normal for a change—if you could call a boy normal who chose to do what Tim was doing on a gala night like this. Ben decided that he could.

He parked in his assigned space, shivered in the unseasonable cold, put on his company face, and went in smiling.

A knot of giggling self-conscious girls greeted him.

"Bit early, aren't you?" he said, glancing at his watch.

"We're the decorating committee," said one.

Ben gagged inwardly at her miniskirt, bangle earrings ("big enough for her to jump through!"), Cleopatra eye makeup, and the long straight hair that straggled down her back. But he nodded pleasantly and went into his office to hang up his coat. The sight of his pipe rack occasioned a minor conflict between id and superego, since he had not had time after dinner for his customary smoke and quiet chat with Jane, but he only sighed and went out again to check over the arrangements.

Near the front doors Helen Chadwick was talking earnestly with Allen Magrue. His expensive black mohair suit looked—on him—like jeans and an old sweat shirt. His hair fell over his eyes and his tie was divided and flapped across his lapels. She pointed to it and he neatened it. But it made no difference. He might as well have been wearing jeans and an old sweat shirt. Occasionally his hand rested on her arm and his face was very close to hers. Jane had found this mannerism disconcerting but Helen's beautiful face glowed with happiness.

Oh my god, Ben thought as he joined them. Do I have a triangle to contend with?

"Aren't they the limit?" Magrue remarked without censure of the girls waiting to admit the mob.

"Weird. Twenty-five years ago girls dressed pretty much alike but they seemed more individual. But in that small group there's every fad in the catalogue and they all seem as dull as dishwater. Maybe I'm getting old."

"Mmmmm," Allen said. He laughed. "I didn't mean that! I'm just glad so much leeway is permitted here. Dress codes are for the birds. Oh—there's Joyce! Excuse me, Helen, Ben. I haven't seen her for three days."

"I'd like a word with her too, Allen. Tell her I'll be looking for her after a while."

Helen's face dimmed. "I'm going to the gym," she said and walked away forlornly.

Ben looked at his watch again. If there really is a god, Jane would have said, that watch would now read eleven o'clock and the dance would be all over! But it was only eight-twenty. Might as well get cracking or they'll get restless and slash some tires, Ben thought in dismay.

He told the girls to open the doors. "But remember," he cautioned them. "Only those with tickets. There are to be no exceptions for any reason, or we'll never have another dance here." But he knew that nothing short of police state methods could ensure the plans that had qualified his consent to this one. He followed Helen down the other corridor to inspect the gym.

"I suspect the decorating committee needed a decorating committee," she said as they looked in.

"God! Did you ever see anything so grim!"

Improperly lighted for nighttime use, the gym's high corners swam away into a sickly yellow-gray dimness that hurt the eyes. The air, and the walls, the bleachers, mats, horses, bucks, even the steel itself—all were redolent of old sweat and the curious odor of athlete's foot. A scattering of paper cornucopias, despairing cornstalks, and bunches of Indian corn tied with floppy bows of orange crepe paper adorned the stacked bleachers. Moons in all the lunar phases hung from miles of streamers that began to jiggle, suggesting the imminent collapse of a peculiar cosmos, for all at once the crowded place was a-roar with gyrating spastic perspiring lunatics: The student band, long-haired and black-booted, had begun to play.

Ben was convinced that he was about to die of depression. "I think I'll just go out and look around. If you don't mind, Helen."

"It's pretty awful," she said, her eyes gleaming with amusement.

He was jostled aside by a couple rushing into the melee, but as this served to speed his escape he did not complain. "I'll—look in later," he gasped, and fled.

An hour later he came upon David Ross on the landing at the south side entrance. "Come on, kids, you're in the wrong pew," David was saying with unusual affability. Ordinarily he would have wrapped the rule book around their throats. "You came to a dance—so dance! Now *up!*" and he shepherded them good-naturedly up the steps, closed the corridor door, and watched them enter the gym.

"Any others down there?" Ben said, wondering why there should have been any down cellar to begin with, if the side doors were being monitored.

"I don't think so. But there's plenty of places to hide in if they want to get cute about it." His eyes were oddly loose in his skull, it seemed to Ben.

"Stick around. I'll go take a look." Anything's better than standing around and watching, he thought. The trouble is, though, it's only nine thirty-five and I've got to patrol for another hour and a half!

He stopped on the landing and opened the outer door to look up and down the side paths. He saw no one but he found that the temperature had plummeted. The air was raw and piercing and smelled of snow. But it was fresh, at least. He took a deep breath, then came back inside and went dejectedly down the rest of the way. It would be warm and beautiful in San Francisco now.

He was sorry that he had allowed the dance to be held. Whatever he was expecting—and he had no idea of exactly what he was expecting—it was axiomatic that trouble had a way of breeding trouble. Given Tuesday, something was bound to happen. He could feel it in his bones.

There may or may not have been a student hiding in the cafeteria, but Ben's first thought was for the south tunnel whose mouth was unaccountably dark.

As he approached it the eye of a large lantern or flashlight swung back and forth, and a furious bellow resounded from its depths. Then the light went out and Mr. Tomasello emerged shouting at a brawny boy whose arm he clutched as easily as if it were the leg of a dead duck. The boy might as well have been one for, in the eyes of the girl whose arm he in turn held, he had irreparably lost face.

"Now get out 'n stay out!" said the Roc, and caught sight of Ben. " 'Lo, Mr. Louis," he offered in a moderated tone.

"What did you catch, Roc?"

"Nuttin' much, I can tell yuh that!"

"Who're you kids? I don't think I know you," Ben said, fixing them with a look into which he summoned every flagging ounce of authority, a look guaranteed to pound the head into the chest. Silence.

And still nothing happened: Ben was in no mood to administer heavy-handed discipline. All that occurred to him was, "For crying out loud, couldn't you think of a *better* time and place?" aggrievedly. "Beat it," he added with an indifference that scared the wits out of them. They ran—in opposite directions—before he changed his mind.

"What's with the lantern, Roc?"

"Some goddam kid went and busted every bulb in that goddam tunnel! Wid a water pistol! They done it before, they shoot 'em through the cages. I was sweepin' up the glass when I see them kids smoochin'."

"I hope you can line up some bulbs, Roc. For what they're worth." He regarded the entrance to the tunnel. "Any chance of putting up some kind of barrier there?"

"What the hell good's a barrier? Anything kids can go round or over ain't any better'n nuttin' at all. We gotta have a door built in, like at the other end, Mr. Louis. An' they should be kept *locked!* It shoulda been done a long time ago." His glance was freighted with meaning and reproach.

"I couldn't agree more. I'll see Mr. Hardy on Monday. Maybe we'll get covered walkways one of these years."

"Sooner the better, Mr. Louis. You tell Mr. Hardy I said so!" And on this injunction Mr. Tomasello departed to locate a batch of bulbs.

Moodily Ben put a dime into the Coke machine, sat on the edge of a table, drank without pleasure, put the unfinished bottle into the case, and went upstairs again by the opposite stairway to avoid going past the gym. Judging by the noise issuing therefrom and the relatively empty rear corridor that traversed the width of the building, the dance was going well. He would look in again later. Meanwhile he could safely smoke a pipe in quiet and privacy. He exchanged a few words with the police officer on duty who was strolling about, bored but not uncomfortable, and then turned back toward his office, anticipating the joy of closing its door against the mass of sound signifying carefree youth. But Simon Wills called to him from the gym door and came over to say good night.

"We seem to be over the hump, Ben," he said as they turned into the long corridor. "I think I'll take off now." He paused as Joyce Bellows and Tony Evans came into the corridor through the side door near Ben's sanctuary. Joyce steered the boy away from the teachers standing guard there and said something to him. But it was plain that her lovely voice had produced an unusual response. The boy's face was stiff with fear and anger, and when she touched his arm he jerked away as though he had been burned.

"I won't, I won't! I don't know! You can't make me! Leave me alone for a change, you—you—" he shouted, backing off. Tactfully the teacher-monitors looked the other way as he wrenched open the door, ran down the steps, and rushed through the outer door into the yard.

"She's been at him even here!" Simon muttered bitterly.

"I'll talk to her. Thanks for helping, Sime. Have a good weekend and—"

"Even at a dance!" Simon continued, staring at Joyce who was staring at the door. "Can you imagine such crass stupidity? Christ! That poor kid! Strong-armed up to the office at a time like this!"

"Up to—! You sure?"

"I'm certain of it. I saw her corral him! Heard her, too! Shall I tell her off—or do you want the pleasure?"

He looked and sounded like the Simon of five years ago, and Ben marveled at his renewed vigor. Apparently Simon had decided that indignation and involvement were better medicines than peace and quiet.

"I'll do it. You go on home. Hope you took a coat—it's a lot colder now."

"No—and my car's a mile away! Damn kids took my space." But his tone, like Allen's earlier, was indulgent and affectionate.

Simon was no fool, Ben thought wryly, even if he liked kids —no matter what! "Do me a favor, will you, Sime? Something else just occurred to me on this night of nights. Ring down to the boiler room and engine room, tell the men on shift to watch out for any kids coming through from that end. Use the office phone. And take care," he said as Joyce came slowly toward them.

"Will do, Ben. You too." Giving Joyce a wide berth, he went into the office. The teacher-monitors left their post temporarily and sauntered toward the front doors.

"You shouldn't have come tonight, Joyce," Ben began without conspicuous warmth. She made a great effort to smile but her expression was a travesty of good humor. "I felt better—and I knew you needed me. Besides, Tony didn't keep his appointment with me Tuesday and I wanted to find out why. And of course the news about Gerald Rosen . . . I can't shake the feeling that *I* could have stopped it. . . ." Her eyes filled with tears.

A troop of girls flew by, giggling and simpering.

"Those girls!" she complained with the touchiness of the sick. "Their behavior is idiotic! And their idea of dress—!"

"Joyce, why don't you go home? Everything's under control. I have to talk to you—the police are hounding me for a list of kids who might be tied up with that gun. But this isn't the time. You're not looking well." What gave her such a feeling of responsibility for Gerald's death? That boy had never gone to the guidance office for anything, not even for program changes.

"Didn't you get anything from the staff?" she said, her face closed.

"Nothing that was worth anything. Nothing bad enough to suggest this business. But you'd know."

"Perhaps. But I can't simply give you a list. Can you imagine the effect on those boys—being questioned by the police because *I* suspect them?"

"I appreciate that, Joyce. You know that. But this is serious and we've got to clear it up. Any upset those boys might suffer because of you would have to be part of their continuing therapy. It can't be helped."

"I'll do things my way, Ben," she said frostily.

"Like taking valuable information out of those confidential folders? To say nothing of taking those folders out of the building?" He was getting angry now.

Her eyes narrowed. "What I took out of those folders was my own business! My own private notes! By law they are *not* part of the cumulative records, Ben!"

"I'm aware of the law," Ben said, controlling his irritation. "And if you want to quote it so will I. Your 'notes' were in those folders. They are therefore part of the records and I want to read them. In the circumstances you'll agree that your knowledge can't be kept under wraps. I've got to have your help—and your co-operation."

Outraged, she cried, "Are you insinuating too that I've with-held it? How dare you! How dare you say such a thing to me!" And then as quickly as she had flared, terror glazed her eyes and her face crumpled.

He gaped at her. Evidently she had been—she was—much sicker than she realized. Nothing could be gained by further discussion now. He was about to offer a soothing apology when Allen Magrue joined them. The little interruption gave Joyce time to regulate her face, which she accomplished as if following a set of instructions.

"What are you two so serious about?" Allen said, giving Ben a friendly poke.

"Allen, would you escort Joyce to her car?" Ben said presumptuously. "She's got to get off home.'"

"It's not necessary!" she said with astonishing rudeness and opened the door. "Ben, if you're going to be home this weekend I'd like to ring you up—if you don't mind. I'll come in tomorrow and go through my records and call you around noon. And there's something else I want to tell you." She went out without saying anything to Magrue.

"I'll see you out," he said to her stiff little back and followed her.

There's something very strange here, Ben told himself. Something very wrong. If those two are in love—with each other—then I don't know anything about love.

He stood where he was for a moment and then hastily went out of the building and away from the lighted doorway, hoping that in his dark suit he would not be noticed. But no one was around except Joyce and Allen and neither turned to see if they were being followed.

He watched them walk to her car and stand there talking, their heads down, not touching each other. And then Joyce seemed to see something or someone, or to think of something, for suddenly she walked away from Allen toward the open door to the boiler room in Building Two. She appeared now to be calling to some-one. Her head was high and she held one hand out, but the racket from the gym was too great for Ben to hear her. He stood behind a gigantic forsythia and kept his eye on Allen Magrue.

Magrue took a few steps toward her, stopped, then continued almost on tiptoe with exaggerated caution. And then he ran toward the boiler room door and out of Ben's sight.

Troubled, Ben returned to the gym by way of the side door and tried for almost fifteen minutes to talk intelligibly under the noise. Everyone in the school seemed to be here and it occurred to him that the side entries and the stairs to the basement might now be unmonitored. Again he went out to check. Two teachers were chatting with his secretary Opal Castle at the side door through which Joyce and Allen had left.

Fine.

He talked with Mrs. Castle for a moment and then hastened to the other side of the building.

There was no one there.

Annoyed with David Ross for leaving before someone took his place, Ben went downstairs a second time.

There were no sounds, no moving telltale shadows in the vast cafeteria. Everything was as it had been left—clean, orderly, undisturbed. The kitchen doors were locked. No one was hiding behind the counters. Or behind the great supporting columns. Or in the custodians' office, because it too was locked.

Good.

But the tunnel?

Ben had good reason for hating the tunnel, and whenever he thought about it genuine rage moved in him. A secretary had once been assaulted there by a senior student but had refused to press charges. She had left the school and the youth had been quietly expelled. Only two people immediately connected with the school knew of the affair, Mr. Tomasello, who in his eternal vigilance had heard her screams, and Ben Louis, to whom he had instantly reported. In handling the matter with utmost discretion Ben had defeated his aim, for he had been unable to convince a penny-wise community to secure this tunnel against common use merely because he said it was a good idea to do so. Covered walkways were expensive and unnecessary, voted the town. The job of the administration was the disciplining of the student body, the elders pontificated. And if *you* can't do it, we'll get somebody else who will, threatened the School Committee. Fearful that the area of discipline would be invaded by nonprofessionals of punitive bent, Ben had let the matter rest.

Well, *goddam Them*, he thought as he went into the tunnel to see if the bulbs had been replaced, I only hope *They* never have cause to regret it!

His hard heels clacked on the ramp and he did not hear Joyce Bellows' pitiable whimper as her assailant struck her.

Just before the point where the tunnel angled sharply to the right, a weak bulb burned.

If he's done that one, he's done them all, if I know Roc, Ben thought. But I'd better make sure.

Bravely he stepped round the corner and in the instant following his recognition of what had happened there, something slammed against the side of his head and knocked him senseless.

Mr. Tomasello's supply closets yielded four twenty-five-watt bulbs, and he needed sixteen more for the tunnel. Bulb-snatching was futile: The protective cages would not accommodate larger bulbs. He put in the four miserable bulbs, one at the dogleg angle, the others eighty feet apart, and went looking for Ben Louis who had become as elusive as a firefly in a bonfire.

"You seen Mr. Louis, Mrs. Grant?"

"He was over at the punch table a minute ago, Mr. Tomasello."

"You seen Mr. Louis, Mr. Crayne?"

"He's here someplace, Roc."

"Mrs. Pinch, you seen Mr. Louis?"

"Well, I'm not *sure*, Mr. Tomasello, but I think he was with the decorating committee, or maybe on that bleacher over there, or else—"

"F'crissake, Mr. Larch, you seen the boss around?"

"Who could recognize anybody in this brawl? Take it easy, Roc, you'll blow a gasket."

"Mrs. Castle, *where's* Mr. Louis?"

"Hello, Mr. Tomasello, how are you? Mr. Louis went downstairs a minute ago to check the basement."

Mr. Tomasello boiled down the steps to the cafeteria, brandishing his lantern and muttering blasphemies. The room was empty.

But Mrs. Castle *said*—

And she was right, as he saw moments later.

Just beyond the sharp angle of the tunnel Joyce Bellows lay on her back with her arms outflung, legs bent and drawn up to one side. Her skull had been savagely crushed from brow to crown as though an elephant had stepped on her head while she was performing a hip-reducing exercise. Whatever expression there may have been on her pretty face was hidden by blood and the shadows cast by the uncertain light of the custodian's lantern.

A few feet away from her left hand lay her open handbag, its contents scattered except for a small pin fastened to the inside of the flap. It gleamed briefly in the lantern's darting light and vanished like a blown candle. At the dead woman's feet was a large brown bulging paper bag. There was a liberal splashing of wet blood on it, and on the floor, and on the ugly paint of the center support. The odor of it was nauseating.

Mr. Tomasello perceived all this in one horrified glance and did not want to linger for an extended inventory. He was anything but squeamish, having grown up on the docks in Sicily and in Hell's Kitchen (although he was by no means an insensitive man, as certain insensitive people liked to think).

Rather, he was stunned at recognizing the head that all but lay on the curve of Miss Bellows' chaste thighs. And near that head was a small statue defaced by bits of flesh and hair and drying blood.

"JesusMary'nJoseph!" he prayed and knelt to put a work-gnarled hand on Ben's heart. The slow but strong beat reassured him. With utmost gentleness he dragged Ben away from the dead body, taking care not to disturb the statue.

I better cover her before he wakes up, he thought, and ran out to the custodians' office, scrabbling in his pocket for his master key.

He was spreading an old tarpaulin over the warm, still body when Ben opened his eyes and groaned.

CHAPTER TEN

Police Chief Art Hudson and Sergeant Sam Lang arrived almost immediately after getting the custodian's call.

"Keefe will be along shortly," Hudson said. "As for you, Ben, you'll need X rays and stitches. Better call his wife, Tomasello."

"Nothing doing!" Ben said in a tone that had caused thousands of students to quake and pray. "I probably have a slight concussion and I may need a few stitches, but I am not leaving this school! That is final! Roc, go call Dr. Muir. Anything he has to do can be done in the nurse's office." He was surprised and gratified by the strength of his voice, although no one sounded normal in the tunnel. Nor did Hudson and Lang and the Roc look any healthier than he. In the poor light they looked embalmed. They all looked terrible.

But not as bad as Joyce. No one looked as dead as she did.

"From what Tomasello says, it looks like you got it just seconds after she did, Ben. And with the same weapon," Hudson said.

"That's my statue. Jane left it in the TV studio and someone took it. She's been looking for it all week," Ben said in a broken voice. Two tears rolled down his cheeks as he grieved silently. And if his grief were not entirely selfless, none who knew him would be unjust enough to fault him on the point.

"She was a good person," he murmured. "A thoroughly good, nice person."

The eulogy was too comprehensive for Hudson. He said sardonically, "Someone else thought so too, Ben. Someone thought she was nice enough to murder!"

A low growl came from Mr. Tomasello's throat.

"Oh—sorry!" Hudson said. "Better call Mrs. Louis," he added quietly to the custodian who gave him a look of vast and spacious contempt before going back to his office to call Jane and the doctor.

"Sam!" Hudson barked. "Don't just *do* something, *stand* there!"

"You name it, chief."

"Get out your notebook and make a list," Hudson said, beginning to set out the contents of the shopping bag.

An expensive cashmere sweater. A package of crayon pencils. A box of charcoal pencils. Two dozen tubes of oil paints. Three paint brushes. Some sandwiches and cookies. Apples, oranges, bananas. Six dollar bills and some coins in an envelope. Two high-quality sketch pads containing rough sketches and unfinished paintings. A scout knife. A half-full box of .22 cartridges.

"Hmmmm," Hudson said, putting everything back into the bag. "Looks like someone's been raiding lockers, Ben. The art supplies are good stuff and could sell for a few pennies. And those cartridges are the first solid piece of proof that *one* of your kids likes to handle guns! Which means exactly nothing! Just like everything else we've found out! Or didn't! Even that statue won't tell us anything we don't already know, namely that it was the murder weapon and that it won't have any prints on it! Surface is too rough. Wouldn't you know it wouldn't be the polished kind!"

Ben said nothing. He was using all his strength to hold his head together and keep his eyes away from the tiny pathetic figure under the tarpaulin.

"Okay, Sam, we'll go through her purse," Hudson said, wrapping a handkerchief around his hand before he touched it. But except for the pin on the flap it was empty. "Notice, Sam? No keys! How was she going to start her car? Tell me that!" he demanded. "Lipstick, hanky, comb, mirror, wallet—and no keys!" He left everything as it was for the medical examiner's scrutiny and returned to a consideration of the little pin. "What was she doing with this?" he muttered. It was a lapel insigne—the caduceus of the Army Medical Corps. "You know anything about this, Ben?"

"No. Probably a souvenir she got from someone. Jane kept my insignia for years. Never wore any other jewelry—not for a long time, anyway." Never could afford to buy her any, he added to himself.

"Miss Bellows in the Medics?"

"I don't know. I'll find out. It would be on her personnel record if she were. I'll call the Superintendent's office."

"I will. I have to call him anyway. And I wish," Hudson grumbled, "I wish we had some light in this godforsaken place!"

He pulled the tarpaulin off the body and put a bulb into the socket of his camera. The flash cast a brief ghostly pattern on the center support and the insulated pipes beyond it. Another flash, and another, and Hudson sighed.

"Sam, cover it up. I'm finished with this. The M.E. can have it, and welcome. I wonder what made that big smear on that center support. . . . Hmmm. . . . You know, the way she's lying there, it looks like she was heading for the old building. It's time I started digging."

Keefe and Tomasello came round the corner just as Ben opened his mouth to tell Hudson that he was wrong. That Joyce, followed by Magrue, had gone into the boiler room in Two, and that she at least had come through the tunnel to Building Three. And, furthermore, that he could not remember seeing Allen Magrue back in the gym before he himself had gone down to the basement again.

He decided, almost too late, to say nothing.

"Well, it's about time!" Hudson said when he saw Keefe. "There's thousands of people up there—"

"And none of them will get away, Art, so relax," Keefe said comfortably, chewing his cigar. "I checked. Between your radio and mine, every door's covered. Not that it'll make any difference, as I get the picture. This looks strictly like a hit-and-run. Whoever killed her had plenty of time to leave long before Tomasello here called in."

"Yeah. Let's get moving. I'll take Ben upstairs to the nurse's office if that's the way he wants it, and see what he knows. Sam, wait for the M.E. He should be along soon."

"Mr. Tomasello, I'd be obliged if you'll come with me," Keefe said. "You can help me get things squared away in that gym, get them all settled on the bleachers—and find the teachers in charge of that bedlam. I'll want Mrs. Castle too. We don't want any panic so we'll do this carefully. Okay?"

Mr. Tomasello, who knew all there was to know about discretion (regarding everything but his temper), nodded with a certain distant condescension. He and Keefe were gone before Hudson and Lang had heaved Ben off the floor.

PART TWO: BEN

CHAPTER ELEVEN

This time the head on a sickroom pillow was Ben's, cleaned, sutured, rakishly bandaged, and as fiercely sore as though every headache in the world had been stitched into it. He sat up with an assumption of nonchalance which fooled nobody: The black stains under his eyes now looked as if they had been painted on.

"My word! A powerful blow!" Dr. Muir twanged, and packed his little bag.

Jane held that he was either a revenant from the Court of Philip IV or an actor whose voice had been dubbed into him for American audiences by a Spanish movie director who had studied at Bowdoin. The more modern his surroundings, the more archaic his appearance, and Jane's fancy clothed him in the laces and velvets of the sixteenth century and put the chased grip of a Toledo sword into his lean surgeon's fingers.

His little beard twitched. "My word! It could have crushed the skull!" Despite all his experience he seemed enormously impressed by the possibility.

"It did," Hudson said bluntly. "One of the teachers, I mean. Smashed it like an eggshell."

Ben winced and Jane glared.

"Soapstone, you said? Yes, well, some people have skulls very little stronger than an eggshell, in point of fact. Fortunately Ben's is as thick as old shoe leather."

Ben winced and Jane grinned.

"You're lucky, Ben," the doctor said severely, suggesting that there had been a miscarriage of justice. "Don't overdo, or you'll have to go to bed and stay there. Whether you like it or not. I want you in the Medical Center for skull X rays tomorrow morning. Don't expect to find anything, though." (Ben and

Jane winced, and Hudson grinned.) "You could do with some rest too, young lady," he added, going to the door. "You look terrible."

"Oh no, I'm fine," Jane said. "If I thought this were the worst thing that would ever happen to Ben, I'd go without sleep for the rest of my life."

The doctor's austere face softened fractionally. "Good night," he said, and left.

"You were damned lucky, Ben," Hudson said. "An inch or two in the other direction and the doc would've been digging it out of your brain. The M.E., I mean, not Muir. What's more to the point is, who hit you?"

"*I* don't know! I went down to check the basement and the tunnel, and just as I saw Joyce lying there, I got conked. Didn't actually know who she was 'til I came to, though."

"Christ, what a case! Two deaths. A gun and a statue. Two other wounds—yours and Bert Shrag's. And no clues, no fingerprints, no anything! My god, Ben, you must know *some*thing! You must've seen her tonight. Do you happen to know when she left—or who she spent time with?"

"As far as I know, Allen Magrue saw her leave. I mean, he walked her out to her car. That was at about . . . ten."

"Ten! Tomasello found you at exactly ten-thirty. And you hadn't been out of the picture for more than a few minutes, figuring back from when he spoke to your secretary. And when *you* spoke to her before that. So what was Joyce Bellows doing during that half hour? Twenty minutes, more likely."

"*I* don't know, Art! All I can tell you is, she was out sick most of the week. She still felt lousy when I spoke to her tonight and I told her to take off. She said she'd come in tomorrow, look through her files, and ring me up around noon to give me some information about some of our problem boys, the ones she knows more about than anyone else on the staff does. And then she went out with Allen."

"And then she came back in. Obviously! You said the side stairs were being monitored?"

"Yes. But in the main corridors, not down on the landings. Of course anyone who saw Joyce wouldn't question where *she* was going," Ben said, telling him something without coming right out and telling him something.

"Obviously!" Hudson snapped. "So when she returned, she went down cellar. Instead of going up and then down. Obviously!"

"But—" Ben began, testing. Now, if Hudson would just tell him to mind his own business, his course was plain before him.

"All *right*, Ben! Let's not have a rerun of two years ago. You run your show, I'll run mine. What about Joyce and this Magrue? Anything between them especially?"

"I don't know. I thought so. The poor guy!"

"But don't you *know*? He's one of your people, after all!"

"Look, Art. He's new. And school's been open for just six weeks. And I don't see my staff members every day. And when I do, they don't sit down and tell me about their personal life. Not usually. And Jane only met him once—"

"And a half," she added.

"All I can say at this point," Ben went on, "is that he's highly qualified and a hell of a nice guy. Anything between them was just rumor. And for my part, I hope he wasn't in love with her. It's a lousy way for a love *affaire* to end, is why." He squinted in thought. "Her sister, Grace Wickham, was visiting her. She might know. Oh—there's something else. One of her old counselees, Tony Evans, was upset about something she said tonight. But he left before she did."

"What's with him?"

"Nothing we don't already know about. He's on a sort of work-study program. Joyce fixed him up with the maintenance staff and he works a few hours a week for them and makes himself some spending money. He's mixed up and miserable, but he's basically a decent kid as far as I know. His mother's been calling me for a week, but I don't know why. I've been too damn busy to find out."

"Well, I will. Ben, didn't anything—Joyce Bellows' behavior or the dance or anything—didn't anything strike you as being particularly unusual?"

"Just that statue," Ben said wryly.

"I don't get it. If she was all that nice a person, why would anyone want to kill her? Jane, what's your impression of her? You must've known her pretty well. You're here a lot."

"As Ben said, she was a very lovely decent person. I think everyone will say the same thing, Art, strange as it seems. Exceptionally well trained for a school psychologist is what they'll also say. She had a Ph.D. in psych' and a lot more graduate study after that, at the University. People thought she was wasting herself at a mere high school, but that tells more about them than it does about her. I remember her saying once that every school should have a resident psychiatrist and a physician and a social worker."

"She must've been crazy!"

"Maybe. Aren't we all? Anyway, she was dedicated to education —which means *the total child*, Arthur Hudson."

"What else?" Hudson said irritably.

"Oh . . . conservative, but not a prude, I'd say. Friendly but highly discreet and professional almost to a fault. My goodness, Ben's worked with her for eight years and finds out just this week that she's got a sister! Ben talked with her Tuesday—Mrs. Wickham, that is—and she said Joyce had met her at Logan the night before. . . .

"I don't know what else to say. I knew her, but not closely. I don't think anyone did. She was always a bit too proprietary about her counselees, though . . . Oh Ben, when I think how worried you were that she'd get married and resign! Who would have thought she'd—she'd leave like this!" Her eyes brimmed over with tears and she wiped them away wearily.

"Look, why don't you take the wounded warrior home, Jane? Keefe and I have plenty of other fish to fry and I'd better get out of here. Unless you can think of something else. No? We have to see this Allen Magrue—odd name, that—and the kid Tony Evans, and the Superintendent, and just about a million more in this cast of thousands!"

"Art, do you think that Luger has any connection with Joyce's murder?" Ben said tensely.

"I was wondering when you'd think of asking that. How the hell do I know? Nobody else knows anything around here, so why should I be an exception?" Hudson said self-pityingly. Investigation into crime always rendered him cranky, and the singularly sweet smile that transfigured his face was never in evidence while he was collecting evidence. "We may get lucky and find some link in those files of hers. It's about time we had a look at them."

"They're confidential, Art."

"They aren't all that confidential! Not like a doctor's! Don't kid yourself, Ben. If we have to push you, we can get a *ducas tecum* without turning a hair. So just give us the key to the files and let us get on with it. We certainly aren't going to broadcast what we find, and you know it."

"I can't give you the key. Jack Hardy has it. Or rather, it's in his safe here. His secretary opens the safe every morning, and when our guidance office secretary, Gert Kane, comes in, she gets the key, opens the files, and brings the key right back to Hardy's office. He's been bunking in with us because there wasn't room until now for him in the Central Office. Half his stuff's been moved over, though, and when he's out I'll have responsibility for the key. It's a stupid arrangement but that's how it's always been done. God! Some guidance file keys are kept in the secretary's top drawer—and *it's* not locked!"

"What about this secretary Gert Kane? Any hanky-panky between her and Bellows?"

"No. She's a blessing. And very loyal."

"Another nice person!" Hudson said furiously. "How many people have the combination to Hardy's safe?"

"Oh—the Superintendent, of course. Hardy and his secretary. I never got around to learning it. Too many other things to do."

"Well, Joyce Bellows must've had her own file key. She told you she'd be in tomorrow to go through her papers, didn't she? She'd hardly expect the Superintendent or Hardy or anybody else to come over on a weekend and open the cabinets for her. Or that safe. Or her office either. And there were no keys among her things. Whoever struck her down and then knocked you out had time enough to grab her keys before Tomasello got there. And it would've been a lead pipe cinch for the murderer to pop upstairs and help himself!"

"You don't know that. He may not try it until afterward, when things are quiet."

"When school is in session, you mean," Hudson said sarcastically. "No. He went up tonight. And the reason I say *that* is we haven't found one thing to help us since Tuesday, and I see no reason why all of a sudden we're going to strike it rich now! I've never had a case like this in thirty years!"

"Mind if I call you tomorrow? I'd like to keep up to date."

"I'll be too busy to chitchat with *you*, Ben! I never saw anything like the way you people like to talk on the phone!" Hudson grumbled as he opened the door. "You're on the phone half your life. But don't try holding out on me if something does occur to you. Loyalty to your people is all very well in its way, very admirable and all that. But this case is bigger and more important than anything else. No matter what you know that you think may hurt one of your fair-haired bunch around here, you'd better tell me. If you do like you did last time—where *concrete information* is concerned—I'll try to keep you informed. Otherwise—"

Jane said wickedly, "You have a bloodstain on your pants, Art."

"Where? Where?" and Hudson bent and whirled and twisted, trying to see every inch of his pristine trousers.

Jane giggled. The spectacle wasn't a patch on what Art Hudson owed Ben for solving the Houseman murder case, but it was an enjoyable down payment.

"A-a-a-r-r-rgh!" said Hudson and went out and came back in again with a vengeful gleam in his big blue eyes. "Looks like you won't make it to Frisco after all, hey, Ben?" and departed.

Ben laughed although it destroyed him to do so, and then his conscience began to throb as violently as his head.

Honor. Loyalty. The duty of a citizen. Respect for the Law. Integrity. Nobility of mind.

Already he had kept five vital pieces of information from Hudson and Keefe. And no doubt he would think of others when his brain had cleared.

Should he call Art back and level with him?

He debated this embarrassing question for a moment. But the answer was very simple, really. He decided not to tell Hudson and Keefe. Later, perhaps. If it became necessary. First he would have to do some investigating on his own.

"Do you think there's a connection, Ben? Between Joyce and that Luger?" Jane said as she supported him down the stairs.

"She may have known whose gun it was, or who put it in Bert's lab," Ben said, intensely nauseated now from the pain and the pain-killers Muir had given him. "But Gerald's death was an accident, like Bert's wound. Whoever left the gun in the drawer did it without criminal intent. I'm convinced of that. Whoever put it there wouldn't be held liable."

"Maybe. But kids don't know the law. And if Joyce knew or

even suspected one of them, he might be scared enough to kill her."

"Sure. But it's also possible that there's someone else involved, someone with no connection to that gun. Someone with a hell of a grudge, though! That was a vicious blow she got. Whoever it was missed me by inches. And the bullet that killed Gerald Rosen missed Bert's heart by inches! A person could die of the relief of knowing that!"

He did not want to tell her anything about Allen Magrue. In fact, he was feeling so sick that he didn't want to talk at all.

"Oh darling, I'm so sorry!" she said as they reached the side door. "I forgot all about it. I found Benjy and told him to drive your car home—and mine's way in back of Two. I couldn't find any other place to park! Do you want to rest on the steps while I go get it?"

"No, I'll go with you. The air will do me good."

They met Mr. Tomasello who was also on his way home after a debilitating day. He looked and sounded like a demented bull, and so preoccupied was he with some unprintable remarks about a goddam fool and burning down the school and clearing up the so-and-so mess that he hardly recognized his revered leader and friend.

Collecting himself, he said, "I'm goin' *home!* 'Nough's 'nough for one day!" and tore off, spreading rubber.

"I'd love to do that," Jane said enviously, "but I don't have the qualifications."

"I'm glad," said Ben, concerned now only with the short view. For, as sedately as Jane drove out of the parking lot, it was even money that he would survive the journey home.

CHAPTER TWELVE

Before eight o'clock on Saturday morning the telephone shrilled in Ben's ear and he groaned and stumbled into wakefulness. He was headachy and sore but surprisingly vigorous after all, he discovered. On the other hand his conscience, so burdensomely healthy a few hours earlier, was tranquil to the point of being comatose. And Hudson and Keefe, through the magical power of projection, were now perverters of the Law, hence untouchables to be avoided at all costs by citizens of integrity and nobility of mind.

The caller, naturally, was Art Hudson, full of wrath and despair. Ben reached for a pain-killer and swallowed it dry.

Tony Evans, Hudson said, had not gone home last night. His mother had no idea of his whereabouts and was still insisting on talking with Ben.

Jack Hardy and his wife had also been out painting the town 'til all hours, Hudson complained, and Hardy wouldn't get here for at least another hour. (Ben smiled: Hardy, an ulcer patient, had been living it up last night on milk and bland biscuits with a degenerate crowd of school administrators after seeing a student performance in another town of *The Importance of Being Earnest*.) Hardy's unmarried secretary had been out too, a fact to which Hudson's fury lent the worst possible connotation. Which meant that the goddam confidential records in the guidance office were still confidential, top secret, and beyond the reach of the Officers of Law Enforcement who were Trying to Do Their Duty and Serve the Public.

The Superintendent was away for the weekend. Neither had his assistant been home. Nor had any of the Central Office secretaries except one—and she was sick in bed with the flu and couldn't talk to anyone. Which meant that Joyce Bellows' personnel file in the Central Office was also unavailable. Which meant that the caduceus pinned to her handbag was still unexplained, assuming that there was anything in the file to explain it! And when, for crissake, was Hardy going to finish his moving and settle down in one place? Too late to do *them* any good, probably!

Nor had the Clerk of Court been home, which meant that a policeman had had to guard the Bellows apartment most of the night until a warrant could be issued—finally!—permitting a search of the papers and effects of the deceased. This, just accomplished, had yielded them precisely nothing. The murderer had used his victim's keys and beat them to it. Obviously!

"I'm calling from her place now," Hudson said. "To look at it, you'd think her right hand didn't know what her left hand was doing! What the hell kind of a person was she, anyway? The only thing we got was her sister's home address—damn near the only one in the book. Near as we can tell, the rest are all you people's!" The Chicago police had informed Grace Wickham of her sister's murder, and she was due at Logan Airport on the eight o'clock plane. She was to meet them at the police station at about nine-thirty. And probably she'd be late!

None of the custodial staff in Building Three had seen Joyce Bellows the night before—except for Mr. Tomasello who had discovered the body.

Last but not least, they had questioned Allen Magrue last night. "In your office, Ben, and it's no wonder your school's in such a state, what with that lousy tobacco you smoke!" Magrue had walked Joyce out to her car, talked with her a minute or two, returned to the dance, and danced. Had been on the brink of asking her to marry him! Didn't know about the insigne on her bag. Didn't know any more about Tony Evans than what Ben had already said. Had seen the boy a couple of times in counseling but had never seen any of Joyce's old reports on the lad. But one thing was damn peculiar! Magrue not only didn't know Grace Wickham. He had never even heard the name! How about them apples!

And that was that, so far.

"Tough," Ben said callously. But new worry for Allen Magrue tore apart the raw, sewn edges of the wound in his scalp.

Hudson was reduced to the ignominious role of suppliant. "What I thought was, suppose you see Mrs. Evans for us. You've got a reason—she's been after you for days. Whereas at this point we can't consider the boy a suspect, and his parents haven't reported him missing so we can't even go looking for him! The mother says he's been out before, with a relative or a friend. But we want that kid. Donnelly got some nice prints from the charcoal in the sketch book—Mrs. Evans doesn't know a thing about the art work, incidentally—and they might be Tony's. If that bag of stuff is his. He may be our murderer! So how about it, Ben?"

"Okay, I'll see her. Want me to meet you at my office afterward? It'll be awhile, though," Ben said hastily lest Hudson suspect his ready agreement. "I have to go for X rays first." And then I've got to get to Allen Magrue before you do, he added to himself.

"Well, we'll be there awhile too, but don't exactly take your time about it. W'll be waiting for your business manager, Hardy. And one of the Central Office gals is coming to that office. So we're expecting some simultaneous action—finally!"

Ben got Allen Magrue's number from the telephone operator and dialed with a shaky hand. No answer. Damn and blast, he muttered. So tense was he that, during the twenty minutes that passed before he was ready to leave for the Medical Center, he projected tons of crimes onto Hudson's evil soul, starting with, "Why, that miserable—he never even asked me how I felt!"

The X rays established that his skull was intact and his brain "within normal limits."

"I always wondered about that, and now I know," Jane said with satisfaction as they went out to the car.

"Yeah. Well, just remember what you said on Tuesday," Ben reminded her complacently. "That I'm smarter than everybody else."

The implication was painful.

"Oh dear," she said. "Oh my goodness . . . Okay, I'll drive you to Tony's house now, and I'll wait in the car like a good wife, but please don't stay too long," she pleaded, "or I'll go in and yank you out by the ears." She kissed him gently and put the ends of the seat belt into his hands. "You look so tired, darling. Remember what Dr. Muir said just now. You've got to rest."

He had taken his place ungraciously in the passenger's seat, unwilling to admit that he felt almost as bad as he had last night, but his condition was unmistakable and they both knew it. The air was crisp and fragrant, the motion of the car soothing. He leaned against the window and fell asleep.

8:40 A.M.

When Jane drew up in front of the Evans' mean dwelling, Ben woke up and looked around absently, forgetting for a moment where he was and why he had come here. Surreptitiously he felt in his pocket for his pills. Then he mustered his forces and opened the door.

"I'll be back soon," he said, getting out with some effort.

"You'd better," Jane threatened. She watched him stumble up the rough path, past a clay Virgin Mary who prayed blindly in her blue and white paint.

A slatternly woman swollen with pregnancy appeared in the doorway, greeted him unsmilingly, and invited him in, and when the door closed behind him Jane fantasized for a heart-stopping instant that she was never going to see him again, that he had vanished forever, that he would never come out. She poked around in the glove compartment for something to read, and discovered a *Mad* paperback, one of their son Benjy's literary favorites. But her eyes strayed restlessly to the house and presently she gave up reading, and waited.

The tiny living room into which Ben walked was so grindingly depressing that he nearly gasped in dismay. It stank of cooking odors and too many bodies. The walls were too close, the ceiling too low, and they seemed to press upon his aching head Procrustean fashion. The floor was covered with dismal brown linoleum tile.

Mrs. Evans said proudly, "I done them tiles myself."

"Marvelous job. Very practical too," he said faintly and sat down without taking off his coat.

Two children stared at him solemnly. Their lips were an endearing mess of milk and crumbs. He smiled at them.

"That's my Mary, the little one, she's thirteen months, and the other one's my Donna, she's two. Say hello to Tony's teacher, babies," Mrs. Evans said adoringly but they backed out of the room.

"That's why I can't come to school," she explained. "My Catherine, she's five, she's sick in bed this week, and my Angela, she's out playing someplace, she's seven, she was sick last week. The rest was all in school. Joan, Debbie, and Tony."

And the next one—another girl, probably—is about to arrive any day now, Ben added silently. He hoped his utter dejection did not show on his face.

"It's a nice family, Mrs. Evans. You're lucky. I'm very sorry I couldn't call you this past week. I've been busier than ever since the tragedy—I've been teaching because one of my teachers had to leave. Now tell me about Tony. Tell me what's upset you."

She was a scrawny woman despite her pregnancy, and pitiably overworked and prematurely aged. She pushed her stringy hair away from her face. "I called those other times to tell you how I felt about—about her. Miss Bellows. But now—it's my Tony, he's gone. He had supper and went to the dance last night and he didn't come back," she said in a tight harsh voice. The amenities were over.

"He's gone off before."

Her eyes flashed resentment. "It wasn't the same thing! He'd hitch a ride to Charlestown to my sister and she'd call me. But he don't go there no more. Now I don't know where he goes! Since he's workin' in the school with the men, he stays out later 'n later. He don't come home for supper, even, and I wait up for him 'til one, two, three o'clock at night—and even then he don't talk to me, he won't tell me nothin'! The only thing he talks about now, he says he's gonna go in the service soon as he can, he's gonna train and be a sailor and go as far away from here as he can get!"

"He's of age. He could, you know."

"I don't want my Tony in the service! I want him to finish school and go to college like all the other kids!"

"Yaaaah!" jeered an unkempt half-dressed wreck of a man passing the door on his way to one of the back rooms. Mrs. Evans bit her lip in embarrassment.

Ben tried to look invisible during that moment. Then he answered with a shake of his head. "We've gone through that, Mrs. Evans. It isn't that he isn't smart enough. He just doesn't want to study, at least not now. We've all tried to help him, encourage him. It didn't work. Some day, maybe. Not now. The most we could do to keep him in school—out of trouble and off the streets—was to make special arrangements in his program. He has no trade, no marketable skills—"

"You're sellin' him short! You put him to work with the men cleanin' up the school, how do you think he's gonna study when you tell him all he can do is wash the floors!" she shouted. "He was doin' okay 'til that nosy Miss Bellows sells him short and treats him like a flunky—like his father's been treated all his life! And she asks him dirty questions and tries to find out what he's thinkin' and what I say and what his father says—and it's disgusting and I want her to stop! And Tony, he does too!" Red spots flamed in her cheeks. "Somethin's been wrong with him ever since she got him a job with that bunch down cellar! Ever since she's been houndin' him, he's worse off than he ever was! I'm tellin' you I want her to leave him alone!"

"If Miss Bellows hadn't done what she did, your son might very well have a police record by now, Mrs. Evans. I only hope you'll let him talk with Mr. Magrue regularly. He asked to. He needs help and we all know that he does. I don't like to upset you further—but I have to tell you that Miss Bellows was killed last night."

She caught her breath and covered her mouth, and her eyes widened in fear, but he knew that this was something she had already heard. And that what she was actually terrified of was her own suspicion of the absent boy.

"What—what happened to your head?"

"I fell."

This seemed to satisfy her, or perhaps she only wanted to believe it.

"Oh," she said. "That's—that's all right then. That's not as bad."

Not as bad as what? As murder?

His head felt as though it were being crushed in a vise, and also as though it were about to fly apart. "I'm all right. But tell me. Did Miss Bellows agree with you about Tony staying home and in school? Or did she think his joining up would be a good idea?"

"She agreed with *me!*" Mrs. Evans said triumphantly. "For once! Tony, he hated her for that!" And all at once, as she realized what she had said, her anger dissolved in a storm of hopeless sobbing.

"Here," she said thickly, taking a rumpled paper from her apron pocket. "I found it in my Tony's things. He never had nothin' like that before, not until he started pallin' around with the men."

Stricken by her wretchedness and bewilderment, Ben took the paper from her shaking hand and opened it.

It was a target, and whoever had hit it must surely be a marksman. For all of the punctures were within the circles, and the neatest one of all was dead center.

CHAPTER THIRTEEN

8:55 A.M.

As Ben went down the path to his car, a dashing well-kept Chevrolet came to a screaming stop and a familiar boy got out. He hesitated when he saw Ben, then squared his shoulders like one facing the enemy and said hello. He was flashily dressed in the latest black-boots-and-studded-jacket mode and there was a large bold *T* on his shirt collar.

"Well, Tim. That was some landing you made. You ought to treat that car with more respect. Whose is it, yours?"

"Nah," said Timothy Lunn. "It's Quinn's. Down the engine room. He let me have it for today. I and Tony, we're goin' in town. He say anything to you?"

"About what?"

"How should I know? Whatever yuh came here for. All you people are the same. Grillin' us night and day!"

"I'd hate to think that's all the reputation I'll ever get from you, Tim. We're not all against you, it looks like. Mr. Quinn is very generous with the loan of his car. Timmy, did you see Tony last night at the dance?"

"Why yuh wanna know?"

"Because he didn't come home last night." The boy's eyes flew to meet his and slid away. "I was wondering if you'd seen him, if you knew what was bothering him. His mother wanted to talk to me—"

"What *she* say?"

"Only that he didn't come home after the dance. Did you talk to him at all last night?"

"Yeah. A bit. He was sore at Miss Bellows. An' Quinn was sore at him. Tony saw her comin' an' he took off. So did I. Bitch!"

"I guess I'm an old square, Tim," Ben said angrily, "but Miss Bellows did a hell of a lot to help you kids. And there are some people who don't think it's out of order to show a little gratitude. Or to speak anything but well of the dead. Or didn't you know she was?"

"Everybody knows. Police all over school last night! Who hit yuh?" He seemed pleased by the sight of Ben's large bandage.

"I fell."

"Sure! Or yuh ran into a door! Lissen, everybody knows you was in that tunnel! With her. I'm no dummy! Can't fool me!"

"I wouldn't try. Look, Tim, do you have any notion where Tony might have gone?"

"What's it *to* yuh? Think he done the murder?"

"I didn't say that."

"Well, I'll say it! He was mad enough, I can tell yuh that! No, I d'know where he is. But when I find him, I'll let him have it! Spoilin' my day!"

He turned abruptly and ran back to Quinn's car, revved up the engine, and sped away.

"Such a lovely boy," Jane said. "His parents must be so proud!"

"Knock it off, Jane. He's another one like Tony. What their families need is massive social work—welfare-psychiatric treatment. I'm not sure which of them has it worse—Timmy who's an only child whose father deserted them, or Tony with six younger sisters and a father who works two jobs and drinks beer and yells at all of them when he's home—and awake.

"I'll tell you something, Jane. If Joyce was trying to keep Tony home—in that house—he had as impressive a motive for murdering her as you could want! I'm not fooling, either. I knew about Tony's situation, but seeing it—! Look at this." He showed her the target as she drove slowly away. "These holes might have been made by a .22 or even a pencil and a lot of wishful thinking! But a Luger's a .354 caliber. It would make much bigger holes."

"Are you going to show it to Art?"

"No. I should. But I won't. Not yet. There's a lot to be said for Joyce's insistence on giving these kids a break before running to the police. If Art knew what she did once for Tim Lunn and a couple of other boys, he'd have booked her along with them! My god, Portia couldn't have pleaded for them better than she did!

She had the Superintendent and Tom Quinn and Tomasello and me crying in our beer—and they wound up under *Quinn's* wing. The guy they roughed up in the south tunnel last year! If she'd lost out, it would have tipped them over the edge. Mrs. Evans knows this, no matter what she thinks about Joyce."

"Well, I'll tell you something, Benjamin Franklin Louis. Something I didn't tell Art last night. What Joyce did for those kids was the right thing to do, right? I mean, it was correct technically, theoretically, psychiatrically, and so forth, right?"

"Right. It was also courageous and generous. Right?"

"Right. But it's right to be courageous and generous. We put a high value on courage and generosity."

"So what's your point?"

"That's my point. She did it because it was right. She always did everything right."

"What are you getting at? A character analysis? Or do you really know something? I think you've lost me."

"I wasn't trying to. Never mind that now. You really look awful, darling."

"You should have seen Tony's mother."

"I did. And it's pitiful. But I'm concerned about you now, and the way she turns to you in your condition with a heartwarming combination of trust and abuse! It's strange the way some people look at the principal of a school. He's either a savior or a magician, or else he's just a stupid civil servant who isn't smart enough to do anything better!" Anger traveled from her head to her toes and the car leaped like a gazelle.

"Easy, baby. Look, I want you to drive home and stay there—and don't argue! I've got lots to do after I see Art Hudson."

He stopped at his house long enough to call Allen Magrue again. Still no answer. Where *was* Magrue, anyway?

He left Jane worried but protesting no further, and drove to his office wishing that two hours had just elapsed so that he could take another pill.

Hudson and Keefe were waiting impatiently for *some*one to arrive, and they pounced on him.

"I didn't learn a thing," he said. "She wanted to complain about Joyce's interference, so-called, with Tony. I told her her troubles were over," he added bitterly, partly because he hated himself for *not* hating himself for lying in his teeth again.

"Well, we found something," Keefe said and showed him a crumpled paper. "It was in Miss Bellows' wastebasket."

It was a tentative draft of a letter, but without date or salutation, and read: "I regret, more than I can say, having to broach such a grave matter, but I have no choice."

"Who do you think she was referring to, Ben?"

"Who or what. I don't know, Pete. In this business it could be one of a thousand different items."

"I don't know about *what*, but it's clear to me she had something on a person," Keefe objected. "Just look at that choice of language."

"And just look at her apartment, Ben!" Hudson groused. "No snapshots or old letters or diaries. Even her library wouldn't specially suggest her interest in psychology. The variety of books was pretty wide. What the hell! Any gal her size could move right in and take over. They all use face creams and nightgowns! There was nothing really personal there. No—no past. Know what I mean? It's like she didn't cast a shadow." Seeing Ben reach for his Saturday pipe, he opened the window before the peach brandy tobacco was even lighted. "And Magrue's remark about not knowing Grace Wickham's name bugs me. Seems to me that even the most reticent person would be bound to say something to her intended like 'I'd like my brother to give me away' or 'I'd like my sister to be matron of honor.'"

"I thought you said he said he hadn't asked her yet."

"Well, I don't care. We're going to see him again. The only trouble is, he doesn't have to tell us anything if he doesn't want to!"

Jack Hardy, the business manager of the Manton schools, came in and apologized for being so late. He was a quiet competent man, and only his valiant sense of humor enabled him to handle a position that many people rightly consider an impossible one. For it involves matters not only as small as the purchase of twenty-five-watt light bulbs but as large as the political and other interference that ceaselessly, often viciously, tells the business manager how many bulbs to buy, and where to buy them, or even not to buy them at all.

"I'll take you up to the guidance office now, Mr. Hudson, Mr. Keefe," Hardy said. "I'm sorry about this crazy split-up of the personnel files and stuff. Next week everything should be all in one place."

"Swell!" Hudson said.

Keefe got up grunting. All of his fatigue and frustration were in his feet, and he could have slumbered for a month and thereafter conducted his business from a sedan chair carried by two other flatfeet.

As they left the office the telephone rang, and Hudson popped back in to listen.

"Uh-huh, mmmmm," Ben said, making a note. "Thanks very much. I appreciate this. Yes, I'll tell them." He put down the receiver. "That was the Superintendent's assistant's secretary, Art. She said Joyce's file shows that she was an army psychologist for practically the whole war and then some."

"So that explains the caduceus!"

"That's all it explains."

"I wonder if she knew Magrue in the service. They're about the same age."

"Well, so am I. Art, come on! It was a big army."

"Stranger things have happened."

"Sure. But Joyce and Magrue met for the first time during the April vacation when I hired him and introduced him to some of the staff he was going to work with. It's—it was her policy that her staff teach one class, so he met the English department head too. And when he and Joyce met, neither of them was putting on any act that I could see. And the next time they got together was at my August staff picnic. My god, Art! *If* that pin meant anything to him, and *if* he killed her, he wouldn't have left it on her bag down cellar. Are you telling me you suspect him of murder just because he didn't know her sister's name?"

"Maybe I do and maybe I don't," Hudson said and went out.

Hardy returned a few minutes later to find Ben pacing with cautious restlessness and trying to corner a darting wisp of an idea.

"Jack, do you happen to remember anything on Allen Magrue's papers that told what salary step he came in on?"

"As a matter of fact I do, Ben. I mightn't have except that he hasn't been here long, for one thing. For another, he mentioned last week that he'd be gone for Reserve training next month. And I remembered thinking it was strange that he was in the Reserve but came out of what was still a pretty red-hot war in December 1944. He had about a year of service to raise his salary an extra step over and above his professional experience."

"No disability pension or anything like that?"

"No."

"Mmmmmmm," Ben said thoughtfully.

"Well, since I'm here I might as well do some work. If the police want me again I'll be on tap."

They did, for they came into the office just then looking worried.

"I don't get it," Hudson said. "There wasn't a thing on Evans at all. Just the folder. No confidential information of any kind, I mean. No records of any counseling sessions with Bellows or Magrue or anybody else. Christ, what a case!"

"Any signs of tampering with the lock?" Ben said.

"No," Hardy said.

"Her desk lock was banged up, though," Keefe said. "And that's funny, now I come to think about it. If the murderer took her keys, you wouldn't expect any of the locks to have been forced."

"We've got to find that kid," Hudson fretted. "And we'll have to see Magrue again. Ben, how did she get on with her staff? Any friction there?"

"I wouldn't say so, no," Ben said, and realized how easy it was to slide into a life of crime.

"There's something funny going on here!" Hudson said. "Well, maybe we'll get something from Wickham. She ought to be at the station by now."

Ben waited until they had gone before calling Allen Magrue a third time. No answer. And then he went out of the building and across the driveway to the boiler room in Building Two.

There was no one in sight and the sound of Ben's heavy shoes on the clattering iron stairway did not flush anyone out of the many corners of the vast room. Noise pummeled Ben's head and saturated the air although due to the return of mild weather only one of the mammoth boilers was working energetically; the other two were firing at a minimum level in order to be kept warm and ready. When all three monsters were hard at it, the only way to be heard was literally to shout into someone's ear. And despite the

change-over from a school generator to Boston Edison, the engine
room was just as bad, Ben said to himself. He had the sensation
of breathing noise into his lungs and becoming unhealthier every
minute.

He wasted no breath or strength in calling out but went across
the room past the roaring metal dragons and into the relative peace
of the storeroom, where he found Stationary Firemen Vanna and
Cooke cleaning nozzles. They looked up without surprise and
smiled, saluting him casually with grimy powerful hands. Both had
unusually large ears, as if these had grown to meet the peculiar
exigency of the job.

"Figured you'd be around, Mr. Louis," Vanna said, plunking the
nozzle into its compartment in a wooden box and selecting another. "Trent gave us the word. Terrible thing! He spoke to her
last night."

I thought so! Ben thought. I knew she came down here.

Vanna's thick fingers held the nozzle as delicately as if it were
made of finest crystal. "Oil sprays through here. Feeds the
burners," he explained, and Ben nodded, thinking that Vanna's
brain was packed as neatly and sparingly as his seaman's duffle
once had been. Ben's own brain felt like a bursting flour sack, but
there was no percentage in worrying about it, he decided, since he
had just died from the neck up anyway.

"What did she want? Did Trent say?"

"She was looking for Tony Evans. Trent said he hadn't seen 'm."

"What do you know about him?"

"A punk. Worked well enough, though," Vanna said.

"We didn't see him often," said Cooke. "He liked the engine
room better."

"You haven't seen the boy this morning, have you?"

"No. Never see much of him anyway. He ain't here weekends,
generally, but if he is, he'd be with Quinn, not our crew," said
Cooke.

"You do much gun practice with him?" Ben said casually.

"Much what?" said Cooke in patent amazement. Vanna only
stared at the paper target that Ben held out. Both shook their
heads decisively.

"I ever tell you I was in the Merchant Marine?" Vanna said.
"Well, I was never armed. Never owned any kind of weapon—

before or after the war. Never even went to a shootin' gallery. Never took my boys to one, neither."

"Same here," said Cooke. "And I'll tell you, Mr. Louis. If I had a gun, that Tony's the last kid in the world I'd put a gun in his hands! Him and a couple others around this school!"

"Yeah. We let them work for us as a favor to Miss Bellows-may-she-rest-in-peace. And Tony worked hard, I'll say that for him. Bad temper though. I don't know what he wants, I'm no sike-atrist. Told Miss Bellows that. We wasn't mad about it, mind you." He pointed to a framed letter on the wall over the work table. "See that? That kid was another punk she sent down to us couple years back. He's one swell kid now! On a destroyer in the Pacific. Fireman with a damn fine rating and a good berth—and we did it!" His eyes shone with pride.

Ben leaned over to read the letter through the smudged glass. It was a literate and grateful testimonial to Vanna and Cooke and Joyce Bellows.

"It's impressive," Ben said sincerely. "I wish we could win 'em all." He stood in thought a moment.

"Why don't you see Quinn? He's in," said Cooke. "We went over to look at the scene of the crime—don't ask me why! Boy oh boy, if the union found out! Technically we're not supposed to even set foot out of here, and Quinn and his gang aren't supposed to come in here either. But he does—we all do, all the time."

"I think I will. Thanks, both of you. Don't mention this to the police though, about my being here, will you? But if anything turns up—like Tony, for instance!—call my home and leave a message with my wife. But call this number first." He wrote down Joyce Bellows' number and his own and then went out into the noise again, and into the narrow corridor to Tom Quinn's office.

A hoarse voice yelled, "Come on in!" over the radio that was playing loudly.

Quinn was at his desk writing with a chewed pencil stump. He looked up and turned off the radio. "Morning, Ben. Figured you'd be around."

"You heard, I take it."

"Yeah. Been on the news since early morning. A lousy thing. She was one nice gal, one of the best. Good to the kids. But I ain't surprised." He shrugged his beefy shoulders as though the reason for Joyce's murder were perfectly plain to him.

"You can't have it both ways, Tom," Ben said, sitting down on the cot.

"Huh? Oh. No, I meant that goddam tunnel. Both of them, for that matter. Not one of us down here hasn't asked for them tunnels to be kept closed and locked. But the people with the say— the ones who don't work here—they don't want to spend the dough to do it. And I don't mean fancy covered walkways outside to take their place, Ben. Just a plain ol' door with a lock—at both ends of both tunnels—and keys for only some of us. Just a coupla doors. And a coupla keys that cost maybe half a buck apiece! Christ!"

"The only thing that's happened lately is breaking the bulbs, according to Rocco." He deliberately left it at that. This belligerent man was extremely nervous, and something told Ben that he would get to the murder in his own good time.

Quinn's lip curled at Mr. Tomasello's name. "Well, I won't speak for nobody but me, then. I got knocked around that time— you remember—in that stinkin' south tunnel. Kids come through the yard door by the boiler room, the one just the other end of this hall. The firemen didn't see them or hear them, but I did. They saw me and ran, and I chased them past the shops and lost them in the tunnel—and then they jump through that goddam center and grab me! But the bastards down Town Hall said if we was doin' our jobs and payin' attention, there wouldn't be no reason to spend good money! That little jerk reporter Al Shedd came nosin' around, but I didn't give *him* any change! Funny about it, though, Ben. In a way it was a good thing and worked out okay. For Timmy Lunn anyways. His father'd been gone about a year then, and he was goin' downhill fast. If Miss Bellows hadn't spoke for him, he'd be in a federal pen by now, maybe! But what good can come out of what happened to her?"

He fiddled with his pencil and Ben waited patiently.

"Somethin' I haven't told nobody," Quinn said hesitantly. "I feel like hell about it. . . . The thing is . . . well, you know I got to leave in a few days. . . ."

"Mmmmmmm," Ben said sympathetically. He was a master at

this technique. But his blood pressure soared like a rocket and his brain now felt like a marble rolling around in his skull.

"Well . . . it's about that gun. The gun that killed the kid upstairs."

The words were like a magic balm, and Ben's head stopped hurting. Again he was silent, exuding the gentle, the loving, the boundless understanding of a psychoanalyst. "Mmmmmmm," he murmured.

"Well, the thing is, I been over to Civil Service for a new berth, see. And I need a good reference. Which I got okay, except for one thing if it comes out. That gun!

"I picked it up during the war, traded it for some food when we docked in Murmansk. The Russkies was hungry. I figured what the hell. They had a bellyful of the Germans by that time, they would've traded Moscow for a can of beans. Naturally I didn't register the gun when I got home. Neither did a lot of other guys who got them. We knew we weren't supposed to keep them but—. So I oiled it and put it away and that was that. Until I got jumped in the tunnel. We didn't get no help from the town and I wasn't about to stay around without protection. You know yourself there's a lot of doors around here that tough punks can come in through. Even in the winter the boiler room door up the stairs is kept open 'cause it gets hot as hell down there. And it's so noisy that even if anybody bangs up and down that metal stairs, you'd never know the difference unless you was standing right there lookin' at it. And we'd had lots of vandalism—paint all over the walls and things, remember? They can get in through a dozen doors after school's closed—and they do!

"So I brought the gun in here and kept it locked in the drawer. And then just like you'd expect, nothin' ever happened and I forgot about it.

"And then I hear about the kid upstairs shot with a Luger, and I look in the drawer—and it's gone! Lock's all scratched around, see?"

"Only that drawer," Ben said, getting up to look at it. He was not as satisfied with the scratches as Quinn seemed to be, but he only added, "Whoever took it knew you kept it there."

"Yeah, Ben. I didn't keep things locked all the time when I was in here, 'cause there's other things in that drawer I use. And I know who saw it and took it. Tony Evans."

It was time to apply a little muscle. "Then why didn't you say something immediately?" Ben said sternly. "We've all spent a lot of time on it. Among other things."

"You gotta understand, Ben. This kid was in a bad way. He's got a tough life and I didn't want to make it worse. Miss Bellows was very particular about that kid, and I was tryin' my best for her. God only knows why he took that gun and put it in the lab.

"Then after the tragedy I was scared to admit it was mine. I gotta get another job, Ben. I couldn't risk it. Maybe it was wrong. I guess it was. But the boy was dead. Nothin' I could do about it. I kept my mouth shut when the police asked around."

"And this morning you decided to open up."

"Ben, I just got scared—all over again! I heard the news and went over with Cooke to look at the tunnel. And I got nervous as hell seein' where they washed up the blood—and I thought maybe she was shot—with my gun! By Tony! He was plenty mad at her, see. I was so upset, I even forgot the police already had the Luger! Which just goes to show! So I come back here, I d'know why. I'm here a lot, though. My wife died after the war and I never married again. The kids here are like my kids, which I never had none. We spent a lot of time together."

"Tell me about Tony. Did you see him last night?"

"Yeah, for a minute. I know most people think he's a no-good punk, and maybe in a way he is. Lousy temper. Blows up like a shot. But he's got another side. Talked about it often—if he was in a good mood. He liked to draw and paint—"

"Was that bag of stuff his?"

"Yeah. Sometimes he'd come in here at night—he has a lousy home life—and look at the magazines and all like that. Sometimes he'd copy the pitchers. Then his face would soften, kind of, and it was—nice. Y' know? I tried to keep him like that but it wasn't easy. Every time he had a blow-up with his parents, he'd come in here like a—like a thunderstorm and stay like that a coupla days. I'm no shrink, Ben, but I think he was—like—jealous. Jealous of all them kids. He said if his mother really loved him like she said, she'd've stopped after three or four and *been* a mother instead of a—a rabbit!"

"And last night?"

"He was in a while, all dressed up. He didn't really wanna go to the dance. It only gave him an excuse to be outa that house. I told him to leave his bag of stuff and go have a good time for a change. I didn't see him again. I took a snooze."

"What did he have against Miss Bellows?"

"He wanted to join up, him and Timmy Lunn. She wanted him to stay home—in that house of his!—and maybe go to trade school. He'd had a real crush on her for a long time, but all of a sudden last spring he cooled way down. Maybe she was right, but *I* went to sea when I was sixteen—and my old lady tried the same way to keep me home. People say kids are different these days, but I don't know. Tony and Tim feel the same way I did then. I just didn't want everybody tellin' me what to do. Seemed like the whole world was against me. I was mad, just the way they are now."

"There's a lot of rules in the service, though, Tom."

"Yeah, but it's different somehow. 'Course I told the kids that. They just laughed—said nobody was gonna push them around! You'd think they was admirals already!" He shook his head indulgently.

"What about Tony and Miss Bellows? Anything else?"

"Oh . . . yeah. He said he wasn't gonna let her bother him no more. I think that was Tuesday . . . yeah, late. After the tragedy. He was jumpy as hell. He said he'd told her one thing too many and was never gonna talk to her again."

"Do you think he had told her about the gun?"

"I—don't know. Maybe. Or maybe she put two and two together and suspected it was him. But he wouldn't be liable for that shooting. Or the boy who done it. It was an accident. The worst that could happen to Tony would be a robbery charge—from me. And I wouldn't of done that! Aside of risking my future, I couldn't louse up that poor kid. It was a hell of a bind, Ben."

"It still is, Tom. It still is," Ben said thoughtfully. There was a disturbing note of evasiveness in Quinn's forthright answers. "Another thing. Seems to me I saw Tim Lunn out back last night playing ball. Did you see him at all?"

"Yeah. He bums around a lot with me. I'm like a father to him. Even let him use my car when he's good. Tony too. They even change their clothes in here for work—chinos like all us guys wear on duty. And like on Saturday we go to the coin laundry together. Sometimes I do it for them."

"That's very generous," Ben said, and got up again to look into Quinn's closet. "Hmmmm. Only one set, though."

"Timmy's. Tony must've took his home last night before supper. He sometimes does on Fridays. Then we go pick him up at home or else he comes back here Saturdays and we go off together. Boy, that'll tee Timmy off! A little thing like that! He'll feel cut out 'cause Tony didn't come in this morning. He's quick to feel put down even when he ain't. But Tony's different. And he does a good job, he earns his pay. That's one good thing. Only—"

"Do you think he killed her?"

"God almighty, I don't know!"

"What about Tim?"

"No," Quinn said firmly as if he were testifying under oath. "Nossir, Ben! That boy was—what's the word?—dedicated to keepin' strictly out of her way! If she went east, he'd go west!"

"Tom, one more question. Did you see Miss Bellows last night?"

"Ben, I swear to god, I never stepped foot outa this office! Not 'til six this mornin'. I only came back when I heard the radio—just about the minute I got home. I was worried about Tony. I thought maybe he'd be back."

It was an equivocal answer at best, but Ben could think of nothing else to say or to ask. He stood up. His blood pressure had jumped again and his head was throbbing. Consequently his expression was grim, and the engineer's hands began to sweat.

"What should I do, Ben?" he said, rubbing his palms on his trousers. "I mean—we didn't have no witness here and—"

"Get a lawyer, Tom. Don't wait. And tell the police. I'm not your judge and jury, although I could tell you a few things—if I had the time. All I will say is this: Sooner or later the police will be back here. It would be better for you to go to them."

He did not ask Quinn to call him if Tony Evans did come by. What with one thing and another Tony would probably avoid Quinn like the plague now, for one thing. For another . . .

Thoughtfully he made his way back along the narrow corridor.

For another, it had been a very interesting statement, he said to himself. Quinn seemed to have done some homework on the law. He probably knew, then, that he really didn't need a lawyer because he couldn't be forced to make a formal statement even if he were formally charged with Joyce's murder.

Well, not quite. If he *were* charged, it would be because there was probable cause to warrant charging him, in which case he'd want a lawyer very much indeed. Because he could well be as guilty as he had hinted Tony was. For the thing cut both ways. Joyce's possible—probable—knowledge that the Luger was his represented more of a threat to his future than it did to Tony's. And he might have killed her if she were going to blow the whistle on him.

Look at it this way. She went down cellar looking for Tony, and spoke to Trent, one of the firemen. No doubt he had told her what Vanna and Cooke would have said, that if Tony were anywhere, he was with Tom Quinn. She would have suspected as much anyway, and gone to Quinn's office immediately. In view of her peculiar mood during the dance, and the argument she had had with the boy, wasn't it likely that she had confronted Tom Quinn with her fully blown suspicions regarding the gun and threatened him then and there with exposure? And wasn't it likely that she had said something like "I'm going back to find Mr. Louis and get this off my chest *right now!*"?

And further, wasn't it likely that he had gone with her, back through the tunnel, arguing all the way, begging for a break? And then killed her because she had remained adamant?

But what about the bag? Tony's bag of stuff.

Quinn said he had told the boy to leave it there and go to the dance and have some fun. Okay. Suppose she had seen the bag there in the office, looked into it, seen the statue in it, recognized it as belonging to me, Ben said. Suppose she had said something like "There you are! Under your influence the boy has become a thief along with everything else! First the gun, now Ben's statue! I'm going to do something about this before anything else happens!" And suppose Quinn, knowing its weight, knew it would make a perfect murder weapon and grabbed it from her. And hit her with it. And then hit me, Ben added with a grunt. And then did two more things—went back to his office or his apartment and changed his bloodied clothes, and then went up to the guidance office to see if any incriminating entries about the Luger had been made in Tony Evans' confidential folder.

It was possible. It was all possible. Although Quinn would have been a fool to kill Joyce. For, apart from any other considerations like the magnitude of such an act, there apparently was no legal proof of ownership of that Luger that could be produced against him. Certainly the voluntary statement he had just made could not incriminate him. And without proof, nothing Tony said would cut much ice.

As for that statement, it had been a very interesting one indeed. Absorbing. Colorful. Insightful. And contradictory.

Because something told him that Quinn had known about the missing gun *before* the tragedy in the lab, not after it. If he hadn't been so worried about his future, he would have risked getting a master key from one of the custodians and opened the lab sometime Monday night. No. More likely the custodian would have insisted, quite properly, on going with him. And he would have had to explain himself. And *there was no way* he could do that, even if he put the blame on Tony, without implicating himself. He would have had to explain why he kept a Luger—a doubly illegal weapon—in his office in the first place. And whether the custodian liked him or didn't like him—and many, resenting his known laziness and self-indulgence, did not—the word would get around. It always did. In fact, it was astonishing that word had not leaked out already through the boys who hung around that he'd had it there so long.

It was the scratch marks on the drawer that had given Ben the strong sense that Quinn was lying. If I know anything at all, Ben told himself, those scratches weren't made almost a week ago, Tuesday, for instance, when Quinn said he had discovered that the gun was missing.

The desk was old and darkened by years of use. But the scratches were brand-new. And it was not that a too eager hand had dug too many too deeply, but that it had left splinters, raw and rough if tiny, standing witness to the act. Whereas, Ben expatiated, a genuinely incredulous discoverer would have felt them, and looked, and felt again, rubbing them down a bit, smoothing them somewhat, and, with a growing sense of outrage and alarm, aged them just enough to give them authenticity. *I* think so, anyway.

Well, no sense upsetting Hudson and Keefe, Ben thought

piously as he went into his office. He remembered all too clearly Hudson's cyclonic burst at him two years before. "Mind your own business and we'll mind ours," Hudson had said. More or less.

All right, he would. And when it occurred to Hudson and Keefe that Joyce had been coming back from Building Two rather than going toward it, they would find out just as much as he had, maybe more. You didn't have to *see* her going toward that boiler room door to wonder whether she might have done so! Pleased with himself, he went to his desk to make five quick calls.

"Don't be so pleased with yourself, Benjamin Franklin Louis!" Jane said prophetically. "You just never know. And you'd better tell Art right away. When are you coming home? You ought to rest." She pulled at the telephone wire as though she were trying to drag him through it.

"I'll be home soon, I think. I'm going to see Joyce's sister. She ought to be back at Joyce's apartment by now."

"What could she tell you that she hasn't already told them?"

"I don't know, but I think I'll get an unabridged version."

Then he called Valentine Shrag, Bert's wife. "Valentine? How's the patient?"

"A lot better, Ben. Helpful, too. I've done several studies of him in his sling and stuff. He looks like a war casualty, poor darling."

It was difficult to picture Bert Shrag as a poor darling, because he was built like a truck and had a face to match. Ben laughed and said, "Look, Valentine, do me a favor. The police are holding onto a bag of stuff that we found in the tunnel last night. I think I know whose it is. Anyway, there are some sketch books in it with charcoals and oils. I'm almost certain they'll be back in school Monday with the boy, please god! I'd like you to look them over and tell me what you think. Okay?"

"Sure, Ben. This sounds intriguing. And very important and significant. You know something," she said accusingly.

"I think so. Tell you some other time."

There was still no answer at Allen Magrue's home.

Then he called Justice Bertram Shrag, Senior, at his chambers. No answer. He tried the house. No answer. "Jesus Christ, isn't anybody home?" he grizzled.

But Grace Wickham, now back at her dead sister's apartment, said she would be glad to see him.

He was halfway out the door when Al Shedd, the reporter, coasted in on his usual brashness, immune from inhospitality.

"What's new, Ben?"

"Not a thing. Try the police."

"I did. Who was that nice-looking dame I saw a while ago at the station? Relation of the deceased?"

"How would I know?"

"I understand the murderer attacked you too. Did you see any-body?"

"No. And I fell."

"*Uh*-huh! How're you feeling now?"

"Fine."

"Anything on that gun yet?"

"Nope."

"Any leads?"

"If there are, *I* haven't been informed."

"Any connection with the murder?"

"Couldn't say."

"Or with that hassle in that same tunnel about a year or so ago? And one before that?"

"Huh?"

"Made you flinch, didn't I! Come on, Ben, give!"

"That depends. If I do, I'll want to see your story before you turn it in. I want something out of it too. But I don't want scandal."

"Covered walkways, I'll bet. Okay, it's a deal."

"Not yet, Al. I'm steering a fine course. It'll be a few days, but I promise you the story. Deal?"

"Deal. But you're not much help now, Ben baby!"

"Can't be helped."

"Someday I'll write you a real nice obit."

"It'll come in handy."

"See yuh!" and the little man sailed out, savoring to the full the fantasy he lived.

Ben gazed almost fondly after him, knowing that two more problems had been solved.

Okay, what's next? Grace Wickham.

He felt as if he were in the middle of a marathon, with miles and miles of running yet to do. And he was right.

He stopped to talk with Mr. Tomasello who was trying to vacuum up the grounds without a vacuum. "What's up, Roc? Isn't the Forestry Department supposed to do that?"

"Yeah. An' if they wanna make somethin' out of it, that's oke wit' me!" and trundled a trash-laden gigantic wheelbarrow away while muttering threats of an immortal character.

Ben could almost see the thunderbolts clutched, Jove-like, in his hand.

CHAPTER FOURTEEN

10:30 A.M.

Grace Wickham was a pretty, graying woman in her early fifties with a controlled manner and quiet bearing. She had been crying, but Ben's impression, after speaking with her on the phone, had been correct. She had not been hysterical, she had not abandoned herself to grief. She would be a helpful and candid witness to one or other crucial aspect of her sister's life—and death.

"It's a family trait," she remarked without self-deprecation. "We were brought up that way. Our parents—Father, actually—didn't believe in great shows of affection or anger. Oh, I don't want you to think that Joyce and I weren't fond of each other! We were. But we just didn't—we didn't trespass, you know. Privacy was perhaps the most important factor in the family. Privacy of the individual. Joyce was always concerned about that. She hated gossip, she rarely confided anything intimate to me about herself or anyone else. Especially after she went into psychology. Many therapists and doctors talk about their cases without identifying anyone, but Joyce never even discussed her cases to *that* extent. She always kept everything to herself. And she almost never commented on anyone anyway. We were almost more like friendly acquaintances than sisters. That's why I wasn't with the police for very long. I purely and simply didn't have much to tell them."

"You didn't see her often, then?"

"Oh yes, I did, Mr. Louis. My husband travels on business a good deal, and one of our daughters is married and lives in New York and the other two are away at college. I come up here now and then when my husband is away, and Joyce often comes—came —to Chicago for a holiday. Or she'd visit the girls at school, see how things were, give us a progress report of sorts. I mean, she never revealed any confidences they made to her, she'd only tell me they were well and happy. That sort of thing. They trusted her. They loved her. I haven't been able to tell them yet. . . ." Her lips quivered. "I only hope they don't see any newspapers until I can talk to them. . . ."

"Tell me about her army service," Ben said after a moment.

"Oh yes. She had her bachelor's and master's in psychology, and by 1943 she was already finished with her course work for her doctorate. Mind you, she was only twenty then! She'd accelerated all through grammar school and high school and she was through college before she was seventeen. It used to bother her that one of her instructors in 1942 was already a Ph.D. at twenty-one! She said if she'd *really* pushed, she'd have been done by then too! Imagine!"

"It's rare, but it happens," Ben said.

"Yes. But I wish . . . Well, anyway, she joined up in 1943, as I said. She got a commission in the Medical Corps and stayed in until 1946 or 1947, I forget exactly. She never wrote much about her work, partly because she was that kind of person and partly because she was so busy. She was working on her dissertation a lot of the time—it was on various kinds of war psychoses—and her university advisers gave her all sorts of leeway because she was so brilliant and had such a wonderful record. She could have gone anywhere in the world and still been able to do the work. It was all done and accepted, finally, and she took her oral examination right after she got out of service, and then she decided to work with children—in school—to try and help them before their problems grew really serious. . . .

"She had an enormous capacity for work. It was all she seemed to care about. I always wished she'd marry and have a more complete life, but she said she had no time for *that sort of thing!* The only thing in her future, she used to say, was her work. She didn't bring anything into her future but her work. She didn't want to be—impeded—by things or by people. You know? People other than the family and those involved in her career."

"That's what the police said after searching here. I guess that was why the pin on her handbag was such a surprise."

"Yes, it was, wasn't it! I saw it too. I asked her why she kept it there. When my husband was in the service, I had a few of his pins. It was considered terribly romantic to wear them, you know. But after the war I put them away in my jewel box. I couldn't throw them away or give them away, but they were painful reminders. My husband was badly wounded during the Battle of the Bulge. So, when I saw the pin, Joyce only said something about its reminding her of something. And as you might imagine by now, she didn't tell me anything more about it and I didn't ask. If she had wanted to tell me, she would have."

"Mrs. Wickham, when she met you at Logan Monday, did she seem to have anything on her mind? Did she seem different in any way?"

"The police asked me that, of course, and I can only tell you what I told them. No, she was quiet as always, but I wouldn't have said she was depressed. But I realized after a very few minutes that she was not well. She was very flushed. That adorable Mr. Magrue was there—she told me his name later—and I thought, 'Oh what a darling! Maybe this time—' But . . . it wasn't that.

"She was more than usually quiet, though, that night, and I didn't think she ought to go to school Tuesday. But when she came home after all, later that morning, I decided to stay until Friday. I'm glad I did. She really had an acute attack of the flu, and it hung on, it wouldn't go away. Not that she hasn't been alone before during an illness, but then she was seldom ill. . . . She was my—my little sister, you see, and I really brought her up. Ever since she was seven, when Mother died. She'd always been extremely dependent on Mother, like a leech. And then to see her die like that—a car parked up the hill from us suddenly lost its brakes and—and—It was a horrible shock to her. She turned to me, but she was quite changed from then on. Father shut himself off—he always had, actually—and he died a few years later. So I became the mother . . . and now, what with my girls away, I enjoyed having someone to take care of. . . ." She wiped her eyes.

"Mmmmmm. What did she say about Allen Magrue?"

"That's such an unusual name, isn't it. I must say I'm curious to know what he said about her."

"He said he loved her, Mrs. Wickham. He said he was going to ask her to marry him. The police told me that this morning."

She looked at him, startled. "But that's—that's quite absurd! I said before that she rarely talked about people. Particularly if she didn't like them. She told me a great deal about you, Mr. Louis—a great deal for her! She had enormous respect for you, personally and professionally. Although," she added smiling apologetically, "she may very well have thought she knew more psychology than you do."

"She did, as a matter of fact. I did disagree with her on one or two matters, though, and I still think I was right." He waited for her to continue.

"Well now, where was I? Oh. She was very cranky Tuesday night. She took a nap and had a light supper, and then she said something about having some work to do—a letter to write—

"Oh good heavens, I nearly forgot!" she cried, and went out of the room, giving Ben a few minutes of unguarded appraisal. They were all he needed. Hudson had been right. No decorating rules had been broken here. Everything was correctly balanced as to color, dimension, placement. The room was cheerful, comfortable, well kept, excessively neat. And entirely impersonal, as though it were a stage setting, or Number A-4 (Middling-High Executive Personnel, School, Male or Female) in a mail order catalogue.

"I'm glad I remembered this," said Mrs. Wickham, coming back with a large expanding envelope tied round by its tape. "I'm sure it was meant for you. It's still a bit wet, I'm afraid, but only a little on the outside. It's that folder Joyce brought home on Tuesday, the one you needed. At least I think it must be for you. The top papers are clipped together with your name on them. I only just peeked to make sure. Isn't it strange that even after Joyce's—even now it's impossible for me to handle her things freely? When you came for it, Joyce said something about giving you the rest when she got back to school."

"Thanks, Mrs. Wickham," Ben said, opening the envelope for a quick look. "Yes, this stuff was supposed to have been handed back—"

Incredulous at what he saw under the staff evaluation forms, he gasped on the plosive but covered his reaction by coughing (which was a mistake, since his head fell into his lap, in splinters).

Mrs. Wickham was out and back again in an instant with a glass of water. "Are you all right? And I haven't even thought to ask you about yourself. I'm so terribly sorry, Mr. Louis."

He took the glass gratefully and washed down a pain-killer.

"I'm all right, thanks. This bandage looks worse than it needs to. By the way, how come the police missed this? Where did you find it?

She looked embarrassed. "In the oddest place, really. Behind—behind the refrigerator. On the floor. When I came back from the police station, I felt so nauseous that I took a bottle of ginger ale out of the refrigerator—to sip it, you know—and it dropped right out of my hand and broke and spattered everywhere. I was cleaning up the mess when you called, and that was when I found it. Do you think she hid it there? It seems so—well, so abnormal to me. And then her reaction when Mr. Wills called Wednesday asking for information or papers that weren't in the files! She was simply hysterical! I've never seen her that way before! She questioned me minutely when I told her he'd called. What had he sounded like? What had he really wanted? And something about his trying to take over . . . Of course she had a very high fever, almost a hundred and three then. I admit I've acted this way when I felt very sick and weak. My husband says I'm a perfectly dreadful patient! Worse than men are supposed to be, he says. But still—what do you think, Mr. Louis?"

"I don't know. I don't know yet. People do strange things when they're sick."

"Yes. And she was very strange all week. Frozen, almost, except for that one outburst. She did everything so—so carefully. So—stiffly. I wanted to call the doctor but she wouldn't let me. . . ." Again she wiped tears away.

"Tell me about Tuesday night," Ben said softly. "You started to tell me what she said about Allen Magrue."

"Oh . . . yes . . . Well, we were chatting for a while. I asked her, naturally, about that attractive man she was talking to at the airport, when I saw her, and she said, 'That was Allen Magrue, one of my staff.' I said it was an odd-sounding name, and what was he like? Was he as nice as he looked? I said, because for a moment I'd hoped she was going to get something else out of life! I couldn't have been more disappointed—or more wrong!"

"Why?"

"Because she said—she said she loathed and despised him!"

"Did she say she'd told him that?"

"Yes, but not—I gathered—in so many words."

"Did you tell the police about this?"

"No. Should I have?"

"I don't think so. I'm glad you didn't, anyway. Whatever she thought of him, I know he's a good man. And from what I've seen, he didn't show her anything but respect and loyalty. But whether he did or he didn't, there are certain factors that suggest that he didn't kill her. I'd stake my own life on it."

"It may sound foolish, Mr. Louis, but I hope he isn't the one. . . . I suppose Joyce and I were more alike than I'd thought. I almost didn't tell Mr. Hudson anything. Not that I had anything to tell, really, but all I could say was how wonderful she was and how much people liked her. He was quite annoyed with me."

"You're not the only one he's annoyed with. Well, after she said that, what happened?"

"She went to her desk and tried to write the letter she'd mentioned earlier. But she threw it away—and then she got up and went to the bathroom and lost the nice supper I'd made her!"

The telephone rang on her last word as though someone had politely waited until she had finished speaking.

"It's for you, Mr. Louis," she said, surprised.

"Mr. Louis? Cooke. Over in Two. We got Tony Evans here. Found him hiding out in the plenum chamber!"

CHAPTER FIFTEEN

11 A.M.

The plenum chamber was a hideous place. Its purpose was something less than sinister: to collect fresh air from outside, heat it over hot coils, and send it through ducts to every part of the three buildings. But to Ben, who was extraordinarily sensitive after walking around for a week bristling with antennae, the plenum chamber seemed to belong to some other world. A world of mystery and horror, of unspeakable rites, unnamable tortures, or the subterranean cellars of the House of Usher. The air was warm and damp. The six-foot blades in the fan mounted eight feet above his head roared ceaselessly. The walls were grimed with soot or thick black dust, so that at a glance—which was all that Ben could bear to take—it was impossible to say whether they were of wooden boards or bricks or mortared stone. And they stretched away into a blue-black shadowy nothingness, like a bottomless pit upended. There was no lamp in the room, but bluish light came from an elusive indefinable distance, as though the particles of dirt were luminescent and restlessly in motion.

His hideout, Cooke had said, leading the way to it. Tony Evans' hideout: his safe retreat from that worst of all possible worlds that was his home.

"Don't come in here often, but I had to check something," Cooke said, playing his flashlight on an old blanket and a flashlight in a far corner. "And there he was! Called you right away. Vanna's got him. All dressed in his best 'n ready to go. Figured you'd want to look in here first—get it over with," he added with a grin.

"Let's get out of this hellhole!" Ben pleaded.

No matter what he had done, the boy's plight was pitiable. He was a tall handsome lad, as tall as Quinn or Timmy Lunn or Cooke, but thin as a reed from growing so fast, and gaunt now from lack of food and sleep. His good suit, a cheap navy serge, was dirty, his face and hands smudged with black, his eyes haggard with fear. He was slumped on the cushioned rocker in the storeroom, where the men on night watch rested and read their newspapers, and he was empty of anger, exhausted. For the moment he had given up the battle, and Ben thought, I'll bet he's glad we found him after all.

"Thanks, fellas," he murmured. "Better fade."

Slowly he went over to the rocker and his head cracked as he squatted, holding onto the arm of the chair. His familiar face and the quietness with which he waited to be acknowledged reached the boy and warmed him.

"Hello, Tony," Ben said. "We've been worried about you."

The boy's lips twitched.

"You feel like talking now?"

"What's to say?" It was a soul-weary observation, not a belligerent question. He might have been a thousand years old.

"Why don't you tell me from the beginning. When you came to school last night."

"O——kay." The word came out on a slow hoarse exhalation. "Only I'm kinda mixed up now. . . .

"I came to the dance after supper but I went to Mr. Quinn's office. He was still mad, though. Because—because—"

"Because of the pistol, Tony?"

"Yeah . . . he was afraid he'd get in trouble. He was afraid Miss Bellows knew it was his. So he told me to leave my stuff an' get the hell out an' go to the dance. So I left it but I took my water pistol. I was so mad, I just hadda carry that water pistol! I went through the tunnel an' shot all the bulbs! I hung around awhile, an' then *she* saw me an' took me up the office an' started in. But I wouldn't tell her nothin' so we came back down. . . ."

"I saw you. You were pretty upset."

"Even there she was at me! We come downstairs an' she's still naggin' me about the gun. I told her about it last month. Didn't mean to—it just slipped out. She remembered about it an' she kept askin' me did Mr. Quinn give it to me or did I steal it? An' why'd I stay away from my appointment Tuesday morning which I had asked for it, she said. An' what was gonna become of me? I couldn't stand it no more! You got any idea how I been feelin' since that kid was shot?"

"Maybe I do, a little bit. What were you planning to do, leave school?"

"Yeah. Me an' Tim Lunn. I figured June but he wanted to go soon as I was eighteen—next month. We was gonna go to sea like Mr. Quinn an' Mr. Vanna an' Mr. Cooke. But she didn't want that. She said it was a bad thing for us an' we should get straightened out first an' I shouldn't give up my art work. She had other plans for Tim. He was real sore when I told him I'd wait 'til June when I graduate. I ain't so sure I wanna go anyways, but— He said she told him she wouldn't *let* him go, but I d'know why. But he said if I chickened out he'd go anyways no matter what! He said no one was gonna stop *him!*"

"I see. What did you do after you ran outside?"

"I went over the boiler room door an' talked to Tim a minute."

"Wasn't he at the dance at all?"

"He came, but he said it was a drag. He hung around out back playin' ball an' talkin' to me 'til *she* showed up."

"And then?"

"When she sees me an' comes over from the car callin' me, I run downstairs an' Timmy he takes off—*he* didn't wanna see her! Some guy was with her. Near her, anyways. Mr. Magrue, I think. I ran to the plenum room and hid."

"Does anyone know you use the plenum chamber?"

"No. Not even Tim . . . A guy has to have a place . . . his place . . . all his own. . . ."

"Yes. That's so. And then?" His head was splitting, but no matter.

"Then when I thought it was safe, I went back. I was gonna get my bag. An' I damn near bump into her when I come aroun' the corner! She was by the engine room door talkin' real loud to someone—I d'know who—Mr. Quinn, maybe—but they didn't see me."

"Was she shouting? Was she angry?"

"Yuh gotta talk loud out there, Mr. Louis."

"Then what?"

"I rushed back in the plenum room. I waited some more, I d'know how long, but it was a long time, maybe fifteen minutes, an' then I figured I'd go hang aroun' the dance again. Mr. Quinn wanted to take a snooze, he said, an' nobody else was aroun' 'cept whoever's on watch in the boiler room. . . . I figured it was safer goin' through the tunnel again, 'cause she might be out in the yard lookin' for me. But she'd of turned back a long time ago from the tunnel when she seen it was dark, see? So I start to go out, an' then I think no matter what I do, she's gonna find me, she's gonna track me down! So I go back an' stay there all night. In the plenum room. An' I think about Gerald Rosen, an'—then Mr. Cooke finds me an' tells me about you an'—an' her—oh god, oh god. . . ."

He was too worn out to sob. Tears ran down his cheeks and he wiped them away with a dirty hand.

Ben took out his spare handkerchief and offered it delicately. Then he stood up and held down the top of his head while he pulled over an old crate. "Okay," he said, sitting down on it. "Then what?"

"I was scared. I couldn't eat nothin' 'cause my bag's in Mr. Quinn's office. . . . I was too scared to go get it. . . . I couldn't of eaten nothin' anyways, I felt too bad. I was goin' over Boston today with Timmy but I didn't even want to do that. He's a creep, always talkin' about goin' in the Green Berets an' shootin' people an' killin' people. I get sick of hearin' it."

"Had you ever told Miss Bellows how you felt about Tim?"

"No. I told Mr. Quinn, before I took the gun. Before he was mad at me. I wouldn't tell her, though, 'cause she was always after Timmy an' a lotta the other guys I go 'round with too. I ain't gonna make it tougher on any of my gang."

"Tony, about the gun. Mr. Quinn said you stole it."

"I never! I never stole nothin'! That's a lie! I bought it. With my own money I made workin'. I was payin' on it a little at a time. I only owed him a couple more bucks. He said I could have it when I joined up. I signed a contrack with him, see?"

He pulled out his wallet and extracted from it a grubby sheet of paper that was signed, dated, explicit. A legal document, in fact.

"He couldn't get the gun back but he wanted this back. My copy. He said he'd get in trouble if I didn't give it back. Well, I couldn't. I d'know why. I was just—mad!"

"But he's your friend. He speaks well of you."

"Not to me he don't! Not the last few days anyways."

"You can't blame him for that—if you broke open his desk—"

"I didn't break it open! It wasn't locked! When he went out a minute Monday night* I took the gun an' stuck it in my pants under my shirt. When I was in there changin' to my work clothes."

"Tony, why? Why did you take it?"

"I d'know. I just . . . I just needed protection . . . I felt—stronger. I d'know . . . I just needed it, is all."

"Why did you leave it in the lab?"

"I done my work. I was lookin' at it an' Mr. Flanagan comes in—an' I can't think! So I stick it in the drawer. But this time *he* locks up an' I can't get back in. I was afraid to tell Mr. Quinn or anybody else. An' then it's too late." Tears of horror flowed from his reddened eyes.

"When did Mr. Quinn find out the gun was gone? When did he ask you about it, and about the contract?"

"That night. Monday night after supper. He called me. I told him then. I had to. I guess he just knew. Then my mother comes in an' says 'Who's onna phone?'—she's always at me!—an' I hang up. An' he's been askin' me for the contrack all week. I finally said I lost it. But he don't believe me."

I was right! Ben told himself. Quinn was lying!

He took the paper target out of his pocket and unfolded it. "Tell me about this. Your mother found it. I saw her this morning."

"That—! I was shootin' this summer with Timmy's .22 rifle. At the Rod an' Gun. I bought the bullets so he let me. It was my best one so I kept it. She's always pokin' in my stuff. That's why I keep the best things in my bag. I ain't got no place of my own at home. Two of my sisters are in the bedroom with me. So I stay in the plenum room a lot."

Ben's heart twisted with pain for this tough punk. "What about the money in the bag?"

"It was my pay for last week. I d'know why I didn't put it in my wallet. I just wasn't thinkin' straight last few days."

A lot longer than that, Ben thought sadly. "Tony, there was a little statue, a statue of a woman, near me and Miss Bellows. Your bag was there too. Do you know anything about that statue?"

* In Massachusetts any time after 2:30 P.M. is called "night" by most students, teachers, and other school personnel.

"Yeah. Mr. Quinn says I stole it but I didn't! I wasn't gonna keep it. I seen it in the TV room when I'm cleanin' up Tuesday. I took it to *dror* it 'cause it was pretty. I was gonna put it back, honest!"

"How did the bag get in the tunnel?"

"I d'know, Mr. Louis. The last I seen of it, I put it down by the door in Mr. Quinn's office, like he told me."

"Did Miss Bellows know what you kept in it?"

"Sure. An' Mr. Quinn an' my gang. But I never did nothin' with the statue after all. I couldn't seem to keep my mind on anything after—Tuesday."

"Okay, I believe you. It was mine, as it happens. Why didn't you ask someone about it instead of just borrowing it?"

"Don't you start in on me, don't start in on me, I'm warnin' yuh!"

To the boy's undying astonishment Ben smiled. "And what'll you do then, hey, tough guy?" he said gently. "Come on, son, I'll drive you home."

"Yah! An' first thing my mother'll say is 'Look at yuh good suit!' Oh god, oh god," he moaned hopelessly.

"You didn't change your clothes last night? After coming to the dance?" The boy shook his head. "According to Mr. Quinn your work clothes aren't in his closet now."

"Well, I didn't change, an' I didn't take them home after work neither. I an' Timmy was goin' to the coin-op on the way to Boston today, we was gonna stop for them here an' then go on. An' I couldn't change when I ran in the plenum room 'cause Mr. Quinn's door was closed an' I was scared he'd really chew me out if I went to get them. I d'know what he'd say if he knew I stayed there. An' I couldn't go no place else. I didn't have no place else to go. So I just laid down on my blanket in the plenum room all night."

"You could have gone home, Tony."

"Yeah. For once I wisht I had!"

After the relatively serene atmosphere of the storeroom, the boiler room was a booming maelstrom. Ben nodded his thanks to Vanna and Cooke and led Tony out into the fresh air.

"What's gonna happen to me, Mr. Louis?"

"If you've told the truth, things won't be too bad. I'll be with you every step of the way, son. No matter what! You'll get your stuff back too. We'll see. We'll talk next week, you and I. Okay?"

"Okay," the boy said dutifully, reserving trust. It was possibly the most poignant response Ben had yet heard from the lad.

He looked at his watch. It was after twelve now, and still he had not talked with Allen Magrue. But there was nothing he could do about it until he had taken Tony home and reported to Hudson and Keefe.

He didn't want to call Hudson and Keefe, he told himself as he returned to his car after a short but difficult visit with the Evans family. And I don't see why I should, he continued as he drove away. Does Macy's tell Gimbels'? No. And Hudson doesn't want to talk to me anyway. He's said so often enough. So that's that. Now, I'll just grab some lunch and go find Allen. I think I'm beginning to see a little daylight, a glimmer. Not that I know yet who did it, but I think I know why. And when I tell Art Hudson, he isn't going to like it. Not after two years ago. Not one little bit.

He grinned, anticipating Hudson's reaction, and then he threw his bandaged head back and laughed aloud although the act all but demolished it.

It was one of those moments, he told Jane later, when he damn near died laughing.

"And if Art Hudson had known what you were up to," she replied, "you would have."

CHAPTER SIXTEEN

12:30 P.M.

"Here's a little something the doctor ordered," Jane said, giving Ben a bowl of hearty homemade soup. "And one for you and one for me and two for Fee." These were rounds of bread covered with liver *pâté*. "And here's your mail."

The mail consisted of a colorful, an alluring, a heartbreakingly beautiful brochure from the San Francisco Chamber of Commerce.

"Oh bloody hell!" he said and sent it flying across the room. Then he got up and retrieved it. "I'll be damned if I cut my own throat over this business!" He folded it carefully and put it into his shirt pocket.

"I couldn't agree more," Jane said with caustic ambiguity. "Feel like telling me what you've found out so far?"

He did, concluding with "I think Quinn had a powerful motive for killing Joyce. Which reminds me. Hold it a sec. I've got to talk to Allen." He dialed so quickly that he left out a digit and had to dial again.

Still no answer.

"Jesus Christ! Where is that guy?"

"Probably having a better time than you are, Ben. Finish your soup or you'll collapse."

"Oh boy, this is good," he said, slurping gratefully, and finished. "Okay, about Quinn. I'll tell you in a word. His job. He's too worried about his future, and why should he have to be if everything's kosher? A guy like him can get a good job anywhere. The only thing he might have to worry about would be losing that surrogate family of his."

"But, Ben, you said he's been trying to stay since before the gun was left in the lab."

"I know, and that's the point. He knew his appeal was just a formality, along with the union lawyer's argument before the School Committee Wednesday night. He didn't really expect anything to come of that business. The point is that he didn't begin *lying* until he found that the gun was gone. He didn't start reading law until then, either. Even if he didn't kill Joyce, his liability regarding that Luger must be considerable. If it got out that it was his, I imagine the effect on his life would be terrific. I tried getting Bertram Shrag, Senior, a while back. If he's not home *this* time—!"

He dialed jerkily, furiously, threateningly, drumming on the table as the phone rang and rang. "Goddammit!" he began, and the judge answered. "Bertram, where the hell were you? Marking your poker deck, for crissake?"

"Already have," the judge said, and laughed. "No, I was out back digging up my tulip bulbs. What's biting you?"

Digging up bulbs! The foremost judge in the Commonwealth? The smartest, the toughest, the shrewdest—

Ben simmered down. "Look, Bertram, what would happen to a guy—one of my maintenance staff—who (a) brought home a handgun from the war, (b) didn't register it, (c) kept it in school and loaded, (d) unlawfully sold it to a minor, and (e) it—the gun, a Luger—killed that kid in the lab in my school?" He reached for pencil and paper.

"I'd say he's got quite a mess on his plate, Ben. What about the murdered woman, the guidance counselor? Did she know about it?"

"I think so. I'm almost certain she suspected whose it was and who took it."

"Why don't you add murder to your little list? Then that poor dumb bastard would have a royal flush. Well, I'll tell you, Ben. It could pile up into a lot of penalties, although I'm not certain of item (a). There's a difference of opinion on the legality of keeping war trophies like guns. I've had words with the DA's people on this. Anyway, here it is. Your man would be up for at least three penalties on three counts. He didn't get an identification card for the gun, which costs a mere dollar a year, too. So that's a penalty of up to a hundred bucks. He sold it to a minor, which results in a penalty of not less than a hundred or more than five hundred dollars. And presumably he didn't report the transfer to the Commissioner of Public Safety, nor did the boy have the written consent of his parents to buy the damn thing in the first place, probably, but I'm not sure about the penalty for that. Also, since the gun was loaded, there'd be another penalty for selling ammunition—not less than a hundred dollars, or imprisonment for not less than six months or more than two years. The big one, though, is a new federal law—with a fine of up to ten thousand bucks and imprisonment of up to ten years for failing to register a semi-automatic—a Luger, for instance—and certain other types of weapons with the IRS."

"God!" said Ben, scribbling away.

"But that's only the beginning of it, in this case, Benjamin, and the easiest part, too. Your guy faces civil and criminal charges. I wouldn't want to be in his shoes! By the way, was the gun shot by the boy who took it or by someone else? And what's the boy's connection with your maintenance man?"

Ben told him about Joyce Bellows' arrangements for the boys on work-study programs and summarized Tony Evans' story.

"Well, there it is, then. A nasty complicated business, I can assure you. Things aren't as tight as they should be, but they're getting tighter since the Kennedy and King assassinations. The boys involved—Tony and this Vinnie Dean—will have to appear for a hearing, and they'll probably have to get some extra attention—psychiatric help and so on—but legally they won't be held liable. But your man is liable. The dead boy's parents, and even the two other families involved—Evans and Dean—can bring a civil suit on charges of negligence. Hell, Valentine can also bring suit because of Bert's wound. But he's also liable for a criminal suit because hypothetically he can face manslaughter charges if gross negligence can be proved. This would be a matter for a judge, and I can tell you right now that if the DA brought the case before me, I'd throw the book at your man in the cellar!

"A gun—a Luger!—in a *school!* And loaded! And unregistered! And sold to a minor without parents' consent! And left in an accessible place! Gross negligence would be a shoo-in!

"Never mind his fatherly motives! The minute he knew that gun was gone, he should have moved his ass to get it back. And he did nothing.

"Put it all together, Ben, and the whole package makes one hell of a motive for murder!"

"And the way Tony tells it, the opportunity was all over the place."

"Yeah. Okay, Ben, if there isn't anything else, I've got to get back out. Those bulbs are uncovered. I don't want to lose them."

"Thanks, Bertram," Ben said automatically, too excited now to think about Shrag, Senior, who (like his son) was as square and solid as a tank and fussed over tulip bulbs with hands as big as bear paws.

He put down the receiver and looked at Jane blankly. "Wow!" he said and read his notes to her. "No wonder Quinn tried to get that contract back from Tony. He also had to find out what Tony had told Joyce. It wasn't the boy who represented a threat to him, not really. It was Joyce who did! Even if he didn't kill her, he's in for a rough time. I wouldn't give two cents for his future if he ever had to face Bertram in court."

"I won't give two cents for yours if you don't call Hudson, Benjamin Franklin Louis," she warned for the second time that day. A rash thing to do, some people would say, if you believed in the power of the word.

"And then there's Allen. He followed her to the boiler room, which is a damning thing against him even if I—"

"Ben!"

So he called Hudson.

"Very nice news, Ben. Thanks. It could be the boy. Get much out of him?"

"Not too much," Ben lied. "His clothes were clean, by the by."

"Mmmmmmm. Well, you've been so helpful that I'll tell you something, although it isn't much. We finally saw Magrue again—"

"Where?"

"At his home. He'd been visiting Miss Chadwick, talking over the battle plans for next week, what with their department chairman out of the picture. They met down at the Square when they were shopping for the weekend."

Oh sure, Ben said. Jane had been right. No doubt about it—Allen had indeed been having a better time of it than he. "So what cooks?"

"The same statement as before. Funny thing, though. He was

still wearing the same suit as last night. Must've slept in it by the looks of him. I wanted to brush him up and fix his shirt collar. All rumpled up. Shame too, because it's the best broadcloth I've—"

"Art!"

"What? Oh. Sorry. He said he said good-bye to Bellows, went back through the outside gym doors, and danced with a few of the teachers including Miss Chadwick. And then Keefe came in and busted up that—that brawl! I'll be damned if I'll call that dogfight a dance! The only thing is, though, I don't believe him."

"Why?"

"I don't know. He's hiding something. I can feel it. Besides, all of a sudden he clammed up. Said he didn't have to talk to us, that we had no cause to ask him anything, that he knew his rights—"

"Look, Art. You said his clothes were clean, didn't you? No blood?"

"He could have changed them."

"Oh come on, Art, he wouldn't have had time. Whoever killed Joyce would've been drenched! The floor was, and the center support. And he'd have had to know the basement, know where he could change—and he'd have had to have a change of clothing ready too, all stashed away, if he were going to kill her. But it was obviously a very quick decision, whoever did it. *He* wasn't prepared. Whatever he may be hiding, he couldn't have done it."

"Did you see him at the dance after she left?"

"No. But I didn't see a lot of other people either. And the ones I did see all looked alike!"

"Well—"

"Well nothing! He wouldn't have had time. And just to remind you of a few small facts, Tomasello found me minutes after the murder. And the place was surrounded minutes after that. And then Keefe saw Allen only minutes after *that*. Of course you can always pull Allen in on circumstantial evidence. It's been done before," he hinted broadly. "I've often wondered why Frank Houseman didn't sue you for false arrest."

"A-a-a-rrrgh! Okay, we'll see Tony Evans now, Ben. It should be very interesting."

Ben put down the receiver and dredged into that part of his brain where Jane said he kept a file of assorted and generally useless facts. Newspaper squibs, she called them. Well, maybe they were. But he could feel something stirring somewhere back of those itchy stitches.

He sat thinking intensely for a few moments and then called Jack Hardy at school.

"You're lucky, Ben. I was just about to leave," Hardy said. "What can I do for you? Don't keep me too long, though. Polly's fixing me a milk-toast feast for lunch. I'd hate to have it stand around spoiling."

"I'll be quick. Jack, did you say there was nothing unusual on Allen Magrue's personnel record? Disabilities? Anything out of the way?"

"There's nothing like that, Ben. Nothing at all."

"How much does a veteran get, a vet with an honorable discharge? I mean when he retires? I know there's something complicated about that but I can't remember the details. It has to do with extra benefits."

"Well, it adds up—if you can live that long in this business! It's fifteen dollars more a year for every year of teaching, but not to exceed three hundred a year. If you have disabilities you get even more."

"What about if you had a dishonorable discharge?"

"Then you just get the straight retirement. But Magrue's in the Reserve. Obviously he has an honorable discharge, no matter what he may eventually retire on. Oh! Are you getting at what I think you're getting at?"

"I just like to know more about penguins than I really have to. Thanks again, Jack. Take care. Sorry I kept you."

"Any time, Ben. Enjoy."

What I'm getting at, Ben told the cradled receiver, is this. Our personnel files record only a teacher's dates of service and branch of service. The State Retirement Board has very little more. But down in Washington—

"What was that all about?" Jane said.

"Just a sec," he said as certain facts began to cluster round a particular one, like crystals round a string, triggering his memory.

Apart from Allen Magrue's being a nice guy and a highly qualified therapist and teacher, what kind of man *is* he? The question brought forth another question. There might be answers to both in that big envelope Mrs. Wickham had given him, but he had no time to read it now.

"Jane," he said slowly, "what did you mean the other night when I told you about Allen maybe being in love with Joyce?"

"Hmmm?"

"You said something . . . something about adding dimension to people. Something to do with Allen."

"Oh, I don't know. I don't remember. . . . Oh, I know! It struck me funny that he should be interested in her. And vice versa."

"What's so goddam funny about that?"

"Nothing. Only I thought they weren't specially interested in the opposite sex. Which is all right with me except that I think it's better our way. Would you care to debate the issue?"

"Do you think you can convince me?"

"Uh-huh. When your head is better. I wouldn't want to win by default."

"Neither would I," he said, and got up to kiss her competently.

"Your head's a lot better already, I can tell. Now tell me what you're thinking about."

"There's something significant about three facts, Jane. Joyce was an army psychologist. Allen was out of the service after about fifteen months, when the war was still going badly. December 1944 wasn't a particularly great month for celebrating, you may recall. And third, according to Grace Wickham, Joyce despised Allen. Why? What did she know about him? Now, there may not be anything on his personnel record here or at the State Retirement Board, but if there were a black mark on his army record down in Washington, it is available and the police could get it."

"But Allen has an honorable discharge and he's in the Reserve, you said."

"Well, not everything off key results in a court-martial or a dishonorable discharge. Or a general discharge, for that matter. But it would be on a man's record. . . ."

"But I have a feeling that in 1944 he got a general discharge."

"But you said—"

"Don't interrupt. The only way he could be in the Reserve after receiving a general discharge would be to bring his case before the Appeal Board at the Pentagon, have it reviewed, and be cleared of whatever charge had resulted in the general discharge. That is one hell of a very tough thing to do. But it can be done, and when it is, all traces of the reason for the general discharge are removed as if they'd never happened at all. In which case there wouldn't *be* anything on the record. Obviously—as Art Hudson would say."

"What is a general discharge? A Section Eight?"

"No. The general discharge is the result of a Section Eight. Section Eight's the old term. It was a comprehensive regulation that covered all sorts of cases resulting in general discharges."

"Such as what?"

"Oh, moral turpitude, homosexuality, mental instability. That sort of thing. There's a new regulation now, since 1950 or 1951, that's specific to homosexuality. I'm not too sure about it."

They stared at each other.

"Oh boy!" Ben said, stunned. "This is one hell of a can of beans I think I've just opened! What could Joyce have had on Allen? And what did he do about it?"

"But, Ben, after what you said to Art—"

"I know what I said to Art. And he seemed to believe it, although he doesn't want to. I think he believed it, anyway."

He put down the notes he had made and looked sick.

"The only trouble is," he said, "now I'm not so sure *I* do."

He dialed a number again, spoke briefly and urgently into the phone, and went out of the house, his car keys in one hand and the top of his head in the other.

CHAPTER SEVENTEEN

2:30 P.M.

As Art Hudson had said, Allen Magrue was even now wearing the dressy black mohair suit that he had worn to the dance the night before. He was well shaved, his thick hair shone, and his skin was rosy from scrubbing and toweling. But the condition of his clothes suggested that he had danced all night in a go-go cage. But I'll bet, Ben said to himself as he went into Allen's apartment, I'll bet he's on the Ten Best Dressed list when he wears jeans and an old sweat shirt.

And then he related part of what he had learned so far and what was on his mind. "Hudson's still after you, Allen. He doesn't know why, but something's bothering him. He thinks you're hiding something. And I do too. I think you lied to him about being in love with Joyce. Why? Why did you?"

"Because with what she knew about me—" The sensitive lips tightened stubbornly.

"Look, Allen! After Hudson sees Tony Evans, I'm sure he and Keefe will be back. You might want a lawyer. The thing is, I saw you follow Joyce last night, although I didn't tell Art that. But Tony saw you too. So did Tim Lunn—and they probably will. There are at least two good suspects so far. Tony and Quinn. But Hudson hasn't closed the applications yet, and you might be another. I thought maybe I could help."

"Oh god . . . I don't know. . . . It isn't easy to talk about, even after so many years. . . . Helen knows, of course," Allen added almost to himself.

"I was way off the mark, wasn't I?" Ben said, facing the news bravely. "It wasn't you and Joyce, as I'd thought. It was you and Helen. You're very lucky, Allen. She's a fine beautiful person."

Allen's face glowed for a moment. "You know what the damndest part of it all is? I almost took a job in New York."

"I know. And I know where, too. Snatching you out of the jaws of that greedy bastard in Eastminster was one of my finest *coups.*"

"If I could have had the program I've got here, I'd be down there now." And Allen grinned slyly.

"I don't think so. My counterproposals were fail-safe, pal. I had everything well in hand. All the angles were covered. You may as well know whom you're dealing with—I don't want my reputation besmirched. I learned pirating under the Morgan of superintendents."

They laughed at and with each other. But two words hung in the air and spread over them like a pall. They sobered quickly.

"Okay, Ben, I'll tell you. You were right. Joyce was about to tell the Superintendent. And you too, I'd say. She made a thing of asking about calling you today." He took a deep breath. "I might as well start at the beginning. Where she started—and finished, unfortunately. I joined the air force in October 1943. I was eighteen and green as grass, just like the kids I have now. I'd been what's called a behavior problem and my relationship with my parents wasn't good. I wasn't being patriotic when I joined up. I was just using a socially acceptable means of running away from home. From my father and mother.

"They're fine people and I love them and understand them better—and myself too. But at that time one of our running arguments was that I follow Dad into engineering, and I couldn't add one and one. At least it wasn't my cup of tea. I didn't know what I wanted to do. But I knew what I didn't want to do—I didn't want to go to MIT and add figures and juggle slide rules. So—

"I went through bombardier training, which is full of math! And then we were graduated after about fifteen months of training and flying and so on. You know."

"Yeah. I was in the Eighth."

"My group was sent to the Pacific. Anyway, we were young and wild and we had a big bash after graduation—

"And that was when it happened. It was a crazy party. We rented some rooms in the local fleabag and started to drink and carry on. Some of the fellows had girls but I didn't. I'd never had one, in fact. I wandered around from room to room getting drunker every minute . . . and wound up in a room where they were smoking pot.

"I tried it and got higher than a kite—and so did everyone else. Then some of them began to get rough. I don't mean nasty, just rough. Tearing each other's clothes off, throwing glasses of water at each other, filling the tub and dunking each other. That sort of stupid prank . . .

"And then . . . it got completely out of hand. . . .

"I was the youngest of the bunch and they knew I was a virgin. They began teasing me, calling me Alice. . . .

"So . . . I rapidly became the goat at that party, in that room, and I was drunk as hell on booze and pot . . . and—and two of them held me down and—another one raped me!"

He clutched his expensive silk tie and his boyish face twisted in pain and revulsion.

"The MPs walked in at that moment and caught us in the act. I was so sick and scared that the full impact of it didn't hit me 'til later. . . .

"I was sent to a hospital for observation and evaluation along with some of the others. Our records were reviewed—mine hadn't been too sharp although I'd gotten by well enough—and then there was a long drawnout testing routine. And I was discharged, finally, with the others.

"We got a general discharge because of mental unsuitability, homosexuality. . . . And that was that. . . .

"It destroyed my parents. It damn near destroyed me. I went home but I couldn't stay there, of course. I went to Detroit and worked in a war plant and made damn good money—enough to go to Wayne University and also into psychoanalysis, which lasted five years. I majored in English and psych'.

"Then when I was ready, I brought the matter to the Appeal Board in Washington. As you know, it was rugged! But I made it. My record was wiped clean, I was reinstated as a second lieutenant, and that was the end of it—I thought.

"I couldn't join up for Korea, though, because Washington took their good old time. But I did join the Reserve. I'm no war buff. It was a matter of pride, I guess. And I felt proud. I still do. . . .

"When I came up here and met Joyce, I liked her and was glad we were going to work together. And there was Helen too. Right from the beginning! I can't believe it yet—how lucky I am to have her! But Joyce remembered me!

"It was my name, she said. Such an odd one. Probably because of the 'Ballad of Dan McGrew,' you know?" He smiled wryly. "When I was a kid we had a plumber named Button. I still remember him and what he looked like—after thirty-five years!—because when he came I used to say, 'Hello, Mr. Button-button-who's-got-the-button!' So it's understandable that Joyce could remember a name like mine after so long, especially in connection with a scandal like the one I was in."

"When did she tell you she remembered you?"

"Just a week ago. Last Friday, in fact. She said it had begun to bug her at your staff picnic. I told her about my Reserve status —and Ben, she didn't believe me! Because I wasn't married. Because I seem to have a habit of touching people or bending close to them when we talk, she said. I never noticed that, did you? Fact is, I'm slightly hard of hearing in one ear, but nobody knows that. Not even the army!

"She told me to resign—to keep things quiet—or else she'd have to go to the Superintendent. I refused, of course. So she said she'd have to 'take steps.'"

"When did she say that?"

"On Tuesday morning, just before the tragedy. We'd gone down to the basement—she was looking for Tony and I was talking with Rocco Tomasello about that flooding in the boys' john. I'd been planning to administer the OQSMA over the intercom to several classes, to save time, but the wires under the lav' had been shorted. Roc and I were talking about when the repairs would be done so that I could figure out another schedule. Joyce and I met down there—and she started all over again. She'd spoken to me Friday, she said, and here it was Tuesday, and what had I done?

"We argued about it all the way back upstairs—and you heard us and said you thought we were having a lovers' quarrel! You weren't the only one. David's been hinting and winking for weeks. God, what irony! Joyce was incapable of love—and I don't mean only romantic love. But we can go into that later.

"Anyway, I was so surprised by your expectations for us that I didn't know what to say. I'm glad I didn't have to. You wanted to talk to her alone, I could see that. And I had a class anyway, so

I took off. But it gave Helen and me something else to think about. Whoever's in charge of the Ironical Department has certainly been having a field day with us!

"But when the police asked me last night about my relationship to Joyce, I grabbed at your assumption about us. Actually I didn't have to say anything like that, I realize now. All I had to say was that, since she'd been out sick, certain department matters needed discussion, and that that's what we'd been talking about. But I was rattled. With what *was* between us, I knew I was a logical suspect. Maybe *the* logical suspect! I should have realized that, being the kind of person she was, plus the fact that she'd been out sick all week, she wouldn't have told anyone that she loved me or that she hated me! At least not until what was for her the very last possible minute, when circumstances of whatever kind forced her to part with a crumb of information—or privacy—or whatever else you want to call it. I know what it should be called. . . .

"For instance, to underline her announcement to me last Friday, she made sure I saw that caduceus Monday at the meeting, two—no, three days later. I damn near fainted when I saw it, although at first I thought that someone she'd known during the war had given it to her as a memento. She'd told me some weeks back that she'd worked with hospitalized servicemen. But it wasn't until Tuesday that she told me she'd actually been in the service! I was astounded that someone could be so close with herself, almost sly. The funny thing is, I've worked with patients like her, and I've noticed the trait quickly in people I'm not close to, but I was slow in catching on to Joyce. I don't know why."

"The same thing happened to me, Allen, and at the same time. But go on. How did she lay it on you? What was her manner like?"

"She wasn't nasty or gloating or anything like that. Anything but, as a matter of fact. She just said in that beautiful voice, 'I was a lieutenant, Allen, and I was on the hospital staff when you were there. In fact I was asked to give my opinion of your case.'"

"I don't get it. Why didn't she believe you—about your Reserve status? Why did she keep pushing?"

"I asked her that. Naturally! After the meeting Monday, I went to Logan to meet one of my brothers. We hadn't seen each other for a year, and he decided to fly from Detroit to Boston instead of direct to Nashville just so we could have dinner together and talk for a couple of hours! We were always very close, the three of us. What we'd lost out on with our parents, we made up for with each other. We were always a team. I was damn glad to see him and we hugged each other and pounded each other a bit—and Joyce saw us. And that did it!

"And, incidentally, after that meeting, I told her I had to get to the airport—and she never mentioned that she was going there too! God! So when I saw her suddenly appear right in front of me there, I was struck again by that closeness, that tightness of hers. I started to introduce Don but she refused to listen or even look at him. If someone hadn't called her then, I don't know what she'd have said."

"That was her sister, on the same plane. Grace Wickham."

"Grace Wick—! My god . . . Ben, did *you* know Joyce had a sister?"

"No. Not until Tuesday afternoon. Not even after eight years."

"So that's why Hudson and Keefe gave me such a going-over! How could I love the gal and know nothing about her family! It makes sense, I guess, their suspecting me. But they don't know Joyce the way I did. I'll tell you about that later."

"What did Joyce say about the Logan meeting? I gather that was part of Tuesday's argument."

"And how! She told me what she thought of me and my—my *boyfriend!* That no matter how much analysis I'd had, it hadn't taken. That I'd regressed or lapsed or something. That as far as she was concerned, my private life was my own, but that in school my position with all those young boys provided a daily temptation! As witness my picking Tony Evans up with such *suspicious solicitude* when he fell last week. She accepted my being in the Reserve, of course. But she was irrational about the rest of it. She didn't believe I was going off *primarily* for two weeks of training —not in November, she said. But you don't pick your time. You go when they send you your orders! Most people think Reserve training is only in the summer.

"But, she said, she'd seen Don and now she'd put two and two together and knew I was really going off with my—my lover! She reminded me that teachers have been caught lying before about taking an illegal vacation and been fired for it. And she said again that it would be better all around if I just resigned. I said I'd do no such thing. So she said she'd have to report the matter although she didn't want to."

"I can't figure it," Ben said. "My picnic was about eight weeks ago. Was she stewing about this all that time?"

"Most of it, she said."

"But why? Why would she wait so long?"

"There are two reasons, Ben. She gave me one of them. That she wanted to be absolutely sure, absolutely fair. And, as Zachary Inman would say, I believe that she believed that. Her very compulsivity is one of the things that made her such a damn fine person."

"And the other reason?"

"Well, the other reason I can only theorize about. She wasn't married either. Her femininity was only skin-deep. I never had a conviction that *she* had a conviction about it. Her clothes were man-tailored and simple in the extreme. And I began to have a growing sense that she suspected herself of latent homosexuality. And if that were true—and later I found that it was—then my presumed perversion scared hell out of her. My being there reactivated, so to speak, the fears she thought she'd buried in herself —about herself. Getting rid of me would quiet those fears. But —on an even deeper level—"

"I think I follow you," Ben said. "On an even deeper level, she thought that if you could be a homosexual, yet successful in a school, with kids, then she was all right too. Your position, your success validated hers, and she could keep on going, just as you were. Which is why she waited so long to tell you she remembered you. Right?"

"I think so. But seeing Don was too much for her. If she hadn't gotten sick—But she did, and she went home and stayed there until last night. And someone stopped her before she had a chance to talk. . . .

"In that lovely sweet soft voice of hers, she said all those terrible things!" His voice broke and he bit his lip and swallowed convulsively.

"And that's it?"

"That's it, I swear, Ben. It's the truth!"

"Still, you needn't have been so alarmed. You had proof."

"Look, Ben. She was a fine, well-trained person. Given her reputation here, whom do you think the Superintendent would believe? I don't mean that he'd overlook my proof. But ask yourself. Wouldn't there be some lingering doubt in his mind? Especially if she put a lousy connotation on the way I talk to people and all that? Wouldn't he wonder just how innocent I'd really been? Wouldn't he wonder whether, if this came out once, it might come out again? And again and again? And cause a juicy filthy scandal every time?"

And Ben's eyes fell away from his, because what he had said was true. The very worst thing on a teacher's record was the slightest hint of moral turpitude. And even worse than *that* was public knowledge of it. And *even* worse than that was the linking of such talk with someone in the field of guidance, which was suspect enough at the best of times.

"I begged her not to do it," Allen said. "But she said she had no choice."

"Those were the words she used in that bit of a letter Hudson and Keefe found in her apartment."

"So I heard. They asked me a while ago if I knew anything that could explain it. I said no, of course. And you can see why I lied. But I didn't kill her. I didn't even go down to the boiler room after her. I knew it wouldn't do any good to try to talk to her any more. I did think of stopping her when she went after Tony, but then I crossed the driveway and went back in through the gym's outside doors and gave Helen the high sign. I danced with a couple of the gals first, and apparently they bore me out from something Hudson said this afternoon. Anyway, when I snagged Helen and told her what had happened, we agreed to see the Superintendent or you this morning. She had wanted me to, several days ago, but I couldn't bring myself to go into the thing, not if I didn't have to. But Keefe came in just as I was talking with Helen, and it wasn't until then that I saw swarms of police all over the place. And then I knew I wouldn't have to do anything."

He was tired now from telling his long story, from the pain of reliving it, and he lay back on the couch and closed his eyes. His arms were outstretched, palms up, fingers curled, unguarded, vulnerable.

Looking at those hands intently, Ben said one more thing.

"You implied that she left you and drove away. Why?"

There was no tremor in the fingers, no jerky reflex of the elbows. If the police tied a lie detector around his neck and followed him around for a week, Ben thought in relief, they'd never find a thing to hold him on. Because—and he was sure of this—there wasn't anything for them to find.

His eyes still closed, Allen said, "I didn't mean to. In any case I was sure she would, in a few more minutes. When she saw that poor kid she'd been badgering out of his mind, she said, 'I'm going to get the truth out of him if it's the last thing I do! I won't tolerate his manner, not after all I've done for him!'

"But he was too quick. They both were. Like a couple of mice scrambling down a hole."

"Both? Who was the other one?"

"Tim Lunn."

"That's funny. I was pretty sure he must have seen you too. But Tony said that Tim took off when Joyce went over there, and that he didn't see him again. And Tim was at Tony's house this morning looking for him. So I inferred that Tim had left the school, not gone back inside it. Well, well. So he was down there too. And *he* had motive and opportunity." He blinked and rubbed his eyes which ached and burned and seemed unable to focus.

"Ben, I'll tell you something I haven't even told Helen yet. You said there were two good suspects so far, Tony and Tom Quinn, right? Well, Tim's a third, with a motive similar to Tony's. If I've got the right picture of the boy so far. I've only seen him a few times, and Joyce refused—she actually refused!—to show me her notes on either kid. Simon was furious about this. As acting chairman he called her apartment Wednesday at my request to see if he could get anything out of her. I was hoping to make tracks while she was out—set up some home visits, see what I could do. In my view those boys were entering a critical state as a result of her continued interference, and I was plenty worried. That's what I came down to see you about on Thursday, but you were busy. I don't know what David was thinking about. Anyway, Simon said someone answered and said Joyce was too ill to come to the phone. That was her sister, I suppose."

"Yes. She left yesterday morning and had to come back today. Go ahead." And now Ben leaned back and closed his eyes as waves of dizziness assailed him.

"Well, as I see it, there are *five* suspects. I'm the fourth—except for opportunity. They *were* down in that cellar. I wasn't."

"And the fifth?"

"David Ross."

Ben was not as surprised as he had expected to be, possibly because he was suddenly unable to think any longer. Exhaustion immobilized him. He felt as boneless as a fillet. And a pulse like a wrecking ball was pounding away inside his skull, making him dangerously nauseous. He took out his pill bottle with palsied hands and asked for a glass of water.

"God, what a fool I am!" Allen said, bringing it to him. "I was too damn full of myself to realize what you looked like. Lie down for five minutes, Ben. Then I'll drive you home. You're flaked out, friend. You've had it for now. We can finish some other time."

"But what about you? How will you get home?" Ben said, stretching out on the couch and closing his eyes again. "And there's something else . . . how you found out about Joyce. . . ."

"Never mind about any of that. Just rest."

There was no point in arguing. He couldn't even if he wanted to, and he didn't want to. Weariness filled him like a cottony stuffing that made his body light enough to float.

Presently, leaning on Allen's arm, he went out to his car and gratefully let himself be chauffeured home.

"I don't know if I should thank you, though, Allen. Raiding my staff, marrying Helen. If it weren't for me, you'd never have met her."

"I hate to say this, Ben. It's terrible to puncture a man's self-image so ruthlessly. But there's something up Boston way that's even more persuasive than you were. That special program at the University that's headed up by *the* Dr. Zachary Inman. It's the next best thing to becoming a psychiatrist! If I hadn't been accepted already, I *would* have gone to Eastminster! And I'd have met Helen anyway. She has a theory about that."

"Oh look, he's asleep!" Jane said, kissing Ben through the car window. "My poor sweet. I guess it's those pills." She awakened him gently.

"Could be," Allen laughed. "But I dealt his pride a low blow. I think it knocked him for a loop!"

CHAPTER EIGHTEEN

4:00 P.M.

"Helen's just taken Allen away, darling, so I'll get over to the store and do some shopping before it closes," Jane said. She folded his trousers and hung them over the back of a chair, then tucked him into bed. "They looked beautiful, just beautiful."

"Who?" Ben said sleepily.

"Helen and Allen. It's funny. They're about our age, but they looked like a couple of kids. Just like Love's Young Dream . . ." She stood for a moment, remembering how her own love had burgeoned and bloomed and was blooming still, and then she bent to kiss Ben's lips. "I won't be long. Go ahead and sleep, darling. I'll be back soon. Benjy's around somewhere. Fee took him for a walk."

"Okay," he said, drowsy from pills. "Would you just do one more thing? Bring me that big envelope I put on my desk. I may look at it later. And my glasses. Thanks, sweet." He snuggled into his nest of pillows and blankets, smiling, relaxed, and feeling only comfortably fatigued now that he was home in his own bed.

The brochure that was still in his shirt pocket crackled as he turned over, and he began to dream about San Francisco. If a dream were all that he was going to have of the trip he had been looking forward to since July, he did not want to miss a minute of it. He squinched his eyes shut and in a moment was floating effortlessly over the Golden Gate into the sunset. . . .

San Francisco was in flames again—the fire alarms were ringing insistently—he had to help—save his TV video tapes—notes—

"Hello? Hello?" he said groggily into the receiver.

"Mr. Louis, this is Mrs. Adams. My daughter is a sophomore."

Slowly he came awake. "Oh. Yes. What can I do for you?"

"Well, Mr. Louis, it's this murder. Miss Bellows, the guidance person. An awful thing, of course, especially after the tragedy Tuesday. Some of us parents have been talking about it—naturally we feel very sorry about it—but we feel it's a kind of reflection of our thinking on this whole area. I mean, we wouldn't want to have all the guidance people *killed*, don't you know, but if our resentment against those kind of meddlers was put all together, I honestly don't think they'd stay very long! We feel this is the responsibility of the home and all that. We don't like those people prying information out of our children and so forth. And we feel this is a good time to review the community's feeling about guidance, and we'd like to present a petition to the School Committee."

"Why don't you come in sometime next week, Mrs. Adams, and we can talk about it. You can bring a list of the people you represent—"

"They don't want to be named, Mr. Louis, if you know what I mean."

"I don't think I do," he said blandly.

"They're afraid the teachers will take it out on their children, Mr. Louis. You can understand that, I'm sure."

"I'll be happy to talk with you, but you'll have to give me something more to go on. Think it over and ring my office someday for an appointment."

She wouldn't, he was sure of that. Nevertheless, the headache moved in his skull like an awakening tiger digging its claws in and stretching.

He closed his eyes again but the dream was gone and would not come back. He stared at the wall, worrying. . . .

When the telephone rang again, he picked it up reluctantly.

"Mr. Louis?" said a belligerent voice.

"Yes, this is he. Who's calling?" It was a man-killing tiger, this headache. He reached for his pills and put them down again. He had taken too many already.

"I'd as soon not say, but it's about the murder. I heard it was a nigger kid that did it. One of those niggers you imported from Boston to give a good education to, in our schools, with our money!"

"I'd appreciate it if you'd be courteous enough to give me your name, sir. You know who *I* am," Ben said tightly.

"That's beside the point! What I'm concerned about—"

Ben hung up.

He was applying a compress to his head when the telephone rang a third time. He answered it with an angry "Yes!"

"Dad! Darling, what have *They* done to you? I just heard the news and I'm worried about you."

Ben smiled happily. This was his daughter Elizabeth calling from Clark University. *They* were all the bastards of the world, the Enemy.

He chatted for a few minutes with his third staunchest ally (the other two, Jane said, were Mrs. Castle and Mr. Tomasello), but his restored calm was soon shattered by a fourth call.

"Yes? This is Mr. Louis," he said. All the nerves and muscles in his body were attached to the sutures in his scalp, and every movement that he made clove his skull in twain.

A hoarse voice said, "I've heard they announced the murderer. You were at the school. Is it true?"

There was something strange about the voice in his ear. It might have been muffled. It might have been reading from a script. And it sounded like Tom Quinn. Or Timothy Lunn. Or Tony Evans.

Ben said, "Do you mean last night or today?"

"Uh—last night, I gu—I believe."

"Who is this? Who's calling?"

But the only reply was a small careful click.

He began to worry again. Should he have told Hudson and Keefe everything he knew? Should he tell them now?

About what? About whom? Allen Magrue? No. If Allen's guilty, then I'm guilty. *Ergo.* For the rest, let sleeping dogs lie.

What about Tony Evans? No. What could I tell Hudson and Keefe that they haven't already found out from the boy? Nothing much, except a couple of minor items like Joyce being in Two last night, and the gun belonged to Tom Quinn. And by now they've also gotten to Quinn—Uh-oh!—and discovered that I got to him first.

No, I'm all right there. All he can say is that I was looking for the boy, and that after hearing his, Quinn's, story, I urged him to go straight to the police. . . . He's a decent guy, a nice guy. . . .

I hope he didn't kill her. . . . But if my theory about him is right, the police will get it out of him. . . .

Did Tony do it? . . . I don't think he could have. . . . I don't see how he could have . . . could he have? . . . would he be likely to kill her *after* shooting out the bulbs and yelling at her and running? *After* ventilating himself and acting out so much of his hostility? . . . I'd feel like hell if he turned out to be the one. . . .

And Tim Lunn? Same thing. They'll have gotten to him already through Tony or even Quinn. Tim Lunn, the war lover, who wants the protection of a United States serviceman's uniform in which he can kill with impunity. . . . An unprepossessing boy, to be sure, but only superficially. There was something of value beneath that studded black jacket. Samuel Butler had said it—that genius is like money, and *everyone* has a little of it. And I believe it. If I didn't, I'd have to find something else to do. And the day I stop believing it, I will!

But could Tim Lunn have killed Joyce? Two character witnesses, Tony and Quinn, said no. When Joyce appeared, Tim fled. Why? On the principle that, if he didn't actually see her, she or the threat she held over him didn't exist or lost its power? And what had she planned for him? And where were her notes on those sessions during which he had made admissions on which her plans were based? There must be some notes somewhere!

I'm going to have to see that boy. Tomorrow morning, for sure . . .

And what about the fifth suspect, David Ross? Should I tell Hudson and Keefe what Allen said? No. In the first place he didn't say anything, and in the second place I'm not responsible for Allen's theories. . . .

Still, there was something peculiar about David last night. Here's a tight compulsive character acting as loose as a goose with kids who Broke a Rule! A real switch for David, I'd say. And a far cry from his performance at the meeting last Monday. . . .

Wonder if he's been drinking? . . . Now that I think it over, he did look kind of sloshed. . . . *Why* would he be drinking? Is he *that* afraid of rigorous supervision and evaluation methods? He was plenty paranoid at the meeting.

Question. How does a paranoic look or sound? When he's heading for a breakup, that is, so that it really shows.

Well, speaking generally, a paranoic is more defensive, more self-protective than a given situation would suggest he need be. His reactions are too great, considering the stimulus. His fear of attack, his resentment of even ordinary criticism or suggestions seem unwarranted by what is known of his ability and past performance. He is massively and increasingly suspicious of the motives of others as regards himself.

He behaves as if he's standing alone against a totally hostile world. A wholly untrustworthy world.

As if there's *no one* to turn to or depend upon.

As if to trust anyone means forfeiting control of the only dependable source of power—himself.

So the paranoic fights to hold onto that control. The more he thinks people are trying to usurp or destroy it, the harder he has to fight them, the more carefully he has to watch them. And test them. And trap them. And fend them off.

And in the process his fear increases and his defensive stance hardens until at last he behaves in a manner quite unlike what he was, or seemed to be, before. . . .

Question. Am I talking about David—or *Joyce?*

With a shiver of apprehension he reached for the big envelope Grace Wickham had given him and took out, first, Joyce's completed evaluations of her four staff members. The forms were intricate ten-paged documents with space for extended comment, but Ben had read dozens of such forms and went through them rapidly.

"Ah . . ." he said.

And then his hands trembled as he opened the private journal Joyce had been writing for her advisers at the University. The candid description of the progress of her doctoral project from its inception and of the people who were in any way connected with it. . . .

"Well now," he said after a while, when he had done. "So I'm paranoid too! It takes one to know one, as they say. . . ."

Shocked to the very core, he needed time to digest all that he had read. Measured and careful as Joyce's words were and had always been, they clearly reflected a disintegrating mind. And he had not suspected it even for a moment. Flu, yes, and the irritability that came with it. But this? No.

He stared at the wall, which had suddenly assumed a strange

aspect. I'll figure the wall out later, he decided, and withdrew into the recesses of his memory to look for something he had read years ago. It had to do with murder and identity in the psychoanalytical sense, and he had not fully agreed with it then.

Probably because I didn't fully understand it then. But I think I do now! he said triumphantly, on finding it.

And now I know the motivation for Joyce's murder! Psychoanalytically speaking.

The only hitch is, it fits at least four of the five suspects Allen listed—and he's one of them! Sort of, anyway.

And if I stretch the rule of probability a little bit, I could even add a sixth!

Feeling uncomfortably and inexplicably warm now, he returned slowly to a more conscious contemplation of the puzzle of the wall. It filled his visual field. And it had become huge and hairy and ardent, and it breathed all over him, tropically, like the very personification of a dog day.

"Oh! Hi, Fee *bubi*. What cooks?"

It was not a rhetorical question. He could hear Jane jumping and clashing in the kitchen. Dinner was in preparation and it would be a masterpiece if his wife were running true to form: The noise she made was always in direct proportion to the excellence of her results.

He hoped that he could taste them. The pain-killers had dried up his taste buds and his tongue felt swollen. He set himself to thinking of the best things Jane had ever cooked. And of Floria Rienzi's spaghetti, down the street. And good scotch whiskey, smooth and fair. And strawberries as big as apples. And mushrooms as big as umbrellas.

It was no good.

The inside of his mouth was a paper bag filled with a swollen tongue that tasted terrible, and he knew that it was all he would taste tonight.

But he could at least enjoy the luxury of a few more minutes of rest. He might even contemplate the possibility of going to San Francisco after all. He took the brochure from his pocket and studied the photographs longingly.

When the telephone rang again, he was certain that the Golden Gate swayed and snapped in the middle and fell into the Bay.

CHAPTER NINETEEN

6:00 P.M.

Mr. Tomasello's esthetic standards were intolerably affronted by the condition of the lawns and walks around the school. Litter was everywhere, and the entire complex—and particularly Building Three, his special *purlieu*—looked like a deserted carnival ground.

Yuh do a job when it's gotta be done, not when yuh get aroun' to doin' it, was his motto. After weighing the complete loss of his cool against a complaint from the Forestry Department and the Building Service Employees Union, he had torn off to the school at eight on this Saturday morning and attacked *his* enemy with a push broom, a leaf rake, a spiked stick, and a gigantic wheelbarrow.

Anger, resentment, and worry over Ben's condition imbued him with a determination that would have kept him going even after he had dropped dead from fatigue (not that anyone had ever known him to be tired). For hours he swept and swept and raked and raked, separating cans and bottles from burnable trash and emptying the wheelbarrow into a forty-gallon container on a dolly, which he had stationed like a sentinel by the boiler room door.

Thomas Quinn, emerging into the areaway at five forty-five, confronted the sweating custodian who was maneuvering the container through the door to the clanking metal stairway. With Quinn was Timothy Lunn, and they looked as much alike as Tweedledum and Tweedledee as they made themselves small against the railing to protect their clean chinos.

"Thanks f' nuttin'," Mr. Tomasello said with poisonous sweetness, bumping the container past them.

"Here! What're yuh doin' with that!" Quinn said. "You're not supposed to do that! The union's pretty goddam particular!"

"So'm I! An' *this* time the incineratin's gonna be done *right!* An' *you* know what yuh can do wit' the *union!*"

Calls himself a member of the working class, Mr. Tomasello muttered with boundless scorn. I bet he don't even lift a finger to wipe his—

"Hey, Roc, lemme help," said Cooke, and together they trundled the container to the incinerator room.

"Thanks, Cookie," said Mr. Tomasello. "I just couldn't stand it no more, that mess out there. Just don't tell the union, though, 'cause that bastid Quinn will get all shook when they slap my hand f' doin' a no-no. I wouldn't want he should suffer!"

Cooke laughed and went back to the boiler room, and Mr. Tomasello opened the fire chamber door and poked at the half-burned stuff inside. Cris*sake!* he said to himself. Some people!

Last night on his way to his car, he had stopped, as was his practice, to check the fire. He had found the ashpit door ajar, and flames and sparks shooting out because of the increased draft. The room was fireproofed, of course, but still, only a goddam fool would leave a fire like that. He had closed the ashpit door, damped down the fire, and left, thinking, I'll be back tomorra anyways, an' when I finish cleanin' up, I'll stick aroun' an' burn everything—an' *watch* it.

Now he applied a lighted match to a twist of paper from the container, peered into the fire chamber, abruptly ground the flaming paper under his work boot, caught something on the end of the spiked stick, and drew it out—and put it back again.

"JesusMary'nJoseph!" he said. Perhaps the school had been—was about to be—made clean again by the work of his hands.

He ran to the boiler room and called Ben.

"This what made you so mad last night, Roc?" Ben said, lifting a partly burned bundle out of the fire chamber and putting it on the floor.

"Yeah! Lazy bastid, whoever he is, can't even wait a couple minutes an' see if it burns right!"

Ben speared something on the spike and held it up. It dangled like a snake. It was a charred leather belt, but the blackened initial on the buckle was quite legible.

T.

So what? There's *T* for Timmy Lunn and *T* for Tom Quinn. Tony isn't the only one.

Using the spiked stick, he poked the bundle apart until a chino shirt and a pair of pants lay spreadeagled on the floor.

There was very little blood on them.

The shirt front was symmetrically decorated with long, almost parallel, dark brown stains that started on the breast pockets and petered out a few inches above the waist.

There were no stains on the front of the trousers.

"I don't think so, anyway. Do you, Roc?"

"No. Hard t' tell, though, 'cause they was plenny dirty t' begin with."

Puzzled, Ben turned them over.

Across the seat was a wide irregular dark-brown smear. And that was all.

"Blood-wise, that is," Ben said, taking a roll of papers out of one of the back pockets. "I think I know what these are! I'll look at them in a minute. Well, Roc, I guess we both know what this means. Maybe you ought to be glad for once that someone bollixed up the job."

"Yuh can see why he did, too! Damn fool can't think straight —don't know who he is, prolly!—'less he checks with his belt buckle two, three times a day!"

"Well, as it happens, you're right, Roc. No joke," Ben said, picking up the trousers. He held them gingerly an inch or two away and measured their length against his own long legs. They would fit any tall man or boy. Tim or Quinn or Tony.

Oh God, no! he prayed, to Someone (but no one in particular).

But the evidence was there, inside the waist band and inside the shirt collar, roughly printed in faded laundry ink.

T. Evans.

He could have wept, for the boy and for himself—a blind stupid jerk who could be so easily fooled. Who had been.

"There ain't *much* blood, though, Mr. Louis," the Roc said loyally. "That Tony, he's a good kid."

"Yeah. Thanks, Roc. I know what you mean. But Tony didn't

murder her a little bit. Oh god!" Miserable and heartsick, he dragged himself to the telephone in the boiler room and then went back to Mr. Tomasello. "We'd better not do anything else, Roc. Officer Cochran's coming for this stuff. He'll be here soon."

He picked up the roll of papers and flattened them out, and his heart rose to his throat and choked him.

They were the notes Joyce had deemed not part of the permanent records and had removed from Tony's confidential folder despite Ben's virtual order that she return them, at least temporarily, because of the shooting in the lab. Two pages resembled a play script, being verbatim accounts of significant parts of one or more counseling sessions. He was about to start reading them when he noticed another name on the last of the pages.

Lunn, Timothy, it said, above a summary dated October through June of the previous school year and ending with a few recent comments.

And he remembered Tony's saying, in that hoarse voice like the one that had called him a while ago, "I wouldn't make things tougher for any of my gang."

"Here, Mr. Louis, siddown on this. I brung it from the boiler room. You feelin' okay?"

It was the rocker from the firemen's storeroom, and Ben sat down thankfully.

"To tell the truth," he said, "I'm not sure I even *feel* my head now. I mean—"

"Yeah. I know. The heart hurts more." Mr. Tomasello stood at the door to watch for the police officer and Ben began to read.

The first page was dated the second week of September, just after the opening of school.

JB: Well, Tony! The schedule took some doing but I finally made it. How are you getting along with Mr. Quinn and the custodians?

TE: Good. I like them. They're—nice.

JB: You're satisfied with the work, then? And the pay?

TE: I guess . . . (with an effort) Thanks, Miss Bellows. It was real nice of you. (obviously wants to talk about something else)

JB: You're very welcome, but that's what I'm here for. To help decide what's best for you.

TE: (shy but eager, with a burst) I'll be seein' Mr. Magrue pretty soon now, won't I? Regular?

JB: I don't think so, Tony. I'm not sure about that any more. Besides, we've worked together for a long while now. You'll do better to keep on with me until you graduate next June. We know each other pretty well by now.

TE: I d'know . . . I'd kinda like to talk to a man, y'know? I got girls all over the place at home! . . . Besides . . .

JB: Yes? Besides what?

TE: I been talkin' with Mr. Magrue a couple times. . . . He—he—

JB: About what?

TE: Well, I don't wanna hurt yuh feelin's, see, but . . . Well, Mr. Magrue he understands things. . . . (his eyes shine)

JB: You don't think I do, is that it?

TE: Some things he knows better 'cause he's a man. He knows how I feel about all them sisters a mine. Boys're better. A guy should have one brother, anyways! An' he knows how I feel about quittin' school an' all. Joinin' the service. . . .

JB: I thought we'd decided about that, Tony. We decided you'd stay and finish, get your diploma, and go to trade school. And work with me this last year, see how much we can get straightened out for you at home.

TE: Miss Bellows, I gotta get outa that house! I can't stand it no more! Mr. Magrue says—

JB: That's nonsense, Tony, and I don't care what Mr. Magrue says! He's only been here a few weeks. He doesn't know the whole picture. How could he?

TE: But—

JB: But nothing! The service isn't for you now. I'm not going into that again.

Comment: I actually displayed annoyance with a client. Must watch this. *Very poor form*. I don't know what got into me! Was also more directive than usual. But client's new attitude is disturbing, shows bad influence already of A.M. Blushed, stammered, on mentioning his name. Dangerous? Suggestive? I agree wholeheartedly that a boy like T.E. should see a male counselor. But—A.M.? Give this further consideration. A.M. deserves benefit of doubt, *if possible.*

The other session was dated a week and a half before the tragic accident in the lab.

JB: I'm sorry I haven't seen you for so long, Tony. I thought you'd be in long ago.

TE: (silence). . . . didn't feel like it. . . .

JB: You didn't feel like talking. Some days are like that.

TE: (silence). . . . My mother . . . (silence)

JB: Does your mother want to speak to me? She can call any time it's convenient for her. Is there something you'd like me to tell her for you? Is that it?

TE: Nah . . . wouldn't do any good. . . .

JB: Depends on what it is.

TE: Nah . . . (fiddles with brown shopping bag)

JB: You've been carrying that bag around a lot lately.

TE: Keep my stuff in it.

JB: It's pretty worn. What about a brief case?

TE: This is good enough. (Suddenly warm and open, like the "old days" last year) Wanna see what's in it?

JB: It's very very good! (spent at least fifteen minutes discussing and analyzing his work; talked about art in general)

TE: It's fun. I like to do it. I got paints and charcoals, for different things, see?

JB: You spent a lot of money on them. What? A water pistol! Now that's an odd combination—art and a gun. You haven't said anything about guns for months.

TE: (silence) . . . (impulsively) I'm gonna get a real one!

JB: A rifle?

TE: Nah. Pistol. Mr.—(bites his lip)

JB: You're excited about it, I can see.

TE: (silence)

JB: You know, Tony, you're a minor, and minors can't own handguns without their parents' written consent. Did you know that?

TE: But Mr. Quinn he said he's gonna—(bites lip)

JB: Well, Tony, that's the law. I'm sure Mr. Quinn knows that.

TE: When I quit school—(threateningly) . . . (silence) . . .

JB: When is that?

TE: (silence) (very sullen)

JB: Have you changed your plans?

TE: He's gonna give me his—give me one when I join up. On my birthday, maybe. December!

JB: You'd find a diploma helpful for getting a good job, Tony. And getting into trade school. And of course your art work will be a nice hobby for you, a nice change of pace from working.

TE: (silence) . . . Can't stand it no more.

JB: What's the matter now?

TE: (takes deep breath; very nervous) *When* can I start seein' Mr. Magrue?

JB: It's time for you to leave now. We'll talk again. I want to check your progress for a while, see how the job goes—

TE: (gives JB an ugly look. Takes bag and runs out)

Comment: A very disturbing session despite art work which is remarkably good. Client probably traced or copied it. Several things to look into here: Speak to T. Quinn about gun. Check with art dep't on possibility of stolen art supplies. Speak to A. Magrue. This will be difficult and distasteful. Check with all T.E.'s teachers on work/behavior thus far. Is my new program for T.E.

really helping him? Influence of T. Quinn may be questionable. Paranoia definitely showing in T.E. now.

A summary of the past three years stressed Tony's difficult home life; his lack of a relationship with his father; his quick and violent temper; his growing feeling of persecution, impotence, and anger; his marginal school performance and indifference to everything but art which he was mentioning with increasing frequency.

The summary on Timothy Lunn was similar to Tony's. It described the emotional poverty of the boy's life, and his anger, frustration, and growing need for violence. The effect on him of his father's desertion (and suspected return to army service, which his mother had never attempted to trace), his attempt to vandalize the school, and his placement under Tom Quinn's wing read like a case study in a textbook. It ended with a cautiously optimistic prognosis.

But the sentences that Joyce had added below, in longhand, were extremely disturbing:

> Since developing a sudden friendship with A.M., T.L.'s behavior has changed radically. He is pathologically suspicious (*principally of me!*), sly, violent. Has developed a passionate hatred of mother, all women. Wants only to leave school, join Green Berets. I have told him that this course would intensify all his problems and that I *will not permit* him to follow it. I broached the need for in-patient observation and evaluation, to be followed by an indefinite period of psychoanalysis. He should be considered a potentially dangerous person with pronounced paranoid tendencies. Follow-up with Dr. Z. Inman as soon as possible, relative to clinic admittance.

Ben pushed Jane's splendid dinner around on his plate as though it were a marinated newspaper.

At seven o'clock Hudson and Keefe came in to scrounge a beer. "We're bushed," Keefe said, falling into a deep chair. He groaned. The chair caressed and soothed only the lesser part of his bulk. The greater part, the pain in his feet, was on the hard unfriendly floor. "When we got the news we were on our way to Larry's Place for supper. Spent half the afternoon with the Evans family, and then we saw Tom Quinn and Timothy Lunn. Art said we might as well stop by and see how you are, while we wait for the lab report on those clothes. Shouldn't be long. Quinn's in a pretty pickle now, by the way. We've got all kinds of things in the works for that guy!"

"Yep!" Hudson almost crowed. "I think we've got everything taped. We can eat later."

Ben crossed his fingers. Had Mrs. Evans told them about the paper target she had given him? If she had, he was in for another tongue lashing from Hudson. Withholding evidence. Disrespect for the Law. Hampering the investigation. Mind your own goddam business.

But the day was not yet over, and he had another surprise.

"I gather," Hudson said mildly, "I gather Mrs. Evans gave you a paper target this morning, Ben. Too bad we didn't have it Monday."

"Yeah. Sorry I forgot about it, Art, but what with my head and all the action in my office—" Ben lied.

"Figured that. You all right? You look like hell."

"Thanks, Jane," Keefe said, accepting a foaming beer. "No, nothing to eat, thanks. I'd as soon wait until we can relax and enjoy it. When we're this close I don't like to eat anything." He took his disgusting stogy out of his mouth and drank gratefully.

"I wish to hell you wouldn't smoke either!" Hudson grumbled. "Dirty habit. Smells up the clothes."

"To each his own, Art," Keefe said calmly.

"Then why don't you smoke when you're all by yourself?" Hudson demanded with impeccable logic.

"You said you've got it taped, Art. What's the score?" said Ben.

"Don't tell me *you* don't know! You're slipping, Ben. If you talked with that kid as long as we did, or even half as long, you know what we know. It's as plain as a pikestaff!"

"I never saw one. Are they nice?" Jane said.

"A-a-arrrrgh! Look. Tony's all to pieces over what will happen to him because of the shooting in the lab. He admits Bellows had been nagging hell out of him about the gun. He also said she was trying to keep him from leading his own life—which means mainly getting out of that house of his. He fights with her and Quinn and even his best friend, the Lunn boy. He sees Bellows coming toward him back of Two. He pops down cellar and changes his clothes and gets his bag. Then he has another argument with her when she catches him down there. She says she's going to see you right away. So he follows her through the tunnel or walks with her, arguing all the way, takes the statue out of the bag and kills her and then hits you.

"Then he goes back and changes to his good suit and goes to her office. If he's seen loitering in the hall up there, he has an acceptable story. They had a fight, he came back to apologize. But if he isn't seen—and obviously he wasn't—he opens the office, gets the papers from her desk—they must have been there because they weren't in the files or in her apartment—wraps them in the bloody clothes, and sticks them in the fire. And he's home free."

"Sure. In the plenum chamber," Ben said bitterly.

"He's just a kid, Ben. He was scared. He was so scared that I felt sorry for him! People do strange things because of fear. I believe you lectured to us poor unfortunate illiterates on the subject a while back," Hudson said sourly.

"It could have happened that way, Art. But why don't you substitute Quinn for Tony? The gun explains his unjustified concern for his job future. Before we knew about that gun and the contract, I wondered what he was bellyaching about, and now I know." He waved the notes he had taken from Judge Shrag and put them down. "Got this stuff from Shrag before supper but Jane wouldn't let me call you. She was threatening to commit me if I didn't rest awhile," he lied. A noble-minded citizen had to lie sometimes, in a good cause. "It all adds up to a better motive than Tony's.

"And then, who'd have a better time figuring out where to change his clothes than Quinn, in the privacy of his office? Remember, he was already wearing chinos. He never wears anything else.

"But Tony was in his good suit—and he was afraid to drop in on Quinn again after being thrown out a little while before. He was also followed very closely by Joyce, so even if he did get his clothes from the office, he wasn't that good a quick-change artist to be ready in a matter of two or three minutes—with murder in mind to boot!

"Also, Quinn knew about the stuff in that bag. He says he was sleeping, and Tony thought he was, but either way, where else would she go down there, when she couldn't find the boy, but to his office? And while she was about it, she'd threaten to expose him because of the gun. Where better to kill her than in the tunnel? He probably told her Tony had gone through, and that he'd escort her because things had happened there before. And that he'd help round the boy up for her because she was still weak and sick."

It was a beautiful airtight case. He wished he could believe it. The only thing was—

"The name inside that shirt and pants, Ben. *T. Evans*. You can't get away from that," Hudson said. "And it's on the papers too."

"That's the way it is, Ben," Keefe said sympathetically. "I was almost fooled myself by the boy and his story. The one thing that bothers me, though, whether it was Tony or Quinn who killed her, is—why is there so little blood on those clothes? Tell me that!"

Fee went over to Keefe to be admired and petted. He knew better than to approach Hudson's immaculate trousers and cover them with his long hairs. Fee too had worked with Art Hudson.

"We thought of giving this buffalo a police medal for his work in the Houseman case," Keefe said, stroking hundreds of hairs out of the thick coat, "but then he went back to the hospital."

"You could have put it in the mail," Jane said reproachfully. "There aren't many dogs like him—and don't say anything, Benjamin Franklin Louis!"

"What'd I say?" he said innocently.

"You had that 'Thank god' look in your eyes!"

Keefe knew everything about wives and decided to stir things up a little. Do Ben good. "I suppose you'll be able to get to Frisco after all, hey, Ben? Now that we've got things sewed up here," he interposed blandly. "Too bad Jane isn't going along. They've got some interesting hot spots out that way."

"Mmmmmm," Ben said, packing his Saturday pipe with immense care. "It's a damn shame, absolutely no question about it. There's no law that says she can't board the same plane, but even if the conference allowed wives, I don't have the money. What with Elizabeth in school . . . Some other time. Maybe."

Jane smoldered in self-pitying silence.

The telephone's sudden ring wiped the grin from Keefe's face, and Hudson jumped up.

"Yeah. Uh-huh. Good. Thought so. That wraps it up, of course, but see what else you can find. Yeah. Thanks. Bye." And he turned to them with that rare sweet smile. "It's her blood, all right. C'mon, Pete, let's go get Tony Evans!"

"Can't we sit and sort of congratulate ourselves a minute?" Keefe said, but he got up slowly and painfully.

As Ben watched them leave, he felt a hand grasp his heart and twist it.

And the telephone rang again. Almost indifferent now, he answered it. And yelled, "*What?* Oh boy! Roc, you're a lifesaver! Round up everyone you can find! I'll be right there!"

He ran out to the car and Jane ran after him.

"That was Roc! Quinn's car passed him going hell for leather back to school! So he went back too!" He drove off, leaving her standing there and gaping at the empty street.

CHAPTER TWENTY

7:15 P.M.

There had been a run of fine weather since the heavy rain early in the week. The shrubs and small trees were fluffy and green. The new-raked lawns looked like a soft carpet. The Forestry Department and the Building Service Employees Union would make an angry protest against Mr. Tomasello's illegal activities with broom and barrow, and they would even be fatheaded enough to deny that the end justified the means. But no system is without its drawbacks and fatheads, and as far as the Roc was concerned, if yuh hadda nabba guy for murder, yuh might as well do it in a clean school.

With an enormous wrench, his *baton*, he had quickly and masterfully marshaled his troops for the battle and was now in the areaway waiting for Ben. Vanna was at the door to the corridor leading past the boiler room to the engine room. Cooke (who had talked it over with Vanna earlier and decided to stick around in case something else happened) was stationed at the boiler room's outer door at the head of the metal staircase. Garvin, engineer second class, was at the engine room's outer doors which faced the back of Building One. From here he could communicate with Cooke if it became necessary. Trent, the fireman who had spoken with Joyce Bellows the night before, was waiting at the Building Three end of the south tunnel.

"Okay, Roc, let's get down there!" Ben said tensely. "He's probably barely started sifting all those ashes—he'll be there awhile—but let's get cracking!"

"Yeah—so I can help 'm! I wouldn't want he should get his hands dirty!"

He hurtled down the steep staircase, but the boilers, even leashed as they were by the mild weather, could still have drowned

out the descent of an elephant. Realizing this, Ben stopped worrying and followed him rapidly although his pace was loosening
the top of his head. Nor did it occur to him to stop breathing and
stay healthy.

They peeked into the narrow corridor which led, on the left, to
the areaway entrance up the steps, where Vanna now stood guard
inside. To the right, at the other end, was the engine room.
Quinn's office was next to it at a right angle. The incinerator
room was almost in the middle but on the opposite side. High
bulbs shone meagerly.

"I'll check his office," Ben mouthed, pointing. "You get the incinerator." He went quickly to the office door and pressed an ear
against it. There was no sound from inside, but then, it was doubt-
ful than Quinn had returned only to take another nap. He turned
the knob to make sure, but the door was locked. He went back to
Mr. Tomasello who was turning the incinerator doorknob with
exquisite care.

The door opened a crack and Mr. Tomasello put an eye to it
as Ben came up behind him.

And there, kneeling in a heap of dirt by the open ashpit door,
was a familiar burly figure, his back turned, his hands and shirt
sleeves filthy with soot as he poked with a stick among the hot
ashes and pieces of stuff that had fallen through the grate.

Intent upon his frantic task, he did not notice the surge of noise
that filled the room as Mr. Tomasello opened the door all the way
and stepped inside. It was only when the custodian growled low
in his throat—a tiny sound—that he whirled and bounded lithely
to his feet, holding the stick like a *rapier*. Which in effect it was,
for it was the spiked stick that Mr. Tomasello had used earlier,
and in that powerful fist it was a dangerous weapon.

He stared wildly at them—at the custodian's square tough body
and Ben's gangling one behind it—and then he lunged at Mr.
Tomasello's belly with the murderous spike. Giving way before the
sudden charge and unable to parry with his wrench, the custodian
stumbled backward into Ben. Both lost their balance and toppled
out into the corridor. And in that instant of confusion their quarry
darted through the door to the corridor leading to the south tunnel and slammed it shut.

They looked at each other in consternation. In that warren of a place there were a thousand corners in which to hide.

"After 'm! Vanna, go to the engine room door!" the custodian yelled. "He might fool us and go round the other way, tryin' for the car! C'mon, Mr. Louis, we'll take the tunnel!"

"What about those shops?"

"Nah, he don't have a master! He can't get in!"

Gasping and heaving, they opened the door and sprinted for the tunnel which was lighted only by the four wretched bulbs that the custodian had spaced so evenly along two hundred forty feet the night before.

They peered into its murky length.

"Shoulda had my lantern!" Mr. Tomasello said in self-reproach.

Ben brought out a butane lighter and set it on High. It would burn like a torch long enough to see them through the south tunnel and back again.

The shadows flickered and danced ghoulishly, laying crazy patterns on the dead air. At each of the square apertures in the center support Ben poked his head and the lighter through to the other side and looked in both directions.

"Even an acrobat can't pop back and forth this fast from side to side!" Ben whispered. "And he's too thick to squinch up in one of these openings!"

Their whispers and their scuffling feet scratched like claws at the thick atmosphere as they traveled the length of the tunnel and emerged into the cafeteria.

Trent assured them that no one had come through in the past ten minutes. "Not a sound either," he said regretfully.

"Gotta get back!" the custodian said. "Maybe he did have a master! C'mon, we'll check the rooms we just passed! An' then the other side!"

It took little time to establish that there was no one in those rooms. Mr. Tomasello knew what each contained and where, among the enormous amount of equipment, the hiding places were.

"But he's somewhere!" Ben said as they came back again to the incinerator room.

Vanna joined them there. He had made an Olympic run down the corridor past the plenum chamber to the front of the building, then back again, and all round the engine room, and back to the incinerator.

"Garvin didn't see him either!" he panted. "But the sound is nuts in this place. He might've been just ahead of me on my way back. Thought I heard something—a second before you came through—but I ain't sure!" He pointed to the boiler room's big swinging doors.

They burst through them and stopped short, momentarily unable to sort themselves out for the final thrust.

High up—at least twenty-five feet above the cement floor—on the landing of the metal stairway was their quarry, clinging to the railing and panting like a trapped animal. Garvin was outside, ready to slam the heavy door shut. Cooke's big body blocked the threshold, and in his hand was a wrench even larger than Mr. Tomasello's.

"Hoi!" the custodian bawled like a stentor over the noise, and stormed up the steps holding his wrench like a cavalry saber as Ben and Vanna followed close behind.

This time the steps clanged under six heavy feet.

The distance narrowed between pursuers and pursued. Their prey had no place to run to, now. Disheveled, smudged with ashes, sweating with exertion and fear, he made a last desperate attempt to escape.

He vaulted the railing and dropped to the cement floor some twenty-five feet below. One scream triumphed over the boilers. And then Timothy Lunn lay still.

CHAPTER TWENTY-ONE

Jane served hot coffee to Ben, Hudson, and Keefe, and then laced it generously and compassionately with brandy. "I wish I could *do* something," she said, "but I don't know what to do."

"Neither do we," said Keefe bleakly.

"I never had a case like this in thirty years!" Hudson exploded. "*Two* deaths, Gerald Rosen's and Joyce Bellows'! *Two* weapons, a Luger and a soapstone statue! *Two* walking wounded, Bert Shrag and you, Ben! *Three* suspects—Tom Quinn, Tony Evans, and Allen Magrue!

"And all of them innocent!

"And how do we find out? When a *fourth* suspect—whom we *didn't* suspect!—comes out of left field and damn near kills *himself!*

"And *clears all four of them* in the process!"

"But if Tim is innocent, why did he go back to school tonight?" Jane said. "There wasn't anything against him."

"Yes, there was," said Hudson. "That *T* on the belt buckle. The lab boys found his name on the inside of that belt. It was tied around the clothes and got the worst of the scorching. They didn't see the name—or they weren't sure of it—until they'd done some more work. They only called here at suppertime to give us the identification of the blood."

"Tim told us the whole bit before they took him to the operating room," Keefe said. "He ducked into that plenum chamber tonight, incidentally. Vanna ran right past it. God, that kid's in a terrible way! What his life will be like if he comes through all that surgery—! He'd been with Quinn all day and they were on their way to Quinn's apartment for supper when he heard Tomasello say something about seeing to it that the incinerator burned properly *this time*. After a while he began to sweat, worrying about that incinerator—and whether by some lousy piece of luck Tomasello would find his belt. How or why, he didn't think about. He was just scared. And also right, as it turned out.

"So he told Quinn he forgot something at the school and asked could he go back for it. And Tomasello saw him. He thought it was Quinn—they look a lot alike—driving back like a bat out of hell. And Tomasello got suspicious."

"Was Tim the one who called me, Pete?"

"Yes. He's one mixed-up kid, that kid. When we saw him and Quinn at school, he knew we'd just come from Tony's house, but that was all he knew. He couldn't come right out and ask if we were pulling Tony in, and he couldn't bring himself to tell us anything either. He said that if Tony had been arrested, he would have come forward."

Hudson snorted with bitter skepticism.

"Well, I'd prefer to believe him," Ben said. "If only because he was destroying Joyce's notes on Tony. He didn't have to. They didn't say anything about him."

"I still don't get it," said Jane. "His belt but Tony's work clothes?"

"They're the same height," Hudson said, "although Tim's heavier. And what happened," he went on with a peculiar light in his eye, "is very simple. I don't mean that it's simple now that we know what he did. Although there's a lot of truth in the whole business about hindsight. I mean that it's simple because what he *did* was simple and—"

"Art, for godsake!"

"Ben, I just wanted you to know how it feels, being lectured at, is all," Hudson said. "Okay. Tim came to the dance—like Tony, he's out of his house a lot—but he never went over there. He started playing handball out back of the boiler room, and when a few of his pals joined him for some touch football he went down to change his clothes. Out of quote respect unquote for his old lady, he said." He stopped to drink some more coffee and Keefe took up the story.

"Quinn *was* asleep, so he changed in the dark. Used his own belt, though, because Tony has only the one and he was wearing it. It was just this morning after you'd seen Quinn, Ben, that Tim found he'd grabbed Tony's things by mistake. That's why he called you late today. You and Quinn and then us—we were all talking about clothes. Specifically Tony's, which weren't where they should have been, in Quinn's closet. He wondered if we were about to arrest Tony for something he himself had done by accident. If we had, he would have spoken up. I believe him too. He was waiting to see if he had to, is all. The call to you was a feeler but you scared him off."

"But how did he get blood on himself if he didn't kill Joyce?" Jane said.

"It happened almost the way Ben figured it for Quinn," said Keefe. "When Joyce Bellows walked over calling Tony, both boys skedaddled down cellar. Tony went to the plenum chamber and Tim hid behind a boiler. He saw her go into the firemen's storeroom and come out. He peeked through those big double doors and saw her knock on Quinn's door, argue with him, take Tony's bag, and go through to the tunnel. He saw Quinn close his door on her. He saw Tony pop out of the other end of the little corridor and pop back again—in his good suit, too. And Magrue never came down through *any* door.

"He diddled around a couple of minutes wondering what to do, and then he decided that if Tony were any place at all, he was back at the dance hiding in the crowd. So he ran through to the tunnel. He also thought he might catch up with Bellows, follow her, and see what she was going to do."

"Quinn was with him at the hospital—very upset about his condition, by the way," Hudson said. "He told us what Joyce Bellows had said and how she'd behaved. He couldn't get over it! But your theory on that was right, Ben. That argument between them was just like you figured it—that he was a bad influence on Tony who had now become a thief along with everything else, as witness the statue. Between her transformation, the awful legal mess he's in now, and his real concern for Tim, he's one miserable character!"

"But what about the blood?" Jane said again.

"Simple," said Keefe. "Tim saw her and Ben lying there. He saw the stuff from her handbag strewn all around and he took the keys. It was his one and only perfect chance to finally get into her office and see what she'd written about him. He may be the war lover you say Joyce said he was, but the sight of all that blood scared the living daylights out of him! There was blood on the keys too, and in trying to pick them up without getting any on his fingers, he lost his balance—and got both palms covered! He picked up the keys but the blood on his hands horrified him and he wiped them on the shirt as he shrank back against that center support. Then he edged away from the two of you, scared out of his mind, and that's what made the smear Art pointed out on the center, remember? And on the back of the pants.

"That's about it. Tomasello missed him by a matter of seconds just as he had missed the murderer. He ran back to Quinn's office, stuck his hand in the closet and got his good clothes. Quinn was on the bed with his back turned, reading a magazine, and the radio was turned up so loud that he didn't see the boy or hear him. He hid behind one of the big engines in the engine room and changed. Then he rolled up the clothes and left them there and went and washed his hands and the keys. He went outside and over to Three, went in a side entrance, and up to the guidance office. There was nothing in the files, as we know only too well, but he struck oil in her desk. He took the papers on Tony because they were right there. He was anxious to know if she'd put anything down in black and white about their plan to quit school.

"Her remarks about his state of mind made him furious and he said a funny thing, Ben. He said, 'She should talk!' Do you know what he meant?"

Ben opened his mouth to answer but Hudson objected vigorously. "It doesn't make any difference!" he snapped. "We know he didn't kill her and that's all we have to know."

If that's the way you want it, that's the way it's going to be, Ben said to himself.

"By then we were on the scene," Keefe continued, "but that kid is as quick as a mountain lion! He slid into the crowd, and when we let the kids go home, he flew back to the engine room, got the clothes, went to the incinerator room, and closed the door. He looked through the notes quickly, then put them into the pants pocket. But they wouldn't stay rolled up, so he tied his belt around them and stuffed them into the fire chamber and lit them. He left the ashpit door open, so they'd burn faster, and then he took off for home. But Tomasello found the fire—again in a matter of seconds. And that's it."

"What happened to him after that fall?" said Ben, who had not been allowed to see him after he had been taken away. The sound of the boy's scream before he fainted was still in his ears, the sight of the broken body was still in his mind's eye.

"Plenty," said Hudson who got restless if he had to sit and listen to essentially irrelevant matters. "In a way, what with one thing and another, he might have been better off dead. He hemorrhaged massively, the doc said, from a ruptured spleen, which has to come out. He has a compression fracture of the spine, and the chances are that he may never walk again. Also one ankle broke. And a wrist, when he fell forward. A boy as heavy as he is, it was like moving bodies colliding, even though that concrete floor wasn't going anyplace! He'll have a tough time being cured of all his hate and violence when he knows he may be in a wheelchair the rest of his life. That poor kid! I don't want to sound like a social worker, but I feel sorry for the boy."

"I'll go see him," said Ben. "There must be something I can do for him. Have to call his mother too."

"Well, I'll tell you something I still don't get," Keefe said. "If Joyce Bellows was as nice a person and as competent, as you say everybody says she was, why did she do what she did? She said nothing to the authorities about that Luger, and she suspected something about it before the Rosen boy was shot. She was still sick last night, but she pushed and pushed on Tony and then Quinn. Why?"

Ben opened his mouth again and Hudson said irritably, "No lectures, Ben! We had enough of that last time. Can't you say it in twenty-five words or less?"

"No."

"Then don't bother. Not now. It's too late and we're all too tired. And tomorrow we're going to have to start in all over again —and we're fresh out of suspects!"

"Got any ideas, Ben?" said Keefe.

"No," Ben said, lying smoothly now.

"Well, don't!" Hudson said. "Just stay out of our way. Go to bed. Take a long rest. You'll be doing all of us a favor!"

"You ought to, at that, Ben," Keefe said seriously. "If you can, you ought to go to Frisco after all. View the topless waitresses they have out there." He sighed. "You're lucky. With the organization you've got at school, there's no reason why you can't leave Wednesday as planned. Whereas we're still in the middle of a mess that we've got to handle—in our own way—no matter where you are. Hell, Ben, why don't you go? Nothing more can happen to *you*."

Jane stared at him. Keefe might very well know all there was to know about wives, after forty years of marital bliss and thirty-five years of criminal investigation. But Jane, who had married into the vast, controversial, varied, crucial world of education some twenty-odd years before, knew everything there was to know about schools, schoolteachers, and school administrators.

So, she stared at Keefe. And then she exploded in mocking prescient laughter.

CHAPTER TWENTY-TWO

Ben slept all day Sunday to prepare himself for Monday and Tuesday because he had definitely decided to leave for the conference on Wednesday.

The decision, which inevitably required making another decision, caused his conscience to come alive again and begin to jab and prod unpleasantly. (He felt it principally in the sutures in his scalp.)

Poor Jane, she's really had the worst of it, he told himself late Sunday morning over a sumptuous breakfast in bed. I'll rest up today. Then tonight we'll get all gussied up and I'll take her out to a swell dinner—give her a big time—show her I care—you know the routine, fella!

Then tomorrow and Tuesday I'll get things in shape at school, tidy up the loose ends, work like hell, give it everything I've got—

And then Wednesday morning—California, here I come!

As for the investigation, well, Hudson and Keefe will have to get along without me. I've done my bit. Allen and Tony are in the clear, and I can't do anything for Quinn except testify, if I'm ever asked to, that he meant well. Which won't cut any ice. I've got to get over to see Tim Lunn too. Bring him something, maybe. Something cheerful. So he'll know we don't intend to write him off. . . .

He slept like a log for twelve hours straight, and Jane and Benjy and Fee ate what tasted like marinated newspapers for supper.

But by the time he woke up to get washed and ready for bed, he had changed his mind again, and he felt a great deal better.

First he made a lengthy telephone call. Then he tied the tape securely about the envelope containing Joyce Bellows' journal and gave it to his son, Benjy, along with the car keys.

"Here's the address, Benj. Dr. Inman's expecting you. And don't stay out too long. If Hudson caught *you* driving after curfew, he'd have my head."

"For what it's worth," Jane said wryly. "But he'd make you change that grubby bandage first."

"It's seen a lot of action," he said, getting back into bed.

And it's going to see some more shortly, he thought. The question is, should I take the initiative and move right in on my guidance staff? Or should I hold off and let them come to me? Depends on when Zach Inman comes, for one thing.

He did not have to wait long for the answers.

He had hardly walked into his office Monday morning when his telephone rang. It was Allen Magrue calling down from the guidance office.

"Ben, you got a minute? We'd like to talk to you."

"I've got more than a minute. I was going to call you. Anybody else around?"

"Simon and David will be right back. None of us has a class now. Things are a bit disorganized. Gert's home with the flu, for one thing. She just called. Helen and I have been working out a schedule so that the phone will be covered. We're canceling appointments for at least an hour."

"Okay, I'll be right up. You sound worked up. Anything special on your mind?"

"I don't know, Ben. I'm not sure. Anyway, a lot of water's gone under the bridge since last Monday. Helen and I thought it would be a good idea for us all to sit down together again and see what the score is."

"I couldn't agree more. Be right up."

He put his coat away, collected his Monday pipe, lighter, tobacco pouch, pipe cleaners, and reamer—his combat gear, so to speak—and poked his head out the door. Poor Mrs. Duffy was clearly prepared to roll up his left flank as soon as he appeared. He closed the door and went back to the desk to ring Mrs. Castle on her extension.

"Opal, I'll be in the guidance office for a while. Would you have the central switchboard relay any calls for that office to you and Mrs. Duffy? Gert Kane's out sick and I'd like at least an hour of peace and quiet up there. Oh—I forgot to thank you for all your help Friday night. You were wonderful. It was very good of you to come."

"I was glad to, Mr. Louis. But I wouldn't exactly say you *forgot*. We've all been very worried about you." She paused, then said slowly, "That's why I—" and stopped again.

"What's the matter, Opal? You're not sick, are you?"

"No. I'm fine, really. Never mind, Mr. Louis. You go ahead. I'll see you later."

He put the phone down, worrying about her. And then he decided that Opal Castle was the last person he had to worry about. She wasn't sick (if she were, he would be inclined to worry about himself), and if she did have something on her mind, she would find a way to deal with it. It was apparently not too important.

He got as far as the door and then went back and called her again.

"Oh," he said when, reluctant and distressed, she told him what she had seen Friday night. "Oh, I see. I missed that. But I think I was beginning to suspect something like it. It'll be risky—you know why—but it can't be helped. Thanks, Opal."

He went upstairs more deeply concerned than ever about the condition of his guidance staff.

Half of it, from a purely personal standpoint, was excellent. Two days ago their situation had been critical, but now Helen and Allen stood before him open-faced, clear-eyed, vibrant with joy. He had already gone to bed on Saturday afternoon when Helen came to pick up Allen. This was the first time he had seen them together as lovers.

"Well," he said. "Well." Never had he seen two people more radiant. He could only give them each a hand, and his warm clasp was infinitely more eloquent than words, possibly because of his regret for all the years these two has missed. His eyes stung with tears.

"Thank you, Ben," Helen said softly, and kissed his cheek. "Thank you for everything."

"Can't you find me something else to do?" he said, laughing, as David Ross and Simon Wills came in.

"You can do something for me, Ben," said an expected but disembodied voice, "but I can't promise to kiss you for it."

"What—? Where—?"

"Here," said the voice. "Over by the table. You can sit down and get started, for one thing. I'm not sure yet whether you'll have to carry me out, for another."

A rubber-tipped cane waggled in the air at the head of the conference table and Ben went over to it and looked down.

Flat on his back, his belly mounded like a carapace in a Tattersall vest, was Dr. Zachary Inman.

Ben grinned. "You feel that you'd like to lie on the floor. You feel it's important to you," he said.

"Well, you see, *Doctor,* I have this pain," said Dr. Inman. "And I might as well tell *you* about it—it's got a long *history.*"

"Oh god! Keep on like that, you two, and you'll have to carry *me* out!" said David Ross. If he had spoken with the belligerence of last Monday or the ease of Friday night or even his usual sharpness—"David's way!"—they would have laughed. But his voice was harsh, and the attempted humor rose on a querulous fearful note.

Ben glanced at Allen's fifth suspect, and then at the sixth, who was sitting and watching quietly. And then he regarded the prostrate psychiatrist. "Listen, Zach, if I thought we'd have this effect on you, I wouldn't have asked you to come."

"Hmph! I wouldn't have agreed to!"

"He walked in just after I called you, Ben," Allen said, laughing, "and dropped like a felled ox, clutching his sacroiliac."

"No," said Dr. Inman. "I was electrocuted by your inflamed condition, Al. Love! Myth!" He disposed of Love with a snort in C sharp. "I'll just take five down here, Ben, while you open the seminar. Carry on."

They took the same places at the table that they had occupied a week ago, except that Simon sat down where Joyce had been, on Ben's right. The doctor's feet were between them, plumb with their elbows.

"Okay, this is the thing," Ben said. "It's time to stop horsing around. We've got to pool what we know and get to the bottom of this mess. Except for Joyce's sister, Grace Wickham, the people in this room probably knew Joyce better than anyone else in the world, for different reasons. And they all come down to the—"

"—same reason. Joyce," said Dr. Inman.

"Yes. Joyce. What she was. And what she did, as a result. And what was done to her, as a result," Ben said slowly, looking from one to the other.

Helen was serious, intent, beautiful, and calm.

Allen, on her left and opposite Ben, was serious, intent, sloppy, and plainly excited.

David looked uneasy, bleary-eyed, and wretchedly tired.

Simon had lost his recent vigor and his face was again a waxen gray.

It all figures, Ben thought, and crossed his fingers for luck. What he had begun to do was frightening him dreadfully. Slowly he filled his pipe, and Simon got up and opened a window.

"Okay," Ben said. "Where do we start?"

"With me, I guess," said Allen. "I was a suspect for a while. Also, I know a few things. And this meeting was my idea, more or less."

"Why were you a suspect?" said David. "I didn't know about that."

"That was sort of my fault," Ben said smoothly. "I was talking with Joyce and Allen Friday night just before she left. Allen walked out to the car with her. To my knowledge, as I told Hudson, Allen was the last one to see her alive. That's all."

"And that little business between you and Joyce last Tuesday morning?" David said. "When you said 'God damn you, Joyce!' —that didn't have anything to do with anything?"

"I told you what that was all about," said Allen. "A misunderstanding about Tim Lunn."

"Which is all beautifully straightened out now!" David said nastily.

"Allen had nothing to do with that," Ben said evenly.

"I'm not so sure," said Allen. "I was pressing her hard. We all were, as a matter of fact. Except for you, Zachary, I suppose."

"Oh, I'm included!" said Dr. Inman. "I took the liberty of disagreeing with her about something Monday night. And giving her a bit of advice besides. We collided literally—at the airport," he added, explaining his use of a cane.

"Was it about something to do with this group?" David said suspiciously.

"Yes. She had a mistaken notion about one of you. She didn't take kindly to being told. Off, that is."

"I'd like to know who it was," said David.

"I told her Helen and I were going to be married," Allen said. "She thought Helen was throwing herself away."

"And she called me from Logan to tell me she wouldn't let me!" Helen said. "I virtually hung up on her."

"Well, for godsake!" David cried, beaming. "Kids, I'm glad for you! I think it's great! Really great news! I'm glad it's you, Helen. I thought it was Joyce and Allen! I guess she was jealous. But who the hell did she think she was—God Almighty?"

"Yes and no. And that was the trouble," Ben said. "We'll get to that later. Allen, you said you knew something. What is it?"

"Well, starting with our meeting last week, I know—we all know —what the reaction was to Joyce's University project—the whole bit on supervision and evaluation of counselors."

"There was really only one reaction," said Simon. "Negative, that is. David's. Everyone else was willing to go ahead."

"I've seen you bugged before, Dave," said Ben, "but never like that! Joyce's audio-video stuff really threw you!"

"This was on Gert's desk Tuesday with a note," said Helen, holding up the little microphone that David had pulled off the cubicle wall. "Gert asked me what I thought we should do with it, but I just let it ride. The note says, 'I don't care how paranoid David says I think he is. See to it that this is put back.'"

"That mike upset hell out of you, Dave," Allen said. "Talk about *bugged!*"

"Where'd you get the idea Joyce thought you were paranoid, David? From her journal?" Ben said.

"What is this, a sensitivity group session?" David shouted. "And when would *I* get a chance to see her journal?"

"David was here very late Monday night," Allen said. "That's the second thing I know. One of the firemen saw him. Trent, down in the boiler room. I asked you about it, Dave, and you said you'd been reading. What the hell were you reading in school in the middle of the night?"

"One thing *I* know," Ben said, "is that the file cabinet locks were okay. So was the one on Gert's desk. But Joyce's desk lock got the treatment."

"And Tuesday morning," Simon said, "when Tim was in here telling Joyce off, you looked like you'd just swallowed the canary.

Quite a switch from your reaction the day before. You were pretty wild at the meeting, Dave."

"That's for damn sure! And don't pull that group pressure crap on me!" David shouted.

"Why not? It worked, didn't it?" the doctor pointed out. "From where I sit, it looks as if you know something too. Why don't you level? You may feel better."

David capitulated quickly. "Yeah. Maybe I will. This week's been hell. I don't have much to tell, though, and I'm pretty ashamed of myself too. . . . Something Flo said before dinner Monday night started me thinking. About how Joyce was going to be sorry for her actions lately. The way she was leaning on the kids. And some other people around here. About being hoist with her own petard. You said that at the meeting, Al, remember?"

"Yes, in another connection. I know what you mean though, and you were right. But go ahead."

"Well, I couldn't sleep, I was so tensed up. It was raining hard but I went out for a walk—thought I'd do some jogging—and I began to *really* think about Joyce, not as someone I knew and worked with, in a personal way, but as a case. I started lining it out in my mind, not what I felt or thought, but what I'd seen. What all of us had seen, if we were looking. And I'm sure we were all looking."

"Why?" said the doctor.

"Because there was something different about Joyce the last— oh—month, I'd say. I couldn't put my finger on it. Not until Monday night. I jogged for about ten minutes, maybe a little less, but it helped—it always does!—and then I had this idea. So I came over to the school—we only live a few blocks away—and went in through the boiler room. It's always open, just about. I've got a key to the office—we all do—and I came up here to do some reading."

"On what?" said the doctor.

"On paranoia! It started out as a pure hunch. I wasn't sure what started it and I wasn't sure just how much I learned—"

"Depends on what you read, for one thing," said the doctor.

"Nothing but the best, according to Joyce! She bought that professional library over there and kept adding to it. Here's a list of what I read," David said, taking a piece of paper from his pocket and passing it over to Simon who handed it down to the doctor.

The doctor's snort was noncommittal. "All right. Now tell us what you think you learned."

"Well, this may sound weird but I got the idea that she was breaking up—I don't know why, I don't know how—and that if I kept on pushing her—if I kept opposing her—if I didn't let up the pressure—well—she'd cave in."

"All the way in . . .

"So I messed up her desk lock a little. To give her a jolt. Make her think she was being hounded, spied on. Feed *her* neurosis a little! I wasn't trying to open the drawer, you understand. That wasn't the idea. So if you're thinking I was after that journal of hers, forget it. She never let it out of her grasp anyway!"

"She did on Monday, Dave. I saw her put it there," Allen said. "I was the last one of us to leave. Before she did, I mean."

"That so? You didn't—"

"No, I never read it. I'd have liked to. But I've got a good idea what was in it. I don't even know where it is, though."

"I do," Ben said. "It was handed over to the authorities." And again he thought how remarkably easy it was to lie (in a good cause, naturally) when you put your mind to it.

"To the police?" David said, appalled.

"To me," the doctor said. "It was quite a document. She was pretty messed up, that was clear. Then what?"

"Well," David said hesitantly, "Tuesday morning I went ahead with my plan. I'm not proud of it, although for once I felt pretty damn smart because I thought it up! I needled her about all the opposition she was getting—and she *was* getting it!—from all sides! Tim Lunn told her to go to hell. And Allen said, 'God damn you, Joyce!' Then all of a sudden Simon got tough and sounded off and told her he wouldn't let her interfere any more with Tim or anyone else. And I gather you told her to mind her own business, Helen. That you didn't need her approval to marry Al. And then Tony Evans wasn't knuckling under any more. He'd refused to see her again.

"So I made some crack about being too paranoid to work with her audio-video stuff and I pulled that mike off the wall of my cubicle and handed it to her. She said something about my being *the one.* I didn't get it at first, but I realized later that she must've spotted the condition of her desk lock and thought I'd done it, looking for her goddam journal.

"That's it. And to tell the whole truth, I've been feeling like hell ever since. Because she did cave in—right in front of my eyes! Gert's too! She had to go home a little later. I've been sick myself, thinking it was my fault. That's what I wanted to talk to you about on Thursday, Ben. It seemed to me that I was choking on it, and the only way to keep it down was to take a couple of belts now and then."

"A couple!" said Simon. "For godsake, Dave, anyone could have spotted what you were up to, sponging it up in the cafeteria Friday night! I saw you stumble upstairs like a Scollay Square bum. It was a stupid thing to do."

That's it! Ben said to himself. That does it!

"I suppose," David said. "But it dissolved that lump in my throat. For a while, anyway. As soon as I got back upstairs, I had to go and puke!"

"That why you weren't at your post, Dave?" Ben said.

"Yes—and boy, was I sick! Haven't had a drop since then. I told the police I had the flu. And maybe I did, actually. Maybe I don't know all that much about this stuff—not as much as you, Al—"

"You're right, Dave, you don't," Allen said. "So stop lacerating yourself and get this straight. Joyce *was* breaking up. You sensed it. I sensed it. Even Tim Lunn did. Given a particular factor, it was bound to happen and it happened. What that precipitating factor was, I don't know. I don't know all that much either. But it was inevitable."

"The precipitant," said Dr. Inman from the floor, "was that virus attack. Paranoics like her can't handle depression. It makes them terribly panicky because they feel they've lost control, that they'll never get out of it, that it'll last forever. And illness always increases depression. The virus had the effect of knocking the keystone out of her defenses. They'd been loosening up, and when she got sick they collapsed like a wall under fire.

"It's like this. She'd seen herself in a certain way. Then Allen entered the scene, and Helen showed an interest in him, which caused Joyce to get jealous and then forced her to change her perception of herself. She struggled to maintain the self-image she'd built up years ago. And all of us balked. Yes, I did too, as I said before. So she struggled harder. But it didn't work. None of us here was going to be used or deprived of his identity just to shore up hers. Which was wrong to begin with."

"But why?" Helen said. "I don't understand *why*."

"Zachary, she had a recurrent dream about disappearing when she was undressed," Allen said. "Did you know about that?"

"No," said the voice. "But with what I do know, I'm not surprised. It's common to the homosexual—"

"The *what*?" David cried.

"I'm not saying she was an overt one," Dr. Inman said, waving his cane in the air. "But she sure as hell suspected she had the potential. And by the way, homosexuality is always linked with paranoia, according to one school of thought, at least. And she was paranoid, all right. I won't get technical, mainly because there isn't time. But it's a tenable theory, from what I learned about Joyce.

"She was overdependent on her mother, which tells us something right there about her pre-oedipal conflict. Further, she witnessed the mother's death when she was a kid, which intensified that conflict and gave rise to great guilt. And that death was caused not by a person or by something natural like an illness that she could perhaps understand, but by an impersonal mechanism, a malevolent agency—a car! On top of that, she had a father who never gave her the time of day, never accepted her as the feminine person she was or was meant to be, and who then died a few years later, leaving her without the means to relate, through him, to other men. So her oedipal complex was never resolved either! Kids, a combo like that is one hell of a mess!

"Well, it added up to a basic and profound distrust of people, of the whole world. People—her parents—and things—a car—had proved untrustworthy, undependable, a source of great pain and deprivation. Who was there to trust but herself? Who but she would never let herself down?

"So she became an overcontrolled, locked-in person. A genuine Madison Avenue type who presented to the world and to herself the picture of the acceptable successful person in the career world. Everything was on the surface. She was programed."

"But—that's what Jane was trying to tell me!" Ben said. "She said Joyce *couldn't* do anything wrong!"

"Yes. She was playing a role. That's why there was no sense of depth in her. No sense of engagement with other people. She *was* married—to her work. And as to that, her achievements—and she *was* brilliant—masked an intense feeling of inferiority.

"As for her apartment, from what Ben said, it was a contemporary museum, showing in still another way that she was as detached from herself, emotionally speaking, as she was from everybody else.

"She had to be. Too much was buried inside her that hurt like hell. So why look at it? And other people could wound. So keep your distance. Simple. That's why even her sister knew nothing about her private life. She really had almost none. She was an obsessive-compulsive, but exceptionally smooth and well oiled.

"Until Allen came! As I've said," Dr. Inman repeated, lying carefully again as he and Ben had agreed last night to do, for Allen's sake. "Her suspicions about him and Helen, of whom she was notably proprietary, opened up all the old fears she had about herself.

"I suspect also that her army work and her doctoral thesis in psychology (which I've read, of course) were an attempt to get a line on a deviation she'd detected in herself long before. Lots of us go into this racket hoping to find out about ourselves. Never mind helping all the other freaks and queers!

"And then everything began to fall apart. Uncharacteristic tantrums followed by increasingly urgent, panicky attempts to regain her cool, along with some profound self-hatred for having been human enough to have lost it. Along the lines of 'How could *I* behave like lesser people!' Or, 'If I can't control myself, what's happening to me?' Then she'd follow up with assertions of her authority, her control. Which didn't work, of course. . . ."

"It sounds so pat," Helen said dubiously.

"Nothing I can do about that," said Dr. Inman. His cane waggled in the air again, faintly apologetic. "There are other interpretations, but the evidence I have suggests this explanation."

"What are we going to do with all her stuff?" David said. "Are we going to keep it? Are we entitled to? And if we do, who's going to use it?"

"I'd guess that's up to her sister," Ben said. "She'll be here a few days, closing up Joyce's apartment. If she wants us to have it, its use will of course be optional. I was going to tell Joyce that, but I didn't get the chance." He found that his pipe was cold, and put it into his pocket.

Allen jumped up excitedly. "I had a thought, Ben. That's what I called about, in fact. None of us used the mikes or tapes last week, right? Well, I happened to look at the footage counters Tuesday morning—"

"Why?" David demanded suspiciously.

"Well, because she'd—she'd undressed in front of the TV camera—"

"She *what?*" David yelled.

"Thought she might've," said Dr. Inman, almost to himself.

"—and I happened to come in just then—a bit earlier than I usually do," Allen went on. "This is what I didn't get around to telling you on Saturday, Ben. Her office door was open and I looked in. I wanted to talk to her about Tim and Tony, and I saw her on the viewer. And the video tape was taking it all in! She didn't know what she was doing, that was plain. She was saying something about seeing and hearing everything that went on here from now on. And then she got the strangest look on her face and began undressing. Automatically . . . almost as if she were in a sudden trance. . . . Well, I stopped the tape as soon as I saw what was happening to her, and I managed to erase it while she was dressing. And then she came out and saw me there! And, well, as Dave said, she caved in! Emotionally the scene was set for what happened when you got here, Dave, with Tim and Simon."

"So?" said Simon, who was breathing with difficulty now.

"So I had a look at the control panels—"

"Big Brother stuff, in her case," Dr. Inman interrupted.

"Yes, that's what I told her. Anyway, when I found out she'd had Tony up here during the dance, I wondered if she'd had a mike on. So I looked at the footage counter this morning on the audio and it was considerably advanced. So I thought about it and then called you, Ben."

"Hmmmm. You didn't play it?"

"No. But now's a good time to see if she did."

"If someone would give me a hand—" Dr. Inman said, but he

rolled over onto his colorful belly and got to his feet with much grunting and panting.

"Physician, heal thyself!" Simon said derisively, following the limping doctor into Joyce's office.

"What? And have a fool for a patient?" Ben said, bringing Joyce's chair from behind her desk. "Here, Zach, make yourself comfortable."

Dr. Inman turned and looked thoughtfully at Simon's white face. "You take it, Mr. Wills. Talk about people caving in! You all right?" He pushed his bifocals up to his forehead for a better look at the older man.

"I'll manage," Simon said brusquely.

But the doctor hooked the cane round Simon's arm and steered him to the chair. Then, with a worried expression on his gnome's face, he stood behind Simon, supporting himself on his cane. The others clustered behind Joyce's desk at the big table which held all the control panels.

"I'll turn the tape back a bit," Allen said. "They couldn't have been here too long. You said you saw her take Tony out of the gym at about nine-thirty, didn't you, Sime?"

"Yes," was the hoarsely whispered reply. "Or a little after."

"And they were down again at about ten of ten, I'd say," Ben said. "We saw them come into the main corridor, right, Simon? Just before you left."

"Right. That's when I made those calls for you."

"So allowing for everything," Allen said, turning on the machine and setting it on *Reverse*, "they couldn't have been at it more than ten minutes, maybe fifteen. So I'll stop it at . . . about . . . here!" he said tensely.

The whirr of the revolving reel ceased. Just before it began to move again, on *Play*, there was a shaking silence in which no one moved or even breathed.

And then Joyce's beautiful voice, soft and persuasive as always, said as from a distance, "—just put my coat away, Tony. Force of habit, you know."

There was a sound of footsteps, each louder than the last, and then she said, "All right, Tony. You don't mind being in our usual cubicle, do you? No, sure you don't! After all," merrily, "we've certainly spent a lot of time here! We're used to talking here, aren't we."

They could have counted to ten, waiting for the boy's reply. Finally he said, "I guess . . . You ain't got that mike hooked up, have yuh? 'Cause I ain't talkin' into no mike!"

"Good heavens, Tony! Of course not! Why are you so suspicious? I must say my feelings are a bit hurt—more than a bit—by your attitude!" Her voice trembled with anger.

"Hmph!" the doctor snorted. "Some lousy trick!"

"Bitch!" Simon muttered.

"It goes along with the notes I found in those pants," Ben said. "I was stunned! She didn't even do as well as a student counselor. She went at him with a sledge hammer."

"Sh-sh!" David hissed.

But the silence continued.

And then the pitch and timbre of Joyce's tone began little by little to change.

"I'm sorry," she said sarcastically, "I'm sorry you no longer trust me enough to tell me the truth, Tony. I won't list all the things I've done for you. I don't like to remind you that you owe me a certain amount of gratitude. But since you've had a few chats— unauthorized illegal ones, I may say!—with Mr. Magrue"—her voice was venomous, and Helen gasped in angry disbelief—"you've decided to do things in your own way. Since when have you been running my department?"

"My god, it's—it's ghoulish!" Helen whispered. "I just can't believe it!"

And Simon said again, "Bitch!"

At length, as though she had heard them, Joyce went on in a more circumspect manner. "I'm waiting, Tony. I want to know about that gun. I want to know about Mr. Quinn. A terrible thing happened—a boy was killed. Another will have nightmares all his life because of the awful thing he did. I've got to get to the root of this dreadful business, Tony. I'm the only one who can straighten it out."

"The Messiah Complex," Ben said.

Again they could have counted to ten or played a round of bridge. The only sounds in the room were the faint friction caused by the tape sliding along its track, and Simon's uneven breathing.

And then Tony said, "I don't know nuthin', Miss Bellows. Honest! All I know, I wanna talk to Mr. Magrue or Mr. Wills."

"That's impossible! That is out of the question! Are you expecting help from *them?* From *either* of them?" Her contempt was unmistakable and shocking.

It covered the sound of a great strangled gasp as Simon threw his head back, fighting for breath. Both hands clutched and clawed at his chest as he tried to get at the terrible pain inside his ribs and tear it out. His back arched rigidly and his legs shot out in front of him. Even though the heels of his shoes were digging into the carpet and giving him some purchase, he was precariously balanced on the back of his neck and the end of his spine. From head to toe the convulsed body shuddered horribly.

Dr. Inman, still standing behind him, saw the seizure begin and slacken, and the sick man's knees start to flex slightly. Grasping Simon under one arm, he thrust the head of his cane down over Simon's belly and hooked one knee lightly but firmly just as the big body went limp. In another instant Simon would have slid to the floor.

"Ben! Allen! Help me!" the doctor cried, groaning as his posture placed an intolerable strain upon his bad back.

So intent had the others been on the tape that they neither saw nor heard what was happening five feet behind them. They whirled, and looked, and seemed to scatter with a *woosh*, like autumn leaves.

Together David and Allen eased Simon gently down while Ben supported the doctor into the chair. Helen ran out and came back quickly with a coat which she rolled into a pillow and put tenderly under Simon's head. His eyes were closed, his mouth was sagging open from the swift immeasurable exhaustion of the attack. He breathed with the greatest difficulty. His color was ashen.

Frightened and shaken, they stared at him. The doctor said quietly, "Coronary. Take it easy. You can't help him that way. Somebody open a window. He needs air."

Joyce was saying, "Might as well go down now, Tony. But don't imagine I'm giving up so easily just . . ."

Slowly Simon shook his head and his bloodless lips twitched.

It was plain that he was smiling, that he would have smiled broadly if not for the agony in his chest.

"No," he whispered. "Don't . . . need that . . . now . . . not for where . . . I'm going . . . something . . . something—tell you, Ben . . ."

His hand moved weakly, groping, and Ben kneeled at his side and held the limp cold fingers. "Easy, Simon, easy. I think I know. Let me say it. Save your strength."

Again the head turned, only slightly this time, and the lips stretched in the faintest echo of an echo of genuine mirth.

"Don't . . . need . . . it . . . No more left, Ben . . . no more . . . used the last . . . of it . . . dance . . . in—tunnel."

"You didn't have a coat, Simon," Ben said softly. "And it had gotten very cold. And your car was all the way the other side of Two. So you called down cellar, as I asked you to do while I spoke to Joyce. Then you must have figured, 'Why not go through the tunnel?' Everyone does. It's warmer. And Opal saw you turn on the landing and go down, instead of outside. Was that it?"

". . . yes, Ben . . . went—to john . . . first . . . then saw David . . . boozing up . . . he went . . . up . . . other side . . . didn't see me. . . ."

"Oh god!" David moaned. "Simon, forgive me! It's my fault! If I'd seen you, stopped you—"

"No!" Simon said sharply, opening his eyes and looking at David as from an immense and always lengthening distance. "No, Dave," he said with an access of strength. "Al's right . . . and our guest shrink. It was . . . the whole thing . . . all of us . . . takes a certain—egocentricity, Dave, to glom all the guilt for yourself . . . not a question . . . of your guilt . . . anyway. . . .

"*Mea culpa*, Ben . . . really . . . mine . . . this time . . . she was—coming through. . . ."

"And she showed you the bag, didn't she, Simon," Ben said. "She told you Tony was a liar, a thief, a washout. That when Quinn and Allen got their mitts on him, when he wasn't under her eye any more, he was going to the dogs, right?"

"Ye-e-e-s . . . going—to see you, Ben . . . I said . . . she'd . . . enough harm. . . ."

The frighteningly distant gaze was shuttered again. They waited.

The unused portion of the audio tape whirred quietly onto the spinning reel.

"Then . . . she told me off . . . stripped me . . . bare. . . . To die—like that—my career . . . all gone . . . a hack . . . presumptuous therapist . . . she said . . . nothing left . . . no identity . . . not even—teacher . . . she said . . .

". . . couldn't stand that . . . man can't—die . . . like that . . . knew . . . hadn't much time left . . . anyway . . .

". . . hit her . . . hard . . . heard someone . . . right away . . . you, Ben . . . sorry . . . so sorry. . . ."

"Easy, Sime, easy. It's all right, it's all right. You rest. Just nod your head if I'm right. You went back up on the same side you came down? Through the cafeteria and out the side door—because you knew no one was down on that landing, right? Which means you saw David go up on the opposite side?"

The assent was the barest tightening of the closed eyelids.

"And Lydia didn't see you come home," Ben said. "So you were able to change your clothes."

". . . no . . . watching TV . . . didn't . . . see me. . . ."

"Don't try to talk any more, Sime. I'll finish for you."

From the edge of the barrier that all but separated them, Simon smiled again.

"No, Ben . . . I'll do . . . own finishing. . . ."

And, very quietly, he was over it and gone.

CHAPTER TWENTY-THREE

Tuesday may have been the day before Ben's departure for San Francisco, but more importantly it was the beginning of the third week of October and Halloween was imminent. It followed, therefore, as the night the day that certain of the holiday's celebrants prepare themselves suitably and in advance with things rank and gross in nature. Yesterday was done. The dead were dead. The living must labor to the end.

Accordingly, Manny Abrams, one of the more refined and resourceful worshipers, took his place in the senior honors chemistry class on Tuesday morning and methodically pursued his plan. He maintained for a time a surveillance of Bert Shrag. But that gentleman spent most of the period resting his healing arm on his desk and noticed nothing unusual about a hardworking lad profoundly occupied with an empty thirteen-ounce tuna fish tin, a broad-bottomed pyrex bowl, and two glass jars.

The boy rapidly assembled the ingredients for two recipes. Into one jar he poured a judicious mixture of ferric sulfide solution. The other he filled with concentrated hydrochloric acid. He capped the jars and labeled them.

Next, he removed the label from the tin and washed off the lumps of glue. When he was satisfied that it was quite clean, he dried it, turned it over, and mathematically marked the center of the bottom. There he punctured it with the corkscrew on his scout knife. Then he put the tin, the bowl, and the jars into a bag and looked at the clock.

Eleven-forty. Just right!

He went out of the lab without being seen and was back again within two minutes.

Mrs. Castle brought in two notes for Ben. The first, from Art

Hudson, informed him that Thomas Quinn was in one hell of a spot. The Rosens, parents of the dead boy, were bringing a civil suit against him for gross negligence. The DA's office was preparing a criminal charge to prosecute and prove same. Further, from the talk among the DA's boys, every judge in the Commonwealth was ready to throw the book at Quinn who was ignorant and well-meaning but certainly not vicious.

So much for that, Ben thought sadly, and opened the second note.

In case I miss you, *Valentine had written,* I looked over Tony Evans' things as you asked me to do. In my opinion he has a definite and pronounced raw talent. Excellent use of shading, very good line, instinctive use of color, etc., etc. I don't want to throw you, Ben, but Tony has what Rembrandts are made of! I gather he has a financial problem now. (He won't if he learns what he has to!!) Is there *any* chance of my giving him free private lessons. He MUST develop this great gift. Let me know. And have a gorgeous trip—you earned it!

Ben called Tony into his office. "You're feeling better about things, I can see that," he said softly, noting a perceptible change in the boy's appearance and demeanor. "Okay, now try this on for size," and handed over Valentine's note.

The boy read it and handed it back silently. But tears were streaming down his cheeks, and for the second time in seventy-two hours he accepted Ben's spare handkerchief and wiped his eyes. But he could not wipe away the signs of wonder and a burgeoning self-respect.

"Okay," Ben said after a moment. "Now then, Mrs. Shrag didn't know you were going to see that note. But you know her and so does everybody else around here. She's an artist of note, she's had successful shows of her own in Boston and New York, and she knows what she's talking about. I want you to keep that note. Frame it and read it every day for the rest of your life. I mean it, I'm not kidding. It'll be better than praying. And go see Mrs. Shrag and get cracking."

The telephone rang but he ignored it, and Mrs. Castle took the call at her desk outside.

"Okay. Now tell me what you think of this plan, Tony. Stay in school—it's only for another few months—and stick with Mr.

Magrue. Let's see if we can rev up your program to suit your ability. It's there but you haven't used much of it yet. A good artist needs schooling. The more you know, the better you'll get.

"And one last thing. Forget about joining up. You know by now why you really wanted to—because you were mad. Get rid of those bullets, forget about guns. If and when the time comes that you have to serve, okay. Whether you do or you don't, with what you've got inside you, you've got better protection than any gun could ever give you.

"And now," Ben said, all choked up himself, "take off to wherever you're supposed to be. We'll talk when I'm back next week. Okay? Fine."

Herbie Sobel picked up the bag from its appointed place in the boys' lavatory (the second stall from the end, in point of fact), and went to one of the blower rooms. Like his colleague in the chem' lab, he too was an honor student, a shining member of the tech'-voc' program. And because of his on-the-job training in wiring, heating, ventilation, plumbing, and all other aspects of the building trades, he himself had made some of the repairs in the high school and there was no corner of it that he did not know.

He set the bag down, fetched a chair, stood on it, and unscrewed the grill that covered the ventilating duct leading to the cafeteria.

He took the bowl and the jar of acid from the bag and got up on the chair again. There was room between blower and grill, so that he could safely set the bowl down and fill it. Then he jumped down again.

FeS in the can. This would be tricky. . . .

He floated the tin on the acid. Then he inhaled a tremendous breath, a mammoth rib-cracking lung-bursting breath, and poured the ferric sulfide into the tin. He watched critically for two or three seconds, and saw the punctured tin begin to sink. Then he pushed the bowl with its sinister freight past the blower and breathed again, tentatively, as he screwed the grill back into place.

He put back the chair, caught up the paper bag, and left. No more than seven minutes had passed.

At eleven fifty-five one third of the student body entered the cafeteria for the first lunch.

Manny Abrams looked at the clock again and conferred upon himself the Westinghouse Science Scholarship and the National Merit Award: the logistics of the operation, from first to last, had been superb. He gave himself up wholly to honors math, as a gesture of thanksgiving (for Thanksgiving) and good will (for Christmas).

The assortment of humanity and teachers pushed and shoved into the cafeteria, went slowly past the food counters, and dispersed noisily, laughingly, to the tables.

The blower blew benignly into the crowded room, according to the intention of the architect that dining be a gracious time of day, a welcome respite in an active demanding program.

The ferric sulfide in the sinking tuna fish tin was embraced by the molecules of the hydrochloric acid. Ferrous chloride salts formed on the bottom of the tin and the bowl. Hydrogen sulfide gas rose, wispy and twirling, and was blown away down the ventilating duct and through the grill at the other end into the cafeteria.

Presently the huge noisy room began to stink of rotten eggs. And as the stench permeated every corner, all became so quiet that a pin could have been heard to drop.

And then all hell broke loose as the students and their monitors and the cooks behind the counters surged out like ocean waves, coughing and choking as they sped. The sensitive types vomited. Several tables were overturned. Books and food were scattered everywhere. The cafeteria was left a shocking mess.

There had been fire drills and bomb drills aplenty. But shortsighted inefficient school administrators like Ben had never made provision for chemical warfare drills.

Mr. Tomasello appeared, bellowing and fulminating, a ladder in his hot grip, an immense screw driver in his back pocket. But nothing was behind the grill on the wall except the baneful stink which gave no sign of decreasing and which, still relatively concentrated at that spot, was potent enough to knock the custodian from his ladder and hurl him unconscious to the floor.

But he was now so furious that no lesser force than a thunderbolt from the hand of mighty Jove himself could have decked him. He climbed down the ladder and went out to the source of the trouble, and then to a telephone.

"*Mamma mia!*" he wept in his frenzy, when Ben, who was talking with Tony Evans, failed to answer his phone. "Mrs. Castle? Lissen, you better get goin' on this goddam quick!"

"Oh god! Oh no!" cried a desperate, cornered, witless Ben.
"You'd better go *now!*" Mrs. Castle advised. "I called Mrs. Louis and told her you'd be waiting for her at Logan. She's packing now. And I changed your reservation," she said, regarding him oddly. "No trouble about that. They've plenty of space.

"And over the weekend I found a sub for Mrs. Cory. She just called to make it official. She's a crackerjack and she can stay for the rest of the year. She'll be here first thing tomorrow.

"Also, the Superintendent called. The School Committee held an executive session last night and voted money for covered walkways and doors with locks for both tunnels. They'll ratify the vote in open session tomorrow night. And they're going to give you a vote of confidence too.

"Also, Mr. Shedd, that reporter, called right after the Superintendent did. How he heard about the executive session last night, I'll never know. He said he's going to do a human interest story on you, with plenty of *schmaltz*, the minute you get back. To make up for the Superintendent scooping him. He said to have a good trip.

"Also, Mrs. Lunn called to thank you for visiting Timmy. She said he said he hopes you'll want to come again. He wasn't very cordial, I gather, but he's feeling better now.

"And here are all your notes and tapes and films for the conference, including the material you wanted from Mr. Shrag.

"And have a wonderful wonderful trip, Mr. Louis!"
"How did you—? How—?"
But he didn't wait to find out. He only grabbed his coat and his rack of pipes and peach brandy tobacco and skulked out of the building and drove away as though the Hounds of Hell were in hot pursuit, with Mr. Tomasello in the van.

"Why did it take you so *long?*" he said suspiciously as Jane came puffing up, laden with baggage.
She looked him in the eye.

"I packed for two. Me and you. I went to the bank and took out all the money. I asked the Rienzis to take Benjy and Fee."

"But—but—"

"In your condition," she continued severely, "I figured you'd need an antidote to those topless wonders out there.

"And I'm *it*. . . . Something?"

Gallantly Ben rose to the occasion. "It's the best idea you ever had!" he said.

And after a moment's reflection he believed it.

N